Tagged for Murder

Tagged for Murder

Elaine Flinn

LARGE PRINT

This large print edition published in 2004 by
RB Large Print
A division of Recorded Books
A Haights Cross Communications Company
270 Skipjack Road
Prince Frederick, MD 20678

Published by arrangement with HarperCollins Publishers, Inc.

This book is a work of fiction. Names, characters, places and
incidents either are products of the author's imagination or are
used fictitiously. Any resemblance to actual events or locales
or persons, living or dead, is entirely coincidental.

Publisher's Cataloging In Publication Data
(Prepared by Donohue Group, Inc.)

Flinn, Elaine.
    Tagged for murder / Elaine Flinn.

    p. (large print) ; cm.

    ISBN: 1-4193-2258-3

1. Doyle, Molly (Fictitious character)—Fiction. 2. Antique dealers—
California—Carmel—Fiction. 3. Murder—Investigation—California—
Carmel—Fiction. 4. Large type books. 5. Mystery fiction. I. Title.

PS3606.F553 T34 2004b
816/.6

Printed in the United States of America

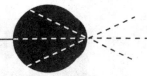

**This Large Print Book carries the
Seal of Approval of N.A.V.H.**

Erma and Curls
You would have loved this

ACKNOWLEDGMENTS

Most writers begin acknowledgments with . . . "I wouldn't be here if not for . . ."

And I shall too, because it's true. I *wouldn't* be here if not for an incredibly supportive family: Joe, my Wild Irish husband of forty-five years whose humor keeps me sane; my son Patrick, who sends me jokes and tries to lure me to Florida to write under swaying palms; my daughters Kelly and Sharon, and daughter-in-law, Karen, who are the real life models of Molly Doyle.

I will always be grateful to Nina Collins, agent extraordinaire, who paved the way for Molly's introduction and who has become a wonderful friend. I offer never-ending admiration to Jennifer Civiletto, my intrepid editor and partner in crime, for keeping me on track when I go too far afield.

To Chassie West, whom I cherish beyond measure, and to the many other mystery writers— too numerous to mention, but they know who they are—who welcomed me into the coven with warmth, support, generosity, and friendship . . . my sincere thanks.

And to Gregor Leazer and Bridget Bolton, whose

generous charity auction bids to be characters are most sincerely appreciated.

And last, but certainly not least, my gratitude and thanks to the many readers who have welcomed Molly, and whose enthusiastic emails, letters, and cards have made all those long hours in front of the computer so very worthwhile.

CHAPTER 1

The woman's screams could be heard all over the exhibit hall. Short, staccato bursts, like an annoying car alarm, silenced those still wandering the aisles of the Carmel Antiques Show.

It was Sunday, the last day of the show, near closing time. Savvy bargain hunters hoping to haggle with the weary dealers lingered in the aisles. They knew one less item to pack was worth discounting a few bucks.

Molly Doyle nearly dropped the pair of Anglo-Irish cut-glass candlesticks when she heard the screams. Molly and a woman offering a hundred dollars less for the candlesticks ran into the aisle. "Hang onto these. I'll see what happened," Molly said as she shoved the candlesticks into the woman's hands.

Running up the aisle, she saw the screaming woman standing in front of Trudy Collins's space. Her heart stopped when she saw Trudy facedown on the Louis IV repro desk she used for sales. Quickly at her side, Molly touched her shoulder and called out, "Trudy! What's wrong?"

1

Not getting a response, she gently jostled her shoulder. "Trudy?" Her hands turned clammy, and she turned to the screaming woman, who was now hyperventilating. "Get some help! I think she's—oh, God! I don't know—just get some help!"

When the woman didn't move, and a small crowd began to gather, Molly searched the faces and was relieved to see the young man who was there to help her pack up after the show. "Robbie! Call 911 and find Randall! He's probably in the cafeteria with Lucero!"

Molly tried once again to rouse Trudy. Gently lifting her off the desk, she nearly fainted when she saw Trudy's face, the cheeks and mouth badly cut and seeping blood.

"Oh, my God!"

Ignoring the startled gasps from the aisle, Molly grabbed Trudy's wrist to check for a pulse. Her hands began to shake when she realized Trudy was dead.

Trying to stay calm, she gently picked up Trudy's dangling arms and was about to place them on the desk when she saw what had caused the cuts on her face. Broken shards of porcelain, as sharp as glass, lay on the desk. When Trudy's head fell forward, she'd apparently fallen on a group of Sèvres porcelain figurines. Scattered among them were what appeared to be oversized sales tags, with magazine cutouts of baroque furniture, porcelain figurines, marble statues, and exotic jewelry. A hole had been punched in the corner of each tag, with a red string attached. More bizarre, a red circle was drawn around each photo, with a red slash across the price.

Carmel's chief of police, Kenneth Randall, had little problem making his way through the crowd gathered in the aisle. Well over six feet, his presence was usually felt before it was noticed. On his heels was Dan Lucero, the district attorney for Monterey County. Returning from a fund-raising banquet for handicapped children, they'd promised to stop by the show to say hello to Molly.

Lucero took one look at Trudy Collins and shook his head. "I'll move these people out of the way."

Randall, at Trudy's side, didn't need to examine her. He'd seen enough in his long career to know she was dead. Nodding to Lucero, he said, "Step back, folks. We need room for the paramedics." Turning to Molly, he asked, "What happened?"

"I don't know. I heard screams, looked in the aisle, and saw that woman in the red leather jacket screaming her head off." Clutching his arm, Molly was near tears. "Poor Trudy! I can't believe this!"

"Okay, okay, I know. This isn't good. Did you touch anything?"

"Her face is so . . ."

"Yeah, looks bad. You didn't answer me, did you touch anything?"

"No. Well, I mean, I just lifted her off the table. I tried to get a pulse."

Randall turned his back to the crowd of onlookers and gave Molly a hard look. "Why the hell did you touch her?"

Stunned by his shortness, Molly said, "I had to do something! I didn't know if she was choking, or having a heart attack, or—or—"

"Okay, simmer down. Just don't go touching dead people anymore. Who helped you?"

Gritting her teeth, Molly said, "No one. I didn't know she was already dead."

Gesturing to Lucero and the security guard now at his side, Randall said, "I want everyone in the cafeteria. Tell them we'll only keep them for a short time. Tell them it's standard procedure, so nobody gets antsy."

"Oh, Lord! What happened? Trudy?"

Molly and Randall turned to see a shaken elderly woman.

Randall headed her off. "Hold up, Bitsy. Don't come in here." Turning her away, he gently said, "You can't help her now. She's gone."

"*Gone?*" Looking at Molly, a puzzled frown filled Bitsy Morgan's face. "But we just spoke . . . just a little while ago. We were going to have drinks with Oliver after she packed up."

Wrapping an arm around her, Molly said, "Oh, Bitsy, I'm so sorry."

"It was her heart, wasn't it?" Bitsy sighed. "She had a bum ticker. I told her time and time again to cut down on the booze!"

Trembling, and angry with Randall for being

4

short with her, Molly said to Bitsy, "I know what a shock this is, but it's best if we get out of the way."

"Here, let me take her." Molly turned around to see Oliver Townsend. The dapper gentleman was dressed in tweed, his paisley ascot slightly askew. He embraced Bitsy, who was sobbing now. "There, there, my dear." Looking over her head, he said to Molly, "I'll take her down to your space. We'll wait there."

Just ahead of the paramedics, Lucero said, "Everyone is in the cafeteria and we've sealed the exits."

"That's probably not necessary," Randall replied. "Looks like a heart attack. But, okay, it's best to be cautious." Turning to the paramedics, he said, "A friend of hers said she had a bad heart. Do your thing, then tell the coroner I'll get with him tomorrow."

Seeing Molly in the aisle, Randall wasn't thrilled with the look on her face. Her jaw was set and her eyes were like slits. He knew that look. He also knew he was in for it. Moving out of the way of the paramedics, he said to her, "You and Lucero take Bitsy and what's his name to the cafeteria." A bit gentler, he added, "Wait for me there, okay?"

Grief and anger pumping through her, Molly said, "Oliver. His name is Oliver."

"Whatever. Just get them out of here."

CHAPTER 2

It was just short of midnight when Molly and Robbie finished loading the aging El Camino truck. By the time Randall let the dealers return to their spaces to pack, the mood in the hall was subdued. The jokes, the friendly ribbing, the bitching about sales, even the weary frustrations of packing everything up were gone. Many of the dealers knew and liked Trudy Collins. A fixture on the traveling show circuit, she was also one of the best estate sale dealers on the Central Coast. Taking only the finest commissions from attorneys and individuals, Trudy Collins did not deal in junk. When she advertised a sale, you'd better drop everything and get in line, even if it was before dawn.

Molly had met Trudy at Daria DeMarco's restaurant one rainy night when she was in the mood for a huge bowl of minestrone. Ushered into the private back room, Trudy was just back from a buying trip in Europe and had stopped in to see Daria. The three women killed two bottles of Château Souverain while trading antique show stories and rehashing Molly's role in uncovering an art scam and her close brush with death. When Trudy described the fabulous contents of an upcoming estate sale and invited Molly to come a day ahead of the dealers and the public, Molly was thrilled by the special treatment. At the sale, she spent over five thousand dollars for the shop in under an hour, and Trudy gave her the same sneak peek for her next two sales. Molly filled Treasures with more wonderful merchandise. Max, who owned the shop, was thrilled, Molly was elated, and Trudy had a new deep pocket buyer.

Now, emotionally drained, Molly parked the loaded truck in the garage and dragged herself up the courtyard stairs to the apartment over the shop. Her eyes red from crying, she headed to the small kitchen. She needed a cup of Café Français before calling Daria at her restaurant.

When Daria answered, Molly took a deep breath and said, "Better sit down. I've got bad news. Trudy . . . Trudy had a heart attack. She's . . . she's gone." Slumping into her sofa, Molly wiped the tears from her eyes and told Daria what had taken place.

"I'm stunned," Daria barely got out. "God, this is horrible. And you found her? Oh, Molly, are you okay? Do you want me to come over?"

"No. I'll be fine. I wanted to call you earlier, but my cell wouldn't work in the hall, and by the time we loaded up . . . well, I just got home."

"Look, get some sleep. We'll talk tomorrow.

Maybe you should call Max. She rented from him. He'll have to know."

"What about family?" Molly asked. "All we ever talked about was merch, merch, and more merch."

"No. Her folks are gone, and she was an only child."

"I'll call Max right away."

Always a night owl, Molly wasn't surprised Max was still up. Her early mentor and boss, Max Roman was one of the elite high-end antiques dealers in San Francisco. Accepting refuge after the scandal in Manhattan, when her husband and his lover decided that faking period antiques was more lucrative than selling the real thing, Molly wanted to throttle Max when she saw the run-down antiques store he wanted her to manage in Carmel. Now he was number one on her nightly prayer list. When he answered, Molly took another deep breath and told him about the tragedy.

"Oh, how utterly horrible!" Max said. "I'm simply devastated. I will miss her so. She was such a delight."

Molly heard a deep sigh at the other end, but wasn't prepared for Max's next words. "I can't possibly come down. I'm leaving for Rio in the morning to visit Pablo. Didn't you get my fax?"

"No. I've been at the show all weekend, Max, and I've only been home for a half hour."

"Oh, dear. I should have called instead." Max soothed, "Trudy was such a gem. Will you handle things for me? I'll call George, my property manager, and tell him to give you his key to her place. You'll have to get something for the funeral. Oh, damn, the house is scheduled to be tented for termite extermination Wednesday. I hope Trudy got all her plants and food out of there. See to it for me just in case, will you? In fact, I'll have George arrange movers and a storage unit until this is all sorted out. Will you and Daria get Trudy's things together for me? I don't want to seem uncaring, but, well, it has to be done."

"Daria said there's no family to . . . arrange things. And someone has to make some arrangements."

"Hmm, yes. Well, I guess that means us. It's the least I can do. Trudy rented from me for years. Have George put you in touch with someone local. This is what friends are for, right?"

Not expecting to have this fall in her lap, Molly was hastily taking notes as Max told her what needed to be done. "Right. Okay, I'll handle it. When will you be back?"

"Oh, sweetie, I'm going to Rio, one can only guess! Order flowers for me. White roses. I'll call soon."

He was gone before Molly could blink. That was Max, always in a hurry, but always a prince. She would love to have been on a plane heading for Rio too. Even seeing Pablo, Max's lover and a royal thorn in her side, would be worth the trip. Although, she had to admit, Pablo had been very apologetic to her lately, and even sent her post-cards and gifts from South America. Letting out another long sigh, she headed back to the kitchen when the phone rang.

"I'm sorry, okay?" Randall said. "I shouldn't have been short with you. You did what any normal person would do. That about do it?" When Molly didn't answer, he said, "Okay, you want to remind me you were a friend trying to help, right? Well, you gotta remember I'm a cop, and I react like one." When Molly still didn't reply, he said, "That's the best you're gonna get from me, so don't give me any more grief. Take it or leave it."

"Not much choice, is there?" she finally said.

"We still pals, then?"

"Yeah, why not." Pausing, Molly added, "If only Trudy could have called out. I mean, I might have been able to get to her right away. If all of us hadn't put up those fancy walls around our spaces, I might have seen her, or something."

"Look, Molly, you probably couldn't have saved her. With heart attacks, it's a toss-up. Did you call Daria?"

"Yes. She took it like a champ. I called Max, too. Trudy rented from him. He wants Daria and me to go over tomorrow and get some of her things. He's heading for Rio tomorrow but is making the funeral arrangements before he leaves. Evidently she doesn't have family here."

"That's nice of him. Get some sleep. I'll see you later."

"Oh, wait. I just thought about Trudy's merch.

10

Can I send Robbie over tomorrow to pack it up?"

"Sure, I don't see why not. Forensics cleared it already."

"Forensics?"

"Routine. Don't go off on me here. Unattended death, we always check things out."

The next morning, Molly walked through the courtyard downstairs on her way to Tosca's. The tiny coffee and pastry bistro at the back of the complex Max owned was often Molly's first stop before opening Treasures. The courtyard was filled with round iron tables and chairs surrounding a large fountain. Vibrant red bougainvillea cascaded over the stucco walls and framed the windows and doors over Tosca's and the new shoe boutique across the way. The soft sounds of the splashing water in the fountain created a soothing melody all day long.

Bleary-eyed after little sleep, and in need of an espresso, Molly set her thermos on the counter and eyed the apple cake Bennie Infama was slicing. It was already seven, and Bennie was late in prepping the pastry case for his early morning customers. Bennie's father had transferred ownership to him last week for his twenty-sixth birthday. Now the proud owner of the tiny café, the five-foot-eight, wiry young man was working both ends of the clock.

"I'll take two slices. No . . . make it one."

"How's a slice and a half? You need the sugar to keep you goin'. Long day yesterday, right? I heard about Trudy. What a shame. How's Daria and Bitsy holding up?"

"Bitsy is devastated. Daria is a rock."

"How about you? You okay?"

Draining her espresso in one gulp, Molly said, "Utterly sad. I'm still in a little shock. But, damn, I'm going to miss her. She was so full of life. She always had a smile and a joke or two to tell." Shaking her head, Molly added, "I just can't imagine she had a bad heart. I never knew."

"Yeah, and she was only in her mid-fifties. So, is that Oliver guy helping Bitsy cope? Man, he watches her like a hawk. When they stop by, he's always on her about too much sugar, or telling her to watch the caffeine. I mean, it's kind of surprising the way she listens to him."

"He's absolutely devoted to her. It's really kind of sweet."

"It's too much, if you ask me. Bitsy's too old for a boy toy."

"Bennie!"

"Just kidding. So, how was the show? I mean, besides, well, you know."

Welcoming the diversion, Molly said, "Oh, hell, I'm not sure I want to do another one. The preparation is a nightmare. Then when it's over, you're either elated over sales or despondent if you didn't do well. Then you have to pack all that stuff up, get it back to the shop, unpack it, and set it out."

"I didn't realize how much work it took. Grab a seat, I'll join you." Molly moved to a small table as Bennie took care of an early customer. Returning with another espresso for her, he said, "I hear Oliver's opening a decorator-type gift shop. Like we need more?"

"Really? Funny, Bitsy never mentioned it."

"You didn't know? He's renting from my father. Bitsy put up the dough for the lease."

The surprised look on Molly's face prompted Bennie to say, "You didn't hear that from me. Is it a secret or something?"

"Maybe Oliver just didn't want people to know he was light on cash." Glancing at her watch, Molly took a final sip, then said, "I have to run. I missed Mass yesterday, and I'd like to run over to the Mission and say a little prayer for Trudy. Then Robbie is meeting me to unpack the truck. By the way, he's been a lifesaver. You've got a great family." Reaching for the last bite of her cake, Molly rolled her eyes. "Then I've got to see what kind of a day my new helper Janet had yesterday. She's kind of loopy, but I can't close the shop when Bitsy's not free."

In the quiet of Mission San Carlos, Molly had a hard time concentrating on the rosary for Trudy. Memories flashed in and out as her fingers moved over the beads. Trudy's breathless calls about an exciting estate sale, to-die-for china and furnishings, always left Molly laughing. She remembered one night at Daria's when Trudy had them in stitches, telling them about misadventures on the show circuit. Completing the rosary, Molly sat back in the pew. "Take care, Trudy," she whispered.

CHAPTER 3

While Robbie unloaded, Molly read Janet's notes on the dismal weekend sales, found the fax Max had sent, and checked the shop for theft. Janet had a short attention span and spent most of her downtime playing computer solitaire. Treasures had a huge display window facing Carmel's main street, Ocean Avenue, and another in the arcade leading to the courtyard. Molly took great care in keeping both windows filled with enticing merchandise and made a point to change them twice a month. The interior of the shop was for showcasing antiques. Oriental rugs covered the stone floor, and brick walls rose fourteen feet to meet a hand-painted ceiling with stars, moonbeams, nymphs, and a smiling sun face. At the back of the huge room, a working fireplace kept the shop cozy on cold winter days. The intricate iron balustrade of pinecones and spraying branches on the inside staircase leading to Molly's apartment had been made in the early thirties by a local craftsman.

When Molly first saw the shop after Max's friend died and left him the complex, she was near tears at how dim it had become during the months it had been closed. Only weeks before, her world had been a prestigious shop on Madison Avenue in Manhattan, with marble floors, five- and six-figure period merchandise, as well as her weekends in the Hamptons and buying trips to London, Paris, and Rome.

But Max gave her a free hand to spruce up the shop, and she'd spent days clearing cobwebs and dust, cleaning dull furniture, spotting worn rugs, and polishing silver until she thought she would drop. Now Treasures was a gem, and even on a day as sad as this, a haven to lift her spirits.

By the time she replaced everything she'd taken to the show, filling in the gaps on the floor, it was almost noon. She sent Robbie back to pack up Trudy's show merchandise and had him put it in her garage for the moment. The bell over the door rang only once, when Max's rental agent dropped off the key to Trudy's cottage. Mondays were always slow, and for once Molly was glad.

By five it was all she could do to stay awake. Treasures had a zero day. She decided to close early, grab a bite to eat, and change into jeans before meeting Daria at Trudy's house at seven. She hoped she remembered how to get there. She'd only been to Trudy's twice, at night each time. While small, Carmel's residential area could be confusing, especially when it was dark. Homes and streets were shadowed by towering pines. The curving narrow roads north of Ocean Avenue often veered around trees in a confusion of short and then long blocks and dead ends. Proudly boasting no streetlights, sidewalks, or house numbers, it could easily be a maze. Most residents gave directions by saying "I'm on Santa Rita, fourth house northeast of Second." When Molly first arrived and began her garage sale routine, she nearly went nuts.

Daria was waiting at the front door when Molly arrived with the key. Words were unnecessary; a quick hug said it all. Once inside, they both stood still for a moment.

"I can't do this now," Daria finally said. "Would you mind if we tried again tomorrow night? We can get a dress then for the funeral home."

"Fine with me. I'm not up to it either." Moving into the living room, Molly looked around. "I'll call the moving company tomorrow and get Janet to come in. I can run over and get things started." When Daria only nodded, Molly said, "Go ahead and leave. I'll check out the rest of the house and see how much needs to be packed. It's not very big so I think the packers and I can probably have everything done ahead of the termite people."

"I forgot all about that. Trudy was going to stay at the Pine Inn while they were here. You sure you don't mind? It's just that . . ."

"I know. You were friends for years. It's harder for you."

Another quick hug, and Molly walked Daria to the door. Watching her leave, she understood how difficult this was for her. Daria let few people see past the battle scars of a tumultuous life, but she and Daria had traded war stories one night while killing a few bottles of vintage wine. As tall as Molly, Daria was of a different species altogether. With jet-black hair gently resting on wide shoulders, her sharply cut bangs and high cheekbones made more than one visiting Hollywood director take notice. Always dressed in rich smoky colors and exotic jewelry, she was the main attraction at her restaurant, in spite of the superb food and rich decor.

Reaching into her large tote for a notepad, Molly moved into each room of the modest-size house and listed all the furniture for the movers. She felt awkward opening cabinets and drawers, but she needed to get some idea of how many boxes would be required. She wished Max had asked his rental agent to do this. Moving into the bedroom Trudy used for her office, Molly shook her head at the mess. The desk looked like a windstorm had blown in and played havoc. Invoices, lists, schedules, and antique magazines were heaped in the middle, and a tutorial for Word was on top.

Molly opened one box among a stack in the corner and sighed. With utter reverence, she picked up a glorious tureen with an ornate ormolu base. It was Meissen from Germany, the oldest porcelain factory in Europe, and, she would bet, nineteenth century and infinitely more rare than the pieces she'd bought from Trudy at her very first estate sale. The yellow background was exquisite, and the painted flowers and gilt cartouches stunning. Examining it carefully, she looked under the ormolu base for the factory incised numbers. Finding them, she shook her head. How Trudy could have left this piece, probably worth at least nine or ten thousand, in a cardboard box was staggering. She carefully set it back in the box, curious to see what the others held.

She wasn't disappointed. In the next box she found a pair of salt cellars. The figures on each, a man and a woman in court dress, with delicate paintings of flowers and butterflies, was fabulous and worth three or four thousand. The next two boxes held a sampling of dinnerware wrapped in newspaper. She quickly realized she'd better supervise the packing. When she opened the closet and found more boxes of sturdier merchandise, she knew she had her hands full. Indo quill boxes, Regency tea chests, Treen bowls, brass and wood candlesticks, and odds and ends of sterling flatware. Satisfied there were no more precious porcelains that needed bubble wrap, Molly closed the closet. Every box would have to be marked and an inventory made. There was no way she could turn this over to a moving company without direction. She just hoped Janet would be free for the next two days. Bitsy, she knew, was in no mood to watch the shop.

Avoiding Trudy's bedroom, Molly locked up and headed back to the shop. If she was going to spend the next two days here, she needed to get her sales reports done tonight and faxed to Max's new majordomo, Marvin. Though not as draconian as his predecessor, Marvin was a stickler for routine.

When she finally completed the reports and the weekend show sales and turned off the computer, she saw that it was already ten-thirty. Holding back a yawn, and in dire need of coffee, she fluffed up a few throw pillows, then turned off most of the shop lamps, leaving a few for night lights. She was heading for the inside stairs to the apartment when she heard knocking on the window. *Now what?* She decided to ignore it. It was probably another sloshed tourist wanting to know where Clint Eastwood's place was. If shop owners had a dollar for every time a tourist asked that question, the town could close up and retire. Molly joked to friends that she was going to make up a little map with directions to the Mission Ranch, Clint's restaurant and mini-lodge, and hand them out to everyone who walked in.

By the time she made the fourth step, the knocking grew more insistent. "That's it!" she swore. Striding down the stairs, she put on her no-nonsense look and was ready for battle. A little girl, not more than ten or twelve, with short dark curly hair and Harry Potter glasses was waving madly at her in front of the main window. Considering the time, all sorts of scenarios rushed through Molly's mind. Was she lost? Had someone tried to grab her? Dressed in a sweatshirt and cut-off jeans, Molly could see she was shivering. Waving her toward the door, Molly unlocked it and opened it wide. "Are you okay?" she asked. "Did someone—"

Before Molly could finish, a woman appeared. "Hello, Molly."

Molly froze. She grabbed the door to steady herself.

"It's been a long time," the woman said.

Molly hadn't seen her sister Carrie, or heard her voice, in almost fifteen years. Yet her eyes were not lying. Not quite as tall as Molly, Carrie's five-foot-eight stance was more forbidding. She'd always held herself with power. Her hair was short and blond now. Her jeans and a Seattle Seahawks sweatshirt seemed incongruous with her long French nails and the knockout diamond rings on both hands.

Pulling the child toward her, Carrie said, "This is Emma, my daughter. I know you're surprised, but it's freezing out here."

Stepping back, Molly could only nod. Catching her breath, she finally said, "Of course, come in." Pulling the door open all the way, she added, "I . . . I'm just so surprised. I can't believe it's you."

Inside the shop, Carrie walked past Molly and looked over the showroom. Molly watched her eyes linger over the highly polished mix of French and English furniture, then move to the lamps

21

made from Oriental vases, past the tableaus of Staffordshire royal figures, old leather books, carriage clocks, and Waterford crystal vases filled with fresh flowers. Turning back, she opened her arms. "Well, big sister, it's really me. How about a hug?"

Molly's feet felt nailed to the floor. The last person she ever expected to see again stood before her with arms wide. A long-buried bitterness shot through her. Giving Carrie a brief hug, she turned to her daughter. The poor child was still shivering, and Molly hadn't the heart not to offer some hospitality. "Hello, Emma. What do you say we go upstairs for something to take that chill away?"

"You live upstairs?" Carrie asked.

Bristling at the condescending tone in Carrie's voice, Molly bit her tongue. "Yes."

"It must be a big come-down after New York."

Stiffening her back, Molly stepped away to lock the front door, then turned to face her sister. "Not at all. In fact, it's very charming and convenient. It's great not to have to commute." Looking at Emma, she said, "Shall we go up?" Nearly bolting up the stairs, Molly almost yanked the door to the apartment off the hinge. Forcing a smile, she said, "Make yourselves comfortable while I make some tea."

In the kitchen, Molly filled the teapot, plugged it in, then set out cups on a tray. Still in shock that Carrie was there, she felt an eye twitch coming on. Back in the living room, she said, "I'll get the heat on and the fireplace going." Turning to Emma, who sat very primly on the sofa, she added, "You're still shivering. Would you like a throw until the room heats up?"

"No, thank you, ma'am. I'll be fine."

Carrie stood at the French doors and pulled the draperies back. Peering down at the lights in the courtyard, she said, "You can call her 'Aunt Molly.' She won't bite."

The dull look in the child's eyes tore Molly's heart. "I'd like that," Molly said. "I've got a comfy chenille throw I love to curl up with when I read. I'll be right back."

Pulling the throw from her bed, Molly didn't have to stretch too far in her memory banks to remember why she and Carrie had rarely got along. By the time they were teens, attitude was Carrie's middle name. Only two years apart, Molly often wondered what in their childhood had prompted her mind-set. Carrie's aggressive attitude had come long after their mother's death, so blaming her problems, which Molly never discovered, on the loss of their mother hardly made sense.

Returning with the throw and tucking it around Emma, Molly felt relief when she heard the teapot whistle. "Instant coffee or tea?" she asked.

"It's really late, we shouldn't stay," Carrie replied. "I just wanted to let you know we were here. It's actually cozy up here." Gesturing to the cushy deep blue sofas flanking the fireplace, and the oversized black lacquered coffee table, she asked, "Is this all yours, or does it go with the shop?"

Molly wanted to lie and say it was hers, but she'd be damned if she let her ego get the best of her. "Max redecorated for me recently, so yes, it goes with the shop. Except," she managed a short laugh, "the planter on the table. It's an old copper footbath I found at a sale last week."

"Nice job. But then, Max always was tasteful." Settling on the sofa next to her daughter, Carrie stretched her legs out. "Actually, a cup of tea would be welcome. But don't light a fire. We won't stay long."

"Cocoa for you, Emma?" Molly asked. "Maybe a cookie or two?"

"Yes, thank you."

Back with the tray, Molly set it on the coffee table. As Carrie helped herself, Molly handed Emma her cocoa. "Help yourself to the cookies."

Taking the cup, Emma said, "This is pretty. Is it an antique?"

Surprised by her question, Molly smiled. "No. It's called an engagement cup. Years ago, when young girls became engaged, relatives and friends of the family would stop by with a pretty cup and saucer, as a memento. There were many different patterns. Mostly flowers, like this one. I find them often now at garage sales so I use them for guests."

"Mother has roses, and I have pansies. You have just ivy. Would you like my pansies?"

"I love ivy, but thank you, Emma." Settling across from them, Molly took a quick sip, then finally asked the question she'd had in mind: "What brings you to Carmel?"

"I've got an interview in The City in a few days, so I thought I'd drop down and say hello. I'm an attorney, by the way."

Not wanting to let on that she knew, Molly said, "Really? How great. And you're leaving where?"

"Seattle. I got tired of not seeing enough sun. It was time to move on."

Carrie's short, terse answers were getting on Molly's nerves. *She shows up out of the blue after all these years,* she thought, *and hasn't the courtesy to at least be pleasant.* "Too bad you've caught us in the middle of a fog bank."

Smiling, Carrie said, "A little more fog in my life couldn't keep me from seeing you. It's been way too long, and I wanted you to meet Emma."

"How did you know I was in Carmel?"

"I saw your write-up in the *New York Times.* Apparently you're quite the sleuth." Carrie laughed. "I lunched out on that for a good two weeks. Even Emma was impressed." Reaching into her bag, she pulled out a mother-of-pearl cigarette case. Nodding to the ashtray on the coffee table, she said, "You still smoke I see."

Her eyes glued to the cigarette case, Molly answered, "Yes and no. I quit every other day. But go ahead." Tearing her eyes from the case, she said, "I left mine near the sink." In the

25

kitchen, Molly reached for the pack in her pocket. Her hand shook as she snapped the Zippo open. Focusing on the flame, her eyes began to tear. The case in Carrie's hand belonged to their mother. Although Molly hadn't seen it in years, flashes of her mother holding it with pride filled her mind. It had been an anniversary gift from her father the year before her mother's death. It had gone missing soon after, and her father had been miserable for weeks.

With effort, Molly returned to the living room. Emma had fallen asleep, and she watched Carrie inhale deeply then lift her head and blow smoke rings. Forcing a calm she hardly felt, Molly said, "So, you're a lawyer! How exciting."

"Actually, it's boring as hell. I should have gone into criminal law. I do trusts and wills and mind-numbing corporate law."

"Well, at least you're meeting a better crowd."

Setting down her cup, Carrie snorted, "Are you kidding? My days were filled with corporate crooks and greedy family members fighting over wills. Give me a drug dealer anytime. At least they're honest about what they do." Stubbing out her cigarette, she glanced at her watch. "It's late and we have years to catch up on, but we can save it for later. Emma and I stopped by earlier, but you were gone. We thought we'd try again before heading back to the hotel."

Before Molly could reply, Carrie tapped Emma's arm. "Come on, time to go."

Snapping awake, the child's knees jerked, knocking the empty cup and saucer to the floor.

"Goddamn you! Look what you've done!"

"Carrie! Don't scold her. It was an accident."

"Don't tell me what to do with my daughter!"

Molly sucked in her breath. "Whoa. Slow down, okay? She couldn't help it. Let's not get into a brawl the first hour, okay?"

"Look, I'm sorry. It's been a hell of a week. We hiked all over Point Lobos today and I'm really beat."

Turning away, Molly smiled at Emma. "Don't worry about the cup."

"I'm sorry. I was just tired. Did I break it?"

Molly was on her feet and picking up the fallen china. "No, honey, everything is fine."

"It's okay, sweetheart," Carrie said, her voice silk now. "I didn't mean to scare you."

Helping unwrap the throw, Molly stood motionless while Emma took her mother's hand. Showing them to the outside door, Molly turned on the light and asked, "Where are you staying?"

"The Inn at Spanish Bay," Carrie answered as she led Emma down the wide, tiled staircase. Turning back, she said, "How about breakfast tomorrow?"

Molly's first instinct was to make an excuse and get out of it. But when Emma looked up at her and nodded, she didn't have the heart to refuse. "Okay. What time, and where?"

Carrie shrugged. "You decide. This is your town."

It was all Molly could do not to say, *You bet your*

ass it is, honey, and you better keep moving on. "I open at ten. How's nine? We can have something quick at Tosca's here in the courtyard."

"See you then."

After her sister left, it took a fair amount of time for Molly to control her desire to slam the tray on the sink. It was chipped enough as it was. In just a half hour it was clear that Carrie hadn't changed. *Why had she come?* It was hard to believe her sister was suddenly interested in reconnecting. But more than that, Molly was deeply disturbed by seeing her mother's cigarette case. The wonderful memories it inspired were tainted by the realization that Carrie had taken it. Especially since she'd known how distressed her father had been over its loss.

Well, why are you surprised? she thought, washing the teapot and cups. *She stole that damned bracelet that sent Dad to prison, didn't she?* The fact that her father was fencing jewelry confiscated from drug dealers by his two brothers on the force was beside the point. Molly later came to realize that it was only a matter of time before he would be caught. But by the hand of his own daughter?

Grabbing the cup Carrie had used, she set it under the hot water, as if to scald away every trace of her. If Carrie hadn't taken the bracelet from their father's used furniture store and sold it to Max, who innocently sold it to Bitsy, who then wore it at a posh San Francisco party, her father might never have been sent to prison.

Those reasons alone should have made her slam the door right in her sister's face. She knew it wasn't right to hate a sister, but at that moment she felt little guilt.

CHAPTER 4

Dressed in fine wool chocolate Armani pants she'd found at Saks on sale, and a matching cashmere sweater, Molly headed over to Tosca's to meet Carrie and Emma. Still angry about the cigarette case, she had to remind herself to stay calm and keep her mouth shut. She wouldn't think of making a scene at Tosca's. She wouldn't do that to Bennie. Or to herself for that matter.

She was on her second espresso, pretending to read the newspaper she'd found on the next table, when Carrie and Emma arrived, twenty minutes late. "Good morning. There are no menus here. Self service and just coffee cake, so we can go up to the counter and—"

"Oh, we've had breakfast," Emma said. "Mother ordered room service."

"We didn't want to hold you up," Carrie quickly added. "Besides, I promised Emma I'd take her to the aquarium. I'd like to get there early. I've got a lunch appointment at the hotel. An attorney friend lives here and he's coming over to discuss some job leads."

Draining her cup, Molly said, "No problem. Stop

back later if you have time." Smiling to Emma, she said, "You'll love the aquarium. I understand it's one of the best in the world."

"Have you been there?" Emma asked.

Molly shook her head. "Not yet, but I'll get there one of these days. You can tell me all about it later, okay?"

Pasting on a smile as she waved them off, Molly nearly broke her spoon in half. Bennie was on his way with another espresso. "The look on your face tells me you need a little something in this."

"That female, by the way, was my sister. I haven't seen her in fifteen years until last night. It was *her* idea to meet, and then she didn't even sit down and pretend to be cordial! And then she splits!"

"Nothing like sisterly love, huh?"

"Don't get me started."

Still rankled over the "poor mouse" innuendos last night, Molly wasn't about to let Carrie think she was hovering near the poverty line and wanted to look prosperous this morning. Hurling her good clothes on the bed, she reached for her jeans, then slipped back into her Ferragamo loafers. Throwing on a cotton turtleneck, Molly hurried downstairs to get ready for Janet. At her desk, she made up another "remember" list. For some reason, Janet seemed to lose them. Switching on the computer, Molly selected a huge font size and began the list in capital letters. First item was to unplug the coffeepot in the small storage room off the main floor. The second was to keep the music soft, and the third was not to accept a credit card or check without a driver's license. She decided to tack it on the wall in the storage room. She hoped Janet would be on time for once. She had an early appointment at Trudy's with the estimator from the moving company and didn't want to be late.

Organized to a fault except for the large tote bags she carried, Molly flipped open the planner on her desk. Managing a shop on her own now brought a slew of responsibilities she hadn't had to contend with in New York, and her life seemed filled with lists. Adding the moving estimator's name and number from a note on her desk, she began crossing out completed tasks when she saw *Lucero's Birthday Party—Daria's—eight p.m.*

She'd totally forgotten about it, and quickly called Daria at home. Before she could say more than hello, Daria said, "I was about to call you. Yes. It's still on. Lucero didn't know Trudy, and it's not fair to him to cancel. So, it's put on a happy face time. We can do it, right?"

"Right," Molly quickly agreed. "Listen, I'm going over to meet the movers. I'll get some clothes and just keep them here until . . . well, until they're needed. You don't have to come. You've got enough to do."

"You're a peach, Molly. I mean that. Thanks."

"Friends in need—"

"Are friends in deed," Daria finished.

★　　★　　★

Molly opened Treasures promptly at ten. Janet, as usual, was late. It was times like this when Molly appreciated Bitsy. With all her grandstanding, rearranging displays, exaggerating the merits of merchandise, and outselling her four to one, she was, at least, a pro. She had to be at Trudy's at noon, and it was now ten-thirty. With other errands to run, she was already off schedule. And she had no idea when, or even if, her sister planned to stop back. Thinking of Carrie made Molly realize it was a good thing Bitsy wasn't coming in. Carrie was obviously not one of Bitsy's favorite people. The two of them in the same room would send off tremors that would be felt all the way to Santa Cruz. Which led Molly to wonder why Bitsy hadn't returned her call yesterday. Oliver had answered and said Bitsy was still in shock from Trudy's death and was in her room resting. When Molly had asked to speak to her housekeeper, Josie, Oliver said she was out shopping.

Smiling at a pair of women entering, Molly said, "If I can be of help, please let me know." A firm believer in not hassling customers, Molly was quick to welcome them and then let them browse. Keeping a discreet eye on the women, she dialed Bitsy's number. It took six rings before Oliver answered. Hearing his voice, she pulled the phone from her ear for a second. *Why on earth did he keep answering the phone? And where was Josie?* "Oliver? It's Molly. Would you put Bitsy on?"

"She's resting. I'd rather not disturb her. This tragedy is taking its toll."

"Of course. I'll stop by later to see her."

"Oh that won't be necessary. I'm sure she'll drop in tomorrow after her salon appointment."

"Great. I'll see her then." Hanging up, Molly was still concerned. Not a day went by that Bitsy either called or stopped by the shop. Keeping her hair appointment meant little. Bitsy's vanity was legend. The seventy-four-year-old dynamo would have to be in an oxygen tent to miss her twice weekly hair and nail appointment.

When Janet arrived at eleven, Molly hid her frustration. There was no point in reminding Janet she was late. It would only fluster her. Very calmly, she took her into the storage room and showed her the list on the wall. "Please do not take it down, okay?" Leading her back into the shop, she said, "Two women were in earlier and might be back. They're looking at those needle-point wing chairs. You can knock two hundred off them but that's all and only if they take the pair." Showing her some new merchandise, she guided Janet to three new displays and explained the finer points of the added pieces. "These little darlings," Molly began as she picked up a small pair of ceramic figures resembling a cross between a lion and a spaniel, "are called Fo Dogs. They're mid–twentieth century and not very old, but the colors are superb." Pointing out the tag to Janet, she added, "They're worth three hundred, but I've marked them at two fifty, so don't let them go for less."

"They're ugly," Janet said. "Who'd even want them?"

Molly couldn't help but laugh. "Ugly? Aw, come on! Collectors love them. They're mythical animals and the guardian spirits of Buddha's temple. It's good feng shui to have them in your home. Traditionally, you place them outside your door to keep evil spirits away."

"Whatever." Pointing to a tea table, Janet asked, "What about that big shiny urn thing? I don't remember seeing it before."

Thrilled Janet was beginning to show some interest in her job, Molly replied, "That's a samovar. It's Russian and used to hold hot water for tea. It works and it's copper."

"Right, copper, I knew that."

Molly grinned and said, "Of course you did. Okay, one more to show you and then I'm off." In three strides she stood before a table. "This," she began with great pride, "is a Harlequin card table. I bought it from Mrs. Kandell last week." Molly lifted a series of three folding tops, and as she laid each down, she gave Janet a tiny smile. "Voilà!"

"Hmm, yeah, okay. It's cute."

"Cute is good, Janet," Molly said, "and add hard to find, so don't take less than what I marked. Okay, I've got to go. Call me on my cell if you need me." At the door, she turned. "Oh, if a Carrie Newsome comes in or calls, tell her I'll be back by five."

35

On her way to Trudy's, it struck Molly that she hadn't heard from Randall either. Then she remembered he'd gone to Palo Alto yesterday to have dinner with his daughter. In her final year at Stanford, they had finally stopped circling each other and made peace. Molly had met her briefly during the Christmas holidays. Randall brought her into the shop to do some last minute shopping. Tall, slim, and absolutely stunning, she'd been charming and promised to be back for another visit.

With little time to do any of her errands, Molly decided to just go right over to Trudy's. She might as well start organizing the mess in her office and pack it up. As she inched her way up the narrow street, she was relieved she could park in Trudy's driveway. Parking in Carmel, even the residential section, was challenging at best. Only one house away, she hit the brakes. A battered old van was blocking the driveway. About to hit the horn, Molly's hand stopped when she saw Milo Kraft on the porch, peering into the windows. She watched him shake the front door, then trot down the front stairs and run around the back. *He must have heard about Trudy. Damn him! What the hell does he think he's doing?* Was he going to rob the house in full daylight? But then, she wouldn't put much past him. Not one of her favorite people, Kraft was an antiques picker who gave an honorable profession a bad name. Pickers played an important role in the world of antiques. They hit the garage and estate sales, the flea markets and auctions, and sold directly to dealers. They were the legs of many a successful shop. But Milo Kraft was a bottom feeder, and made no bones about the fact he had access to fake collectibles of any kind. *You name it*, he'd told her when she first came to Carmel. *I can get any Tiffany lamp you want, desk sets too. All the Dirk van Earp copper you can think of, even Wedgwood Fairy stuff. Give me a list.*

She'd shown him the door in quick order and told him never to come back. Every time she ran into him at a garage sale, he gave her the finger. Naturally, she gave it back.

Ready to call Randall, she stopped searching her tote for her cell phone when she saw Milo Kraft going down the driveway to his van. Before she could blink, he was off and turning the corner. She decided not to call Randall. What could she tell him anyway? Kraft really hadn't done anything illegal.

Molly no sooner pulled into the driveway when the moving company estimator pulled up behind her. Inside, she handed him the list of furnishings, then showed him the rest of the house. She hesitated at Trudy's bedroom, then went in. "I've got to get some clothes for the funeral. I'll be just a minute."

Reaching into the closet, she quickly found a black suit, then changed her mind and pulled out a scarlet coat dress with black velvet lapels Trudy was fond of wearing. "Red is good luck in Japan,"

Molly said to the estimator. "She was going there next month on a buying trip."

Busy making notes, he hadn't heard her. Molly smiled. "You'd have knocked them dead in this, Trudy. No pun intended." Draping the dress over her arm, she said to him, "Okay, I'm fine now. Let's see the rest of the house."

Opening cabinets and closets, he said, "If you pack up her personal papers, and get her office stuff together, we can do this in about six hours. How's tomorrow around nine?"

"That's fine." Molly walked him to the door and locked it behind him, in case Milo Kraft decided to make a return visit. Dropping the dress on the sofa, she headed for Trudy's office. Staring at the mess on the desk, she realized she didn't have a box. Then she wondered who was supposed to contact Trudy's clients and pay any bills that might be due. What was she supposed to do with the invoices, bills, bank statements, and regular paperwork that needed attention? She decided to throw it all in a plastic bag and ask Lucero later. He'd be able to find out who Trudy's lawyer was and hand it over.

Finding a box of plastic trash bags in the kitchen, Molly remembered the termite people would be there in a few days and decided to empty the refrigerator first. After that, she set the few houseplants on the patio, then returned to the office and filled two large bags. Remembering there was a plant in Trudy's bedroom, Molly went back to get it.

Not wanting to linger earlier, she realized she'd left the double doors to the walk-in closet open. About to close them, she noticed a shelf full of wigs, of different colors and styles. Molly smiled. Knowing Trudy traveled frequently for shows, out of town clients, and buying trips, she assumed she took them along to make bad hair days fun. Stepping in closer to move a wig back from the edge of the shelf, her foot hit a suitcase on the floor under Trudy's jackets. She bent down to move it and was surprised at its weight. Pushing it aside, she noted a smaller one behind it, and found it just as heavy. Staring at the packed suitcases, Molly pondered whether to open them. Dismissing them as irrelevant, she checked her watch and realized she'd been there over two hours. Setting the plant outside the deck off the bedroom, she closed the door and called Janet from Trudy's office telephone.

Miracles do happen, she decided when Janet reported that all was well and had made three small sales. Setting down the phone, Molly noticed the blinking message light. Eager to be out of the house, she was happy to see it had a drop-in tape. The messages wouldn't be lost if she took it home. She could play the tape later, jot down the callers, and notify them of Trudy's death.

Placing the plastic bags filled with Trudy's paper-work in the back of the truck, she gave up doing her errands. She wasn't comfortable taking Trudy's personal files, and having them stolen in the open truck bed was a problem she didn't need. She returned to the shop, pulled into the alley, and parked the truck in the garage. Taking the answering machine with her, she went up the courtyard stairs to the apartment, set the answering machine on the counter, then went down to check on Janet. Molly smiled at the couple browsing and headed for her desk. When she didn't see Janet, and realized the music wasn't on, she thought Janet must be in the storage room changing discs. Stepping into the small room, she found Janet sound asleep on the tattered overstuffed chair. Careful to keep her voice low, Molly whispered, "Damnit, Janet! Wake up!"

Jumping from the chair, Janet nearly knocked her over. "Oh, gosh, I guess I dozed off. I mean, that darn Kenny G music you have just makes me drowsy, you know? I was going to change it, but I guess I—"

Furious, Molly said, "How long have you been in here?"

"Oh, I don't know. Uh, just after you called, I guess."

"That was over an hour ago!" Storming out of the room, Molly saw a woman leaving, and smiled at the couple coming her way. "Was there something that caught your eye? I'd be happy to help, if I can."

The man laughed. "We always knew Carmel was different, but a shop with no salespeople is really unique. We've been here for about fifteen minutes. We could have robbed you blind."

Flustered, Molly tried to smile as they walked to the wide open door. "My salesperson was ill. I, ah . . . I'm so sorry you were on your own. Please stop back when you have time."

Closing the door, Molly called for Janet to come out from the storage room. She'd never had to fire anyone, but she knew she had little choice. Back at her desk, she faced the young woman. "Look, this just isn't for you. Maybe you might think about working someplace that's more . . . more energetic. I'll call the office in the City and have your final check sent down, okay? We'll pay you for a full day today, but this isn't working."

"Okay. I'll just grab my backpack and go then, huh?"

"I think that's best. Oh, did a Carrie Newsome or anyone else call for me?"

"Uh, well I think I missed a call or two. I was outside having a smoke and didn't get back in time."

So much for feeling guilty, Molly thought as she glanced at the message light on the answering machine. It wasn't blinking. "Why is the machine off?"

"Hmmm, well, I might have turned it off by mistake when I tried to catch the phone."

"Did Bitsy stop in?"

"I . . . I don't think so. Maybe when I was, um, resting my eyes?"

CHAPTER 5

When Molly hadn't heard from Carrie by six-thirty, she closed the shop, then rushed upstairs to shower and change. About to leave, she was startled by a scratching sound on the French doors in the living room. Opening it, she was greeted by a gorgeous black and white cat. The soft mewing was so endearing, she immediately bent down and petted it. Cats ruled Carmel. The population outnumbered the human residents two to one. And that was a low estimate.

Before she could check for a collar, the cat slipped past her into the apartment. *Great, that's all I need now.* Closing the door behind her, she headed for the kitchen, assuming the cat had followed her nose and gone there. Finding it empty, Molly searched the living room and hoped the cat hadn't decided to hide under one of the sofas. On her knees, she checked both and found only dust balls. Next she tried her bedroom. No luck there. That left only the second bedroom, which she used to store merchandise that needed cleaning. Sure enough, the cat had found the large empty carton she used to carry merchandise up and down the stairs. Seeing it already curled up with its eyes closed, and knowing rain was on the agenda that night, she hadn't the heart to scoot it out. Instead, she tore open a new bag of cloth baby diapers she used to polish silver and tucked them around the purring cat. Shaking her head, she turned on a small lamp, then headed for the kitchen for the bag of cat food she kept on hand to feed the strays who gathered on her balcony each day. Returning with food and water, Molly realized she'd need a litter box, so she pulled out another box, shredded up some newspaper, and hoped that would work while she was gone.

The party for Dan Lucero was slated for eight. It was seven-thirty, and still no word from Carrie. Molly wasn't anxious to spend more time with her, but would at least have made the effort for Emma's sake. She knew Daria wouldn't mind if she'd brought Carrie to the party. She also realized that a meaningful reconciliation would have been dicey even if she hadn't seen her mother's cigarette case. Grabbing her raincoat and Lucero's gift, she looked at her watch once more. She had fifteen minutes to get to Daria's. The restaurant was only four blocks away, and since she'd missed her early morning walks on the beach for the past week, she decided to walk.

She was barely in the private banquet room when Randall stood towering over her with a grin on his face and a drink in his hand. "Ah, she comes bearing gifts. Look out, Lucero, she must have really ripped you good on those chairs you bought for your office."

Ignoring the dig, Molly brushed past him toward Lucero. "If you can't say something nice," she said over her shoulder, "then don't talk at all." Handing Lucero the gift, Molly smiled. "Happy birthday." She gave him a quick peck on the cheek. "And many more in good health. Open it later. I don't want to hear any more of Randall's wisecracks."

Giving Molly a hug, Lucero grinned, then said, "I'll drink to that. Thanks."

Molly edged her way to the bar through the crowd packed with people she didn't know. Somehow, Randall had gotten there ahead of her and was talking with two couples. After he made the introductions, he said, "I tried to get you today and no one answered the phone. You closed?"

"No. But I should have been. I was at Trudy's getting some clothes for the funeral, and I had to meet a moving estimator. Janet was outside smoking and missed two calls, then I found her asleep."

Turning to the two couples, Randall nodded, and led Molly away. "You have no business going to Trudy's house."

"Excuse me, but Max happens to own the house, and since Trudy has no relatives here, he asked me to get a move organized to put her stuff in storage. Daria, by the way, invited me to go with her to get a dress for the funeral home, only she . . . she, well, I went back today to take care of it." Turning away, she said, "I've had a stomach full today, so lay off."

"How the hell did you get in?"

"With a key?" Moving to the bartender, Molly said, "Jack Daniel's, please. Straight up."

"Add some soda to that. She's a lousy drinker," Randall said as he moved closer to her. "Listen, Molly, I'm having the house sealed tomorrow. Please tell me you didn't touch anything except the door handle."

"Sealed? Why?"

"Never mind. Standard procedure."

Thanking the bartender, Molly ignored Randall until she'd downed a good third of her drink. "I got a dress, and . . ." She was about to add the plastic bags from Trudy's office, then changed her mind. She didn't feel like being yanked outside and yelled at.

"And? And what?"

"And it's not standard procedure, and you know that I know that," she said, quickly recovering.

Turning away, watching the crowded room, he said, "New rules. Come down from on high."

"Bullshit," Molly whispered. "You don't have an 'on high.' You're it."

Giving her one of his squinty looks, he grinned. "You got that right. So butt out. It's none of your affair."

Grabbing his arm, Molly persisted. "What's going on? I have a right to know."

Randall laughed. "Really? Since when did you join the force?"

"Trudy Collins was my friend, that's enough for me."

"Is Randall giving you heat again?" Lucero said as he joined them. "Come on, give Molly a break. She gave me a good deal on those chairs for my office. In fact, I'm thinking of redoing my condo, and I'm shopping with Molly Doyle. Oh, I almost forgot, that guy that's staying with Bitsy . . . uh, what the hell is his name?"

"Oliver," Molly answered.

"Right. Oliver. He called Daria and sent their regrets. Bitsy's got the flu or something." Glancing around the room, Lucero said, "Every judge in the county is here, and half the lawyers. You think it's my sparkling personality or my job?"

"Neither," Randall said, "it's the free booze and Daria's food."

"I'd say it's your personality," Molly said. Giving Randall a nod, she added, "Your friend here could take some lessons."

Molly sometimes felt Randall could read her mind, and she was desperate to put some distance between them. Feeling anxious about the plastic bags in her truck, and certain Randall wasn't telling her the truth about ordering Trudy's house sealed, she slipped away from them when they turned to the bar for refills. She found Daria talking with two women who looked familiar. It took a moment, and then Molly remembered seeing them in the shop. One of them, she recalled, collected Victorian hat pins, which she didn't happen to have, and the other collected Belleek, the very thin and iridescent parian ware from Ireland. Being introduced all around, Molly discovered that both women were married to local judges.

The topic of conversation soon turned to golf. Daria took Molly's arm and nodded to the women, saying, "Excuse us. I want Molly to meet an old friend."

"That's always a good line when you want to split," Molly said as they moved away.

"I just can't take too much of the golf and society stuff. I hear it every day as it is. Listen, thanks for going back for a dress. I'm still reeling."

"I know. Me too. I got that red dress she loved." About to tell her Randall was having the house sealed, she saw Randall and Lucero coming their way.

Giving Daria a hug, Lucero said, "How about making my birthday complete by saying you'll marry me. Hell, even Father Jim said if our great-grandmothers were cousins, it's too far away to make us relatives."

"Get over it, will you?" Daria said.

"I'm serious." Winking at Molly and Randall, he added, "They can be our witnesses. We've even got two or three judges here right now."

"Not tonight, I've got a headache." Daria grinned as more well wishers joined them. She took advantage of the welcome distraction and huddled with

47

Molly, giving her the lowdown on some of the women in the room.

When the group moved on, Lucero nudged Randall and said, "Check out the blonde coming in with Ted Banks. Now that's what I call a knockout."

Molly nearly spilled her drink when she saw the newly arriving couple.

"I wonder where Ted's been hiding her," Lucero said.

"Could be she's the reason for the divorce," Daria said. "Maybe Molly's seen her around. Has she ever been in the shop?"

Molly took a deep sigh and gulped down her drink. "That's my sister, Carrie."

Eyeing the woman, Randall said, "Is that right."

"She showed up last night when I got home. She has a daughter too, ten or twelve I'd guess."

"I take it you're not too pleased to see her?" Daria said.

"Except for meeting a niece I didn't know I had, I'm not sure. It's been so many years since . . . well, since things went sour."

"Does that mean you don't think she's my type?" Lucero said.

Visions of her mother's cigarette case prompted Molly to say, "I don't think you'd want to find out."

"Well, put a smile on," Randall said, "they're heading in our direction."

Carrie was all smiles and outstretched arms when she approached Molly. The quick hug she gave Molly didn't keep her eyes from taking in her friends. "This is a small town! I had no idea you'd be here, Molly."

Pulling away, Molly said, "I have to admit I'm surprised to see you too." She watched Carrie's body language as her sister was introduced to Lucero, Daria, and then Randall. Lucero got the deference any lawyer owed a D.A., including a seductive smile. Daria, with her own strong aura, got a quick nod, but Randall got the full power of her attention. Holding onto his outstretched hand, Carrie said, "I'm staying in Pebble Beach. If I need a cop, can I call you?"

"I'm strictly Carmel. Try 911. The Sheriff's Department is real quick."

The flat tone of Randall's voice made Molly want to laugh. Instead, she smiled at Ted Banks. "I guess you're the attorney friend Carrie said she was meeting today."

"That's me. I'm hoping to convince her to stick around. Now that I know she's got family here, that makes my argument more valid."

Linking her arm in Ted's, Carrie said, "When Ted insisted I meet some of the area's heavy hitters to decide, I certainly didn't expect my big sister to be among them."

Stunned, but not enough to bite her tongue, Molly said, "Well, *little* sister, life is full of surprises. Where is Emma?"

"Another sister?" Ted laughed.

When Carrie didn't answer, Molly figured she'd

49

neglected to mention she had a child. "Oh, no, the two of us were all my poor father could handle. I'd hate to think what it would have been like with another Doyle girl. Emma is Carrie's daughter. I was so surprised to meet her." Turning to Daria, she said, "I had no idea I had a niece, and she's just adorable." Smiling at Carrie, she asked, "Emma's what? Ten? Twelve? Hard to tell these days. Girls mature so fast."

Carrie's smile failed to match her eyes. "Emma is twelve." Turning to Ted Banks, she said, "Twelve going on thirty. I swear that child is old beyond her years. Reads constantly! I hardly know she's around."

In spite of wanting to wipe that earlier smirk off her sister's face, Molly didn't want Emma to pay for Carrie's stupidity. It was clear she had left Emma alone at the hotel. Being a lawyer and in full knowledge of the child endangerment laws, the last thing Molly needed was to have the district attorney and the police chief know Emma was alone. "How lucky you found a sitter," Molly said.

"Yes," Carrie replied, "the hotel recommended a lovely young woman."

"Well, folks," Daria said, "I need Molly for a few minutes. Nice to meet you, Carrie." Taking Molly away, she leaned down and whispered, "She left the little girl alone, right? You saved her ass damn quick there. You didn't tell me your sister was here."

"I didn't have time. She showed up out of the blue last night."

Surprised to see Carrie, and worried about Emma alone in a hotel room, Molly completely forgot to tell Daria that Randall was sealing Trudy's house. Spending the rest of the evening avoiding Carrie, Molly glued a smile on her face and went out of her way talking to people she'd never met. When Randall finally caught up with her an hour later, he said, "So, the kid is all alone in a posh room at Spanish Bay, huh?"

"How do you know where she's staying?" Molly asked.

"She gave me her room number."

"What?"

"Yeah, said she'd like to get to know me better. Hell, I might take her up on it. Could be novel having dinner with a woman who doesn't want to argue all the time."

"You're lying. Besides, you're not her type."

"Yeah? What makes you think that?"

"You're too bossy. Carrie needs to have the upper hand."

"I think it runs in the family."

Staring him down, Molly said, "She didn't really, did she?"

Randall saw the twitch over Molly's eye slowly begin to pulse. Keeping a straight face, he said, "Would you really care?"

"Randall!"

"I overheard her tell someone."

When the party began to wind down toward eleven, Molly was tired of watching Carrie fawn over every man in the room. And when her sister had made a crack earlier about the simple black dress she was wearing, Molly barely hid her annoyance. "Oh, Molly is always the perfectly groomed lady. I find simple clothes boring, don't you?" She'd said it to Daria, who was wearing a to-die-for Chinese embroidered tunic over silk pants, which made Carrie's sequined jacket look gauche.

"Not at all," Daria had replied. "Elegant women can get away with simplicity. It never works for me." Pretending not to hear the exchange, Molly had to hold back from hugging Daria.

An hour later Molly figured it was a reasonable time to leave without looking like she was bothered by her sister's presence. Covering a yawn, she said, "I'm going home." Setting her drink on the table, she added, "I'm a working girl, and I need my sleep."

Randall, who had been sitting quietly while Daria and Lucero greeted guests, said, "Don't give her the satisfaction. You belong here. She doesn't."

"That's the nicest thing you've said to me all night."

"Besides, you can't drive. You're close to being looped."

"I *am* not. And I walked." Giving Randall a look, she added, "And that's not why I'm leaving."

Shoving a cigarette between her lips, Molly smoked up a storm all the way home. She knew leaving was the coward's way out. She should have stayed until the end. But she was damned if she'd let Carrie get her game going again. When she stopped in front of the shop, she stared bleary-eyed at the front window. There was no point to stay and be further goaded into snapping back. Carrie would love that. How many times had she pulled this before? Almost to the day she'd turned fifteen, the smart mouth came alive. It didn't matter where they were; family holiday gatherings, friends over for dinner or barbecue. It never stopped. The oneupmanship became part of the menu. *If she was hoping I'd leave with my tail between my legs, she won.* Molly wasn't sure which bothered her more, that or her obvious flirting with Randall. Every time Carrie got near them, she'd be sure to touch his arm.

She told herself she ought to just turn around and go back. But feeling the effect of several drinks, she decided discretion was the better part of valor. Daria would understand. Lucero probably wouldn't notice, and she didn't give a damn what Randall thought. But it was the last time she would let Carrie get under her skin. She'd discovered a wonderful life here, and no one, especially Carrie, was going to ruin it.

Peeking into the spare bedroom at the cat, all thoughts of her sister faded away. Moving slowly to the big carton, careful not to spook her new boarder, Molly stretched out on the floor and petted him. She thought about the kitten she once had when she was a child. She'd loved the little gray with brown stripes and had named it Tiger. When her mother became allergic and they'd had to give it away, she'd cried for days. Listening to the loud purring, she smiled. "Guess you've moved in, huh?" Holding back a yawn, she eyed the big black and white, then said, "I think I'll call you Tiger."

CHAPTER 6

Molly fumbled for the ringing telephone and looked at the clock beside her bed. It was seven and she'd overslept again. The days were flying by too fast. She could hardly believe it was already Wednesday. The blaring voice on the other end made her sit up like a shot.

"Why didn't you give me a heads-up about the exterminators?"

"Don't yell! I forgot about it!" Pulling the phone away from her ear, she took a deep breath and said, "I had enough on my mind."

"The damn house had a tent around it when we showed up this morning to seal it."

"You should have done whatever you do yesterday. It's not my fault you're too late!" Slamming down the phone, she got out of bed, pulled on her sweats, and stomped to the kitchen to turn on the coffee. "Damn cop! I don't need this. I really don't," she blurted. Looking out the kitchen window, searching for a Zen moment, Molly stared at the towering pine trees. Gently swaying from the breeze coming in from Carmel

Bay, and cloaked in a light fog, the delicate scent of wet pine was soothing. Something was up if Randall was sealing Trudy's house. Maybe it was a new procedure when a person died without family nearby to take care of things. She wanted to believe he was telling the truth, but she had a feeling he wasn't. The only other reason was too bizarre to consider. She told him she hadn't touched anything. How was she going to explain the plastic bags in the garage? He was going to kill her for sure.

The soft mewing startled her. And then she remembered her new guest. Behind her, sitting still, like a well-behaved child, the cat was staring up. "Good morning, Tiger. I forgot all about you." Picking him up, Molly laughed as he licked her chin. "You need a grooming, pal. If you're going to stick around here, we've got to give you a bath. But not now. I've got a ton to do today."

Heading for the shower, the ringing phone caught her halfway. Running back to the bedroom for the portable, ready to tell Randall to go to hell, she was surprised to hear Carrie's voice. "Your police chief may be an ex-big-time cop, but he's a lousy liar. Did he really think I'd believe you left the party because your shop alarm went off? I think you were drunk, Molly dear, and I hope it wasn't because I showed up."

So Randall felt a need to cover for her. Now she had little choice but to go along with his story. "Oh, come on, Carrie! Randall wasn't making excuses for me. By the time the officer and I checked to see if anything was missing, it was late, and I didn't feel like going back."

"He's really a hunk. You could do worse. Listen, I've got to take off for an interview in San Francisco, can Emma spend the day with you?"

"Today?" She hesitated a moment, annoyed as hell with the imposition, and finally said, "Sure." Distracted by the knocking on the French door in the living room, she added, "Hold on. Someone's knocking—oh, she's here already? Ah, Carrie, it might have been—" Before she could finish, Carrie hung up.

Molly unlocked the door and saw Emma standing there in the heavy drizzle with a suitcase in her hand. *Damn, Carrie!* she thought. *How dare she have this child standing on my balcony in this weather! What if I'd said no?* "Well, good morning. Hurry in, you'll get soaked."

"I promise not to be a bother," Emma said. "I have my books to read. And I just had breakfast downstairs at that cute place where we met you yesterday. So, you won't have to worry about feeding me." By the time the poor child got this all out, she was nearly breathless.

"Don't be silly, you're not a bother." Stepping out on the balcony, Molly looked down. "Go on in, I'll just run down to see your mother for a moment."

"She left an hour ago. She dropped me off here and told me to be upstairs at eight sharp."

"Oh, really. Well, then, uh, make yourself comfortable. I've got to shower still." Staring at the suitcase, Molly said, "That isn't filled with books, is it?"

"No. Just my things. Mother said she might have to stay overnight."

"Oh. Overnight. Well, if that's the case, I hope you won't mind sleeping on the sofa. My extra bedroom doesn't have a bed, and it's filled with—"

"The sofa is fine. It's so comfy, I fell asleep the other night, remember?"

Indeed Molly did. She also remembered Carrie's sharpness with Emma when she'd knocked the cup of cocoa on the floor. "Swell. Look, Emma, why don't you pull out one of your books while I get ready for work, and then you can come downstairs with me while I open. Sound like a plan?"

Emma gave Molly a tentative nod, then said, "Is it still okay if I call you Aunt Molly?"

Leaning down, almost eye-to-eye, Molly said, "I'd certainly be pleased if you did. After all, I *am* your aunt, and I am so happy to know you finally."

"That's nice of you to say that. I'm happy to meet you too. You could call me Em if you want."

"I'd love to."

"But not when Mother's around. She doesn't like it. She says nicknames are tacky."

"It's a deal."

Touched by the child's sweetness, Molly hurried

into the bathroom to shower. Toweling off, she replayed their telephone conversation. So, Randall had made up an excuse for her, did he? She was surprised to find she was actually touched. And then she remembered Emma's suitcase. Carrie didn't bother to mention she wouldn't be back today. Typical. Finishing her makeup, she hoped Carrie didn't get the job. Strapping on the inexpensive Timex she wore at the shop, she edited that thought. Better San Francisco than Carmel.

Molly found Emma with Tiger curled up on her lap. "I love cats. I wish I had one."

"I had one once, but that was a long time ago. This little prince just adopted me last night."

"Mother said they were dirty and were full of fleas. Oh, I almost forgot the other thing I was supposed to say. I promise not to do anything that might make you angry."

"I don't think that will be a problem. You're one of the best mannered young ladies I've met in a long time." Giving her what she hoped was a reassuring smile, Molly added, "Let's run down to Tosca's. I usually stop there every morning before I open. I'm addicted to espresso and Bennie's apple cake."

"That's what I had."

"Great. Think you can handle another?"

When Emma nodded, Molly laughed. "Ah, a girl after my heart. Come on, let's go."

⋆　　⋆　　⋆

Molly saw Randall sitting inside Tosca's and considered turning back, but it was too late. He'd seen her and was waving her over. "Looks like a friend wants us to sit with him."

When Molly introduced Emma, she was pleased to see Randall rise. Molly smiled and waved at Bennie, who was already on the way with espresso for her. "Thanks for taking care of my niece this morning. I didn't know she'd be here this early." It was a small lie, but she didn't want them to think the poor kid had been dumped on her doorstep.

"No problemo. Your sister told me she was going to be staying with you for a while, so I let her come in before I opened."

"Did she?"

"Yeah, she said she had to go up to the City for a few days, then down to L.A. It's great for you to have family around, Molly."

When Molly saw Emma's face redden, she quickly said, "It's a great chance for Emma and I to get to know each other."

"Yeah, quality time, I think they call it," Randall said.

Giving him a look, Molly said, "Well, what brings you here this morning?"

Fiddling with his cup, Randall replied, "I had a few things to go over with you, but I guess it can wait."

"Am I in the way?" Emma asked. "If this is adult time, I can move to another table."

"Adult time? What on earth does that mean?"

"That's what Mother tells me when she wants me to leave the room."

Randall's smile was surprisingly gentle. "Nope, nothing like that. I just had a few questions for your auntie here. Nothing important." Rising, he said, "I've got to see some people. I'll stop by later."

Watching him leave, Molly wondered if Randall knew she'd taken Trudy's files. Could someone have seen her leaving yesterday with those plastic bags in the truck? Then again, why would he know unless he was questioning people? More to the point, why would that even be necessary?

Besides being a welcome distraction, showing Emma around the shop turned out to be more fun than Molly had expected, especially when she looked up and saw the whimsical painted ceiling with it sun, moon, and fairies.

"Oh, this is so pretty. I didn't notice much the other night," Emma said, looking up at the ceiling. "I could spend hours here and never be bored." Glancing around the showroom, she asked, "Does all this belong to you?"

"Not everything. My boss, Max Roman, owns the shop and the building. A few of the pieces are mine. He lets me put my own buys in with his merch."

"What?"

Molly laughed, then explained, "Antique dealer lingo. Short for merchandise. And we often call our precious things 'stuff.' Keeps us grounded."

"Is it okay if I look around?"

"Be my guest. I've got some computer work to do, so have fun."

Molly watched her stop, fold her arms, and stare at a display of leather-bound books on a Regency chest, then move to a silk-covered Louis XIV style chair. Emma gently ran her fingers over the fabric, then quickly pulled them away. After a moment, she leaned over and examined a small silver hunt cup sitting next to a gilt-framed photo of Isadora Duncan that she had found in an old magazine. "Is everything here an antique?" Emma asked.

"No. Some are 'almosts.' I mean not a hundred years old yet."

Pointing to a group of desk accessories, Emma asked, "What's that inkwell made of? It looks kind of pebbly."

"Ah, one of my favorites. It's called 'shagreen.' Would you laugh if I told you that pebbly stuff came from the bottom of the sea?"

Emma's eyes lit up and she gave Molly a big smile. "I'll try not to."

"Deal. Shagreen is the skin of a dogfish. It's a species of shark, and it's a close relative to the stingray. The true color is off-white, and often dyed before it hardens. It was used in the seventeenth century for fine objects, and then became popular again in the Art Deco period of the 1920s. This dark green color was the most popular." Picking up the inkwell, Molly explained, "Now this group is English, and the reason you can tell is because they usually used ivory or silver where the material was joined." Showing Emma the fine seams, she added, "And the English preferred to sand and polish the surface, while the French didn't. It was very expensive to work with because the skin had to be treated almost immediately or it would rot. Since it's so durable, many pieces have survived. The French made beautiful furniture with it and it was very expensive."

"If it's a fish, how come it's called shagreen?"

"It's from the Turkish *saghri*. They first used it when they discovered it was excellent for sheaths and sword handles."

"Oh." After thinking that over, she said, "Do you ever wonder who used to own these things? I mean, what kind of people they were?" Before Molly could answer, Emma turned back to the photo. "If they were happy people? With families?"

The wistful tone of Emma's questions were not lost on Molly. She moved to the girl and placed an arm around her shoulder. "I wonder all the time. And then I wonder about the artisan who made the object. Who was the furniture maker? The glass blower, the potter? The artist? Who painted those lovely flowers or figures on the porcelain?" Giving her a gentle squeeze, she said, "Oh, yes, I wonder . . . with every new piece."

Thinking that over for a minute, Emma wandered over to a French armoire. Running her fingers over the brass escutcheons, she asked, "Where do you get all this . . . stuff?"

Molly let out a long sigh, then said, "Ah, the major question! Well, I go to estate and garage sales, Max sends a lot down from the City, and sometimes people will call me with things they want to sell. A lot comes from auctions."

Molly was surprised to see Emma's face light up. "I'd love to go to an auction someday," she said. "I bet it's fun."

"It's the best show in town."

"But I probably will have to wait until I grow up. Mother only buys new things."

The child's genuine interest in many of the items surprised Molly, and helped keep her mind off Randall's wanting to talk to her. When her first customer of the day arrived, Emma quietly headed for the storage room with a book. "Mother said to be sure not to get in the way."

"You're not in the way. Just get that out of your head. You can read out here."

"People might wonder why I'm not in school. I don't want you to get in trouble."

Molly couldn't fault her logic. She certainly didn't need to have Social Services on her case. "Good thinking. How about going upstairs, then? You can check on Tiger, read, or watch TV."

Watching her climb the stairs, Molly called out, "There's not much in the fridge, but help yourself." When Emma turned and smiled, Molly was struck by how similar the tilt of her head and tiny smile reminded her of her mother, as well as the color of her hair and the oval shape of her face. It was a wonder she hadn't noticed the resemblance earlier. But then, she'd been so absorbed with seeing her sister again, it wasn't a wonder Emma had been relegated to the shadows. Turning away, she fought back the lump in her throat. What irony that Carrie, who was so indifferent to their mother, should be the one to have a child so like her.

The next ringing of the bell over the door snapped Molly from her reverie. Fixing her shop smile on full throttle, she nodded to the woman arriving, who immediately put up her hand and tersely said, "Don't bother, I'm just going to browse."

Molly kept her smile in place. "Please do." She turned away and sighed. Could this be the portent of the rest of the week? The sadness of Trudy's death had its own compartment in her mind, but she hadn't dialed up for the rest of the surprises. Carrie showing up out of the blue, with a child, yet. The two bags of personal papers in her truck she neglected to tell Randall about, a cat who decided to move in, and babysitting a child she didn't know. Of course, having Janet screw up didn't help either.

Heading for the storage room to slip in a soothing disc that might defrost the woman wandering around the shop, she stopped suddenly by a display table and stared at the spot where three leather books and a pair of sterling salt

65

cellars once reposed. The few sales yesterday were for two lamps and one vintage tapestry pillow. Slowing moving toward the display window facing Ocean Avenue, purposely keeping out of the way of the browsing woman, Molly discovered another missing hole in her layout. A pair of good English brass candlesticks were gone. Feeling a flush of anger creep up her neck, her eyes searched the room, hoping the missing items might have been picked up and set down elsewhere. Customers often did that with something that interested them, only to find something else, and then just set the piece down wherever they happened to be.

Molly moved around the shop, discreetly eyeballing every table, chest, and any surface she might use for display. Knowing every piece in the shop like the back of her hand, she felt some relief to know everything else was still in place. The missing items had probably been lifted when Janet was napping in the storage room. Her visions of throttling Janet were interrupted when the woman tapped her on the shoulder. "I'm interested in those leather wing chairs, but not at your price. If you'll let them go for half, I'll take them."

Surprised by the woman's audacity in thinking she'd go from four thousand to two thousand, Molly bit back a terse remark and said instead, "I couldn't possibly go that low." Giving her a weak smile, she added, "I'd lose my job."

When the woman shook her head and left, Molly was about to call her back, but stopped. It was too much of a knock, but she could have countered and didn't. Furious with herself for being so stubborn, she made a beeline for the storage room and lit a cigarette. Puffing madly, she didn't care if anyone walked in on her. She reached for the can of air freshener, began spraying the small room, and nearly choked on the fumes. When she heard the bell ring again, she stubbed out the cigarette and tried to get a smile back in place.

"Oh, it's you. I could have finished my smoke, damn it."

"I ought to run you in," Randall said. "You can't keep breaking the law and think I'm going to ignore it."

"Arrest me, then. Maybe some time in your jail will teach me a little humility."

"It's been a day already? You haven't been open long."

"I just blew a huge sale." Going back into the storage room, she lit another cigarette. When Randall followed her, he helped himself to coffee, then plopped down on the tattered chair. "You need to get another chair in here."

Fanning the smoke with her hand, Molly laughed. "When I find one as lovely, I will."

"I need to get Trudy's show merch. Where is it?"

Molly knew she should have realized that was what he'd planned to talk to her about at Tosca's.

If he wanted Trudy's stuff from the show, something was definitely up. She didn't dare let him in the garage. Now that he knew she'd been to Trudy's house, he might wonder about the plastic bags in the truck. "In the garage. But," she quickly added, "Robbie forgot to bring back the key after he left them there."

"How about giving him a call. I'll wait."

Setting her cigarette in the ashtray, Molly turned away and poured a cup of coffee. "He's fishing with his father," she lied. "I'll leave a message." Facing him now, she said, "That okay?"

"A day trip, or what?"

"Gosh, I don't know."

"*Gosh?* You sound like a little kid about to swear you didn't eat the last cookie."

"I'm trying to modify my vocabulary, okay? I've got a child around for a few days."

"By the way, you skated over that little surprise pretty well. So your sister dumped the kid on you, huh?"

"She's not a *kid*. I hate that term. Kids belong to goats. She's a child. And yes, she damn well did, and when she gets back, I'm going to tell her—"

"She's not coming back," Emma said as she stepped inside the storage room.

Molly's face collapsed. Turning to face Emma, she blurted, *"What?"*

"Mother left a letter in my suitcase. I just found it when I opened it for my new book." Handing it to Molly, she said, "She put five hundred dollars with it, and the telephone number of the people I stay with when she goes out of town. She said they would take me if you didn't want me."

CHAPTER 7

It was hard for Molly to keep shock and anger from her face as she read the letter. In a typical lawyer's tone, void of emotion, it offered little apology. Carrie stated that she had never been cut out to be a mother and Emma was better off without her. It was apparent, she went on to say, that Emma was taken with her, and considering Molly's marital predicament, and her age, she would probably never have children, so now she was offering her a housebroken, ready-made daughter. She concluded by saying she was taking a job with a law firm that had an office in Japan, and would be out of the country for some time.

The stoic but dignified look on Emma's face tore at Molly's heart. Opening her arms, she embraced and hugged her. "Oh, Emma, I'm so sorry." Feeling the child's stiffness, Molly squeezed harder. "Of course I want you." Pulling back, she said, "In fact, I'm looking for a new assistant. Think you might want the job?"

When Emma finally managed a smile, Molly said, "I can't pay much, but room and board is included. And I can throw in a daily ration of Bennie's apple cake."

Emma murmured, "Is this a trial run or a real deal?"

"As real as it gets. Okay?"

"Okay. I liked you right away, so maybe it'll work."

"Ditto. Uh, what about your father? I mean, what if he—"

"He died a long time ago. I never knew him."

Randall's discreet cough reminded them of his presence. Wiping the tears hovering at the edge of Emma's eyes, Molly said, "Then I guess we're clear." She turned to Randall. "We need to talk to Lucero and make this legal."

Randall cleared his throat again, touched by Emma and proud of the way Molly had handled it. "Considering how much he owes you, he'll do it personally. How about I set up a meet for to-night? We can celebrate with dinner at Daria's." He laughed. "Hell, I'll even buy. How's that sound, Ms. Emma?"

Easing away from Molly, Emma said, "I'm good for it."

"You are, huh? Okay! Oh, and Molly, get me that key."

"Right, the key. I'll do it."

When Randall left, Molly said, "It helps to have the chief of police and the district attorney as friends." They both stared at each other for a moment, then broke out in giggles.

"That felt good," Emma said.

"It sure did!" Brushing back Emma's dark curls, Molly said, "First thing we have to get settled is something called honesty. I'm royally pissed with your mother for doing this to you. But I'm happy it happened here, with me."

Folding the letter in half, Molly put it in her pocket. "I guess you know the letter was addressed to me."

"Yes, and I'm sorry I opened it. But I had to know." Sitting cross-legged on the floor, Emma added, "I was afraid she was telling you to send me back to Seattle."

Noticing Emma's smile was gone, she thought about that for a moment. "And if she had?"

"Well, I'd have to figure out some way to talk you out of it."

"But how could you know what was in the letter?"

"Mother told me it wasn't working with us. So I figured it out."

Molly was shocked. "She told you that? Oh, my God!" When she saw a frown deepen Emma's forehead, she wanted to cry for her.

"I've known for a long time she wasn't the mother type. I've learned to deal with it."

Emma's perception, and what appeared to be unemotional acceptance of her mother's short-comings, bordered on being spooky, and it totally unnerved Molly. "Good God in Heaven!" she nearly screeched.

"Aunt Molly, please, get hold of yourself. It's not the end of the world."

As she watched Emma head for the staircase to the apartment, it wasn't hard to notice the slump in her shoulders or the way her hand dangled over the iron railing as she slowly climbed each stair. Molly's heart cried for the child, but she knew that further discussion would only make matters worse.

It wasn't easy concentrating on selling antiques that afternoon, but she did manage to sell a very nice butler's secretary for $2,800. Bearing in mind that the sum constituted a fair day, she decided to close at five-thirty instead of seven. Time enough to check on Bitsy, get the plastic bags from Trudy's locked in the storage cabinets in the garage, and decide what to do to prepare the second bedroom upstairs for Emma. Emma, she discovered, had only two pair of jeans, three shorts, four tee shirts, one sweatshirt, a nightie, and three books in her suitcase. She hadn't a clue where the rest of Emma's clothes were. And she didn't want to ask. She feared that what she saw was all there was.

Just before leaving for dinner, Molly called Bitsy. Relieved to finally get her, she was concerned by the weakness in her voice. "Oh, darling, stop worrying," Bitsy said. "It's just one of those nasty flus. I'll bounce back in a few days."

"Is there anything I can do?" Molly inquired.

"Oliver and Josie are taking good care of me. I'm so happy Oliver is here. He's been marvelous. The man can't do enough for me. I guess the shock over Trudy and this little bug just got the best of me. Any news about the funeral?"

"Ah, no. Not yet. I'll let you know as soon as I hear."

"Who's arranging it? Frankly, as well as I knew her, she never mentioned family."

"That's what Max said. He's made arrangements. I'll check with Randall. Maybe he can give us some information."

"Randall? What the hell has he got to do with Trudy's funeral?"

Molly wanted to kick herself for bringing Randall's name up. Bitsy Morgan was the doyenne of the Carmel grapevine. While not a malicious gossip, she wasn't above letting her wide circle of friends know she had an exclusive bead on the comings and goings of the village. "Uh, nothing. I just meant he could tell me who to call."

When Bitsy didn't reply, Molly said, "Hello? You still there?"

"Yes, darling, I'm here. This damn phone is acting up again. It keeps going on and off. The joys of living in Pebble Beach! Some of the telephone wires are older than me. I'll have Oliver look into it for me."

When Molly hung up, she hoped she'd convinced Bitsy nothing was up. Checking her watch, she called Emma. "Time to go."

As they walked to Daria's, Molly said, "Okay, here's the plan. I've got a dresser and an Art Deco brass twin bed in the garage that will look great in your room. They need a little sprucing up, but between us, we can have it ready in no time. I'll get Robbie over tomorrow to haul it upstairs. Sound good?"

When Emma didn't answer, Molly looked around and saw the girl a few feet behind her, staring across the street. "Emma?"

Turning slowly back to Molly, Emma said, "I thought I saw a man Mother was talking to the other day at the aquarium."

Following Emma's gaze, Molly's eyes narrowed when she saw Milo Kraft talking to an art gallery owner. "Do you mean the man in the shirt and tie?"

"No. The one with the dirty hat. I didn't like him. He gave me the creeps."

Taking Emma's hand, Molly quickly said, "Hey, it's getting late. We have three more blocks to go." Not wanting Milo Kraft to see them or recognize Emma, she added, "It's getting cold, better put your hood up." Walking as fast as Emma's legs could manage, Molly tried to digest the impossible connection between her sister and Milo Kraft.

As they entered Daria's, Emma's mood seemed to lighten. Her eyes lit up as she took in the stunning restaurant. "Oh, wow! This is like the movies. All the hanging lights look like diamonds dripping from the sky. And there's big vases of flowers everywhere! I can't go in here in jeans!"

Thinking about Milo Kraft, Molly almost didn't

hear her. "Don't worry. We're having dinner in Daria's private room." Leading Emma down a plush carpeted hall, Molly paused for a moment to show her the oil paintings on the wall. "The artist is a friend of Daria's. Her name is Mackie O'Brien and she'll be coming back from Europe next month. I wanted you to see what a fine artist she is."

"Do I have to know about artists if I decide to be an antiques dealer?"

Surprised, yet pleased by her interest earlier, Molly smiled. "It helps. Thinking about the future, are you?"

"I'm keeping my options open."

When they entered Daria's sanctuary, they found that Randall and Lucero had already made a dent in a huge platter of antipasto. Both men rose, and Randall introduced Emma. Then Daria appeared, and they quickly made Emma feel at home.

Eyeing the lovely room with its Country French furniture and bistro posters, Emma asked Daria, "Do you live here too?"

"No. This is my getaway room. And it's for my special friends when they want to relax and sometimes talk private stuff."

Looking at Lucero, Emma said, "Like tonight, I guess. Are you the man who's going to help me stay with Aunt Molly?"

"I sure am. But it's going to take some doing. So for now, if anyone asks, you're on school vacation. That way you won't have to hide out."

Turning to Molly, Emma's eyes glistened, "Then I can come downstairs sometimes and learn about antiques."

Molly blew Lucero a kiss, then said, "Yes."

"Not tonight, please," Randall said. He pulled a chair out for Emma. "Come on, squirt, sit next to me. I'm starved and I don't want to get your Aunt Molly started on merch, okay?"

Taking her seat, Emma said, "You can call me Em."

"Em, huh? Okay, that's good." Winking at Molly, he said, "By the way, did you get that key back?"

"It's on my desk whenever you're ready."

"Good. I'll be by first thing in the morning."

As each course arrived, Daria and Lucero thankfully kept the conversation going, explaining the various dishes to Emma. Molly's brain was on overload trying to figure out how her sister knew Milo Kraft, and it was all she could do to nod and smile. While their meeting at the aquarium could have been a coincidence, it was highly unlikely. Milo Kraft didn't seem like an aquarium kind of guy. Molly caught herself stabbing at her food every time her mind asked, *How did Carrie know Kraft?*

Her mental probing was interrupted by a sudden outburst of giggles from Emma when Lucero said to her, "Except for your curly hair, you even look like Harry Potter! Is this a book I should read?"

"Hey, don't get cute, Lucero," Randall said, "it's a hell of a book."

"You've read it?" Molly asked.

"Sure. Every one." With silence and dropped jaws as a response, Randall laughed. "What? You thought I couldn't read?"

"But . . . *Harry Potter*?" Daria asked.

Paying attention to his pasta con pesto, Randall said, "Why the hell not? It's not just for kids. Adventure is adventure, no matter how you slice it."

"I could learn to love you," Emma said with a straight face.

Giving Randall a tiny smile, Molly added, "It won't be easy."

Looking up from his dish, Randall eyed Molly for a moment. "Never said it would be."

Holding Randall's hand as he walked them home, Emma said, "I think I'm going to like living here. Carmel is so pretty and clean. I love all the pine trees, and having the ocean down the street. It's nice and quiet and it feels kind of cozy." Lifting her head, she said, "I can even smell the smoke from people's fireplaces. And all the shops are snuggled together like old friends. Best of all, there's no noise at night."

Glancing at Randall, Molly said, "The people are pretty great too. You met some of the very best tonight."

Molly's mood was broken the minute they stopped in front of the shop and Randall said, "I'll be by around eight tomorrow morning to get Trudy's stuff. That work for you?"

"Perfect," Molly replied.

★   ★   ★

Pulling a pillow and blanket from her bed, and sheets from the linen closet, Molly moved Tiger to Emma's lap and set up her bed on the sofa. "We'll get your room put together tomorrow, and then we'll go shopping after I close. You need some clothes, I see."

"I have the money she left. We can use that."

Referring to her mother as *she* was not lost on Molly. Had Emma already relegated her mother to a distant planet?

"That's yours. Save it for something special." Holding back a yawn, Molly said, "I'm ready for bed. If you want to read a little, go ahead. But don't stay up too late. I get up early. In fact, once we get your room done, we'll try to get to the beach for a walk if I don't oversleep."

"Is the beach here cold?"

"The water is like ice. It's also very dangerous, so you'll have to stay with me and not get near the surf. Deal?"

"Deal. Is it okay if Tiger sleeps with me?"

"Since he's purring away like crazy on your lap, I think he's already decided that."

Cranking open the window over the sink in the kitchen just slightly, Molly returned to the living room and found Emma with an open book propped on the blanket and yawning. "If you listen real close, you'll hear the surf crashing down at the beach. I open my bedroom window a little at night and it puts me right to sleep." Emma's nod told Molly she was already on the way. It was no wonder, she thought. It had been quite a day for them both.

It was almost four A.M. when Molly shot up in bed and swore, "Shit!" Somewhere between shivering with only one blanket, rubbing her feet to keep them warm, and one eye on the clock, she remembered that Trudy's answering machine was still on the passenger seat in the truck.

Throwing on her sweats, she quietly eased out of the apartment through the French doors in her bedroom, tiptoed across the balcony, and hurried down the freezing tile steps to the courtyard. She was in and out of the garage in less than ten minutes. Clambering back up the stairs, she prayed Emma hadn't heard the squeaking door. In her bedroom again, she wondered where to hide the machine. Placing it in the back of her closet, she climbed back into bed, sweats and all. Snuggling under the blanket, warm at last, she finally began to doze, then shot up in bed again. The French doors in her bedroom had been unlocked when she went to the garage. Staring at the doors, she mentally backtracked to the last time she'd opened them, and couldn't remember.

CHAPTER 8

Randall and two of his officers were standing by the garage door promptly at eight the next morning. Molly greeted them with a cheerful smile and unlocked the doors. Robbie had placed Trudy's boxes and props at the far end of the garage, so Molly had to move the El Camino. Back in the garage, she pulled out a red marking pen and drew an X on Trudy's boxes. "This way," she smiled at Randall, "you'll be sure to get everything."

"Clever. God forbid we should take some treasure of yours and deprive you of ripping off some unwary customer."

"So true," Molly said.

Emma, standing next to Molly, quickly said, "I like him, Aunt Molly. Can we keep him?"

"He's all yours, Em."

"That's all I need. Two smart aleck broads to give me grief."

Watching the two officers load the boxes into a van, Emma said, "If your policemen would take that brass bed and small chest over in the corner upstairs for my new bedroom, I promise

I'll talk to Aunt Molly about being a little nicer to you."

Molly's jaw dropped, and Randall burst out laughing.

Standing with her arms crossed, Emma asked, "Deal?"

"I'll even help them," Randall said, trying to keep a straight face. "But just this once, okay? These men are police officers, not dockhands."

"I understand," Emma said. "But isn't *serve* part of their job?"

Randall turned away so she wouldn't see the grin on his face. Heading over to the two officers at the van, he turned back and said to Molly, "Get her out of here before I run her in."

With the brass bed and dresser in place, and all the merchandise-in-waiting shoved aside, Molly and Emma surveyed the room. "We need sheets, blankets, and pillows for starters." Molly said, "and a lamp so you can read." Pausing for a moment, she added, "And a night table and desk. I think we better make up a list and hit the garage sales this weekend. We'll get your bedding tonight after I close."

"Can we have dinner at Wendy's?"

"Are you kidding? We eat real food around here."

"Like we had last night?"

Molly laughed. "Uh, well, not quite that grand."

While Emma was upstairs cleaning the brass bed, Molly rushed to open on time. Performing her morning ritual of spraying air freshener, light dusting, and a quick vacuum, she was ready to unlock the door just a few minutes past ten. When she heard the bell over the door ring, she felt the great jolt of excitement another day of selling antiques always brought. The smile on her face dimmed when she saw Bitsy Morgan move to a tall ebonized planter she'd bought at Trudy's last sale. "I'd put a real plant in here, darling. These silk things just attract dust."

"My God! You look terrible," Molly blurted.

Bitsy's eyes barely flickered. "This flu was the nastiest I've ever had. I'm still not up to par, but I couldn't stand staying at home one moment longer."

At her side, Molly took Bitsy's arm and steered her to the first chair at hand. "Get off your feet and I'll bring you some tea."

Sinking into the soft folds of a leather armchair, Bitsy waved her off. "If I drink another cup of that damn stuff, I'll scream. Oliver swears up and down about its powers, but I'm getting to hate it." With what seemed like an effort, Bitsy smiled at Molly. "Even that instant coffee junk you drink would be better." Patting the Chanel bag slung over her shoulder, she said, "I've got a little something here to zing it up."

Back with a tray and two cups of coffee, Molly set it on a low table and held Bitsy's cup while the older woman pulled out a silver flask and topped it off. Taking a quick sip, Bitsy sighed. "Ah, I almost feel human now."

Shaking her head, Molly asked, "Have you seen your doctor?"

"Honey, it's just the flu. I'll bounce back in a day or two." Setting down her cup, Bitsy leaned in closer to Molly. "What the hell is going on with Trudy's funeral? Why haven't arrangements been made yet? There hasn't even been a notice on the obit page."

Bitsy's perfectly made-up face couldn't hide the haggard pallor of her skin, and Molly was becoming more worried by the minute. "Max made arrangements. It's just that . . . well, her body hasn't been released yet."

"Why the hell not?" Bitsy demanded.

"I don't know."

"Well, I'm going to call Randall and—"

"Aunt Molly? Excuse me, but I've run out of brass polish," Emma said as she came down the stairs.

Oh, no! Molly thought. *Not now!*

Bitsy's eyes were glued to Emma. "*Aunt* Molly? Well, I'll be damned and gone to hell if that isn't the spitting image of Maeve Connovan!"

"Uh, look, Bitsy, I haven't had a chance to tell you that—"

Bitsy's eyes never left Emma. Under her breath, she said, "The bitch was here, I take it."

Giving Bitsy a sharp look, Molly said, "Emma, this is Mrs. Bitsy Morgan."

Emma offered her hand. "How do you do. I'm Emma Newsome."

Taking the child's hand, Bitsy said, "A bit surprised, but I'm happy to meet you."

"I'm sorry to interrupt, but I'm cleaning my brass bed and I've run out of polish."

Bitsy's eyes flashed at Molly. "Don't tell me Carrie has moved in!"

Ignoring her, Molly said to Emma, "Take a look in the storage room on the bottom shelf of the cabinet. There's another can of Brasso. Be sure to shake it good, okay?"

"It was nice to meet you, ma'am," Emma said.

"Hmm, yes. Yes, very nice, dear."

Giving Bitsy a shake of her head, Molly whispered, "Calling her mother a bitch in front of her was a bit rude, don't you think? Wait until she gets upstairs. I'll fill you in then."

Snapping open her bag, Bitsy pulled out her flask again. Taking a quick sip, she said, "You damn well better."

When Emma was safely upstairs and out of earshot, Molly told Bitsy of Carrie's arrival and the letter. Every time Bitsy was about to interrupt, Molly had to stop her. "Just let me finish before you blow a gasket. I know how close you and Mother were, and how much you blame yourself and Carrie for Dad's arrest, but it's done. It's over. Let's leave it, okay?"

"Typical Irish family legacy. Always a bad penny in the mix. How she even managed to spawn a child will haunt me to my grave. And the spitting image of your mother! Oh, how that galls me!"

Reaching for her cigarettes, Bitsy said, "Lock the door. We've got to talk."

"I can't lock up. I just opened. And bad pennies are in every mix, so leave the Irish out of it, okay?"

"Put a sign on the door. The town's dead today. It's raining and there's empty parking all over Ocean Avenue."

Molly locked the door, turned Bitsy's chair away from the window, grabbed the can of air freshener and an ashtray, then joined her. "Before you start in, Lucero is looking into the legality of Emma staying with me. And I don't want you bad-mouthing Carrie in front of her. She's got enough to deal with at the moment. She was crying this morning and tried to hide it when I found her in the kitchen trying to make coffee for us."

"Are you through?"

"Not really, but go ahead. I can't wait for my new orders."

Less bawdy than usual, Bitsy's laugh seemed strained. "Since when have I—oh, don't answer that. Are you out of your mind? You can't keep this child here. She could be as good a con as her mother for all you know."

"That's unfair."

"Yes, but it might also be true."

Molly dug out a cigarette from the pack in her pocket, along with her Zippo. Inhaling deeply, she looked away from Bitsy for a moment, then lowered her voice. "It might. She's certainly had a good teacher. But I don't think so. She's smart and incredibly mature for her age, but . . . no, she's okay. I'd bet on it."

Stubbing out her cigarette, Bitsy realized Molly was not in a mood to argue. "Well, I bet on you, and I won, so who am I to argue?" Rising with difficulty, she leaned over and kissed Molly on the forehead. "You've been dealt a few bad hands in your life, darling. I just don't want to see you catch another."

"I won't. After all, I have you at my table."

Bitsy smiled. "Yes, but it's getting crowded."

"I like crowds. And I expect you to be in the middle. If you don't see a doctor, I'm going to drag you to the E.R."

"Don't be silly. Oliver and Josie are taking good care of me."

"Speaking of Oliver, what's this I hear about you backing a store for him? I know it's none of my business, but how well do you really know the man?"

When Molly saw Bitsy's lips tighten again, she knew she'd made a mistake bringing Oliver up. But she didn't want to see her taken advantage of at this stage of her life. "Okay, tell me to butt out."

"Look, Oliver's had a few bad hands of his own. I'm just fronting his key money and first and last rent."

"Bitsy! That's thousands! What about his merch? Are you carrying that too?"

Before Bitsy could answer, they both turned at

the hard pounding on the door. "Shit!" Molly said. "Hide that ashtray and shoot some spray for me. I'll get the door."

When she opened the door and saw Oliver Townsend, she said, "Oh, I'm glad it's just you. Come in. Bitsy and I were having a quick smoke."

Pushing past Molly, Oliver's voice was terse. "She's not to smoke!" Turning around, he was nearly in her face. "You know she's been ill!"

Inching back, Molly said, "She's also seventy-three years old. If she wants to smoke, it's her business, not yours."

The flicker in his eyes was not lost on Molly. Walking over to Bitsy, he took hold of her arm, linked it in his and said gently, "It's time for your nap. You agreed to an hour, and it's up."

Molly was dumbfounded as she watched Bitsy meekly nod. As they passed, Bitsy blew her a kiss. "Call me when you know more about Trudy's funeral."

Molly watched how carefully Oliver led Bitsy to the door. Pausing for a moment, Bitsy half turned around. "Say good-bye to Emma for me, will you? And think about what I said."

Nodding, Molly's eyes followed them out of the shop. At the door, she wrinkled her nose. Something was burning. Rushing back to the chair Bitsy had been sitting in, she saw the ashtray had fallen on the leather cushion and Bitsy's cigarette, which hadn't completely been stubbed out, was burning a hole in the leather. Grabbing the ashtray, she quickly dumped her coffee on the seat. A few four-letter-word combinations crossed her mind as she ran to the storage room for a rag. Now she had a single, and expensive, repair job. She wasn't angry with Bitsy, only more worried. A seasoned and successful dealer in her day, Bitsy knew how to care for fine things and how difficult they were to come by. One was not careless around merchandise. Especially a smoker. Something was physically wrong, and Molly was afraid it was more than the flu.

Wiping up the spillage, she prayed she was wrong. She'd grown to love the old bat, and didn't want to think about her not being around. On her way back to the storage room with the wet rag, she stopped at her desk and made a note to call Josie in the morning and remind her to get Bitsy to her doctor.

The morning seemed to fly by like the pages of a calendar in an old movie. Molly made four sales, broke a small Royal Doulton teapot reaching for a large majolica jug, and spilled water from a vase of wilting red tulips on a newly polished breakfast table. Emma surprised her around two by fixing sandwiches. They had a quick picnic in the storage room, and Molly tried to keep a straight face when Emma asked if she really liked tuna and mustard. "Actually, it's rather nouvelle, wouldn't you say?"

"No. It's rather awful," Emma replied, "but you have to work with what you have."

That comment stuck to Molly the rest of the

day. It seemed apparent Emma had managed to do that very thing. With events happening so fast, Molly had little chance to wonder just what the hell she'd gotten into. Bitsy's prompting had opened up avenues of questions she hadn't had time to explore. A runaway sister, a niece she knew absolutely nothing about, and, by the way, who was Emma's father? The boyfriend Carrie had run off with, she remembered, was Tommy Cameron. Who was Newsome?

Spending the rest of the day making a half-dozen small sales to tourists, checking on Emma's progress, and worrying about everything under the sun, Molly began to fade around four. She was the sudden guardian of a twelve-year-old girl. She was hiding two bags of the personal papers of a dead woman. She was lying to Randall, she fired Janet, lost a four grand sale, and snapped at Oliver Townsend. *It's amazing how much trouble I can get into in just a few days. Oh, and I now have a cat.*

Noting there were few ingredients in the refrigerator to fix a proper dinner, and ruling out Lean Cuisine, Molly decided Emma's idea about Wendy's might work. Shortly after seven they headed for Sand City. Next to Monterey, and just fifteen minutes north of Carmel, its vast shopping complex had turned a tiny community into one of the largest tax earning bases in the county. Eyeing a local Mexican food chain she'd heard Randall rave about, Molly decided to go ethnic, and stopped there first.

Luckily, Emma loved Mexican food. From there they went to a mattress outlet for Emma's bed, and then headed for Target to complete their shopping list. By the time they loaded two carts with bed linens and towels, Molly glanced at Emma's jeans and said, "Follow me." In the children's department, she said, "No low-slung hip hugger jeans or midriff tank tops."

"Of course not. I wouldn't be caught dead in those things."

Breathing a sigh of relief, Molly nodded. "Right." When they got to the checkout counter, Molly nearly fainted when she signed the slip for her credit card. The $478 she'd just spent, besides the new mattress, would have to come out of her savings. Before leaving the shopping complex, Molly drove over to Office Depot and bought two sets of fold-up cardboard storage boxes. She figured that would be enough to pack up Trudy's office records.

Not in the mood to lug all the purchases up the stairs, Molly pulled into the garage and woke Emma, who'd fallen asleep as soon as they'd gotten in the El Camino. "We'll get this stuff in the morning, okay?"

Emma's drooping eyes gave Molly her answer. After seeing her to bed, she opened the French doors in her bedroom to let Tiger out for a stroll, then unplugged her telephone and set up Trudy's answering machine. Randall was going to want everything, including the answering machine, and not knowing how long he would hold onto Trudy's things, she thought she'd better get her messages. On the floor with a notepad, she hit the play button. Holding back a groan when she saw there were fifteen calls, Molly turned the volume low, ready to note each one. If it rained again tomorrow, traffic in the shop would be light and she could return the calls then. She wasn't looking forward to being the bearer of bad news to so many of Trudy's clients and acquaintances. Many of the calls were from local friends who by now knew about her death. So far, she had only four callers who hadn't left a number.

Making notes on the next three messages, she hit the pause button and got up to let Tiger in. It was already ten-thirty, and she longed for bed. When she saw Tiger jump up on her bed and get comfortable, she almost joined him. Only two calls left. A few more minutes wouldn't matter. Tapping on the play button again, she turned the page, ready to make the next entry, and froze when she heard the message.

"It's me," the caller said angrily. "Things are beginning to unravel. It's over at my end. I want my money, damnit! No more excuses. This is your last warning, and I mean it. I'll blow the gig to high heaven if I have to. And you know what he'll do if that happens."

Molly's hands were shaking so hard she almost hit Delete. Collapsing against the closet door, she paused for a moment in disbelief. She had to play it back to be sure. *It couldn't be her. God, please! Don't let it be her! Why the hell did I take this damn thing home? Why didn't I tell Max to let his property manager take care of packing Trudy's house?*

Her hand reached for the tiny crucifix she always wore. Clutching it through the fabric of her tee shirt, she closed her eyes. Saying a quick prayer wouldn't make that damn machine disappear. She might say one for guidance, but she knew what she had to do. Not bothering with the last message, she went back to the beginning, hitting Skip until she came to the threatening call. She turned up the volume, then closed her eyes again. As she listened, she prayed her sister was in Tibet, hiding in a monastery, instead of Japan.

Numb, she rose, unplugged the machine, and replaced her own. Returning it to the closet, Molly closed the door and undressed for bed. She threw on the sweats she'd worn last night, climbed into bed, and sat in the dark for several moments. How the hell did Carrie know Trudy? What was the money for? What gig? Who was *he*? And then she remembered Emma pointing out Milo Kraft. Was he the man Carrie referred to?

There was just no getting away from it. She had to know. Her gray sweats blended in perfectly with the thick fog that blanketed Carmel as she quietly made three trips up and down the stairs with the plastic bags and the storage boxes she'd bought.

Tiptoeing past Emma, sound asleep on the sofa, she carefully made her way through the dark living room to the kitchen. She'd need a full thermos of espresso to see her through this. Gingerly pulling out the instant espresso she kept for late night sessions cleaning merchandise, she plugged in the electric teapot and alternated between clutching her crucifix and drumming her fingers on the counter. If she'd had decent nails, she thought, they'd be gone by now.

First thing was to get the boxes set up. Back on the floor again, Molly emptied both plastic bags and used the boxes to sort. By the time she was finished, she had boxes for bank information, paid bills, incoming bills and invoices, photographs, file folders, and auction catalogs. Three computer discs were set aside. She was surprised to find so many manila envelopes with photos of shows, estate sales, and odds and ends of merchandise. Deciding the photos would be the easiest to deal with, she began with those. Each envelope had a date, the name of the show or sale, and the city. Toward the bottom was a short list of what appeared to be abbreviated names, followed by one or two sets of initials.

With envelopes dating back four years, Molly placed all but this year's in the appropriate box. Opening up an envelope labeled San Diego, she ran through the photos. A dozen or so were of Trudy's show layout, and clearly illustrated her talent for display. She found a short list of what Trudy had used for backdrops and props, and an inventory of what had been sold. There was also a shot of Trudy, wearing a short red wig, looking up as she unpacked a box. That explained the wigs she'd seen in the closet. They were for shows. The long hours and hard work played havoc on looking your best.

Next, she opened the Pasadena envelope. More of the same, except this time Trudy wore a black wig. Then she found a few photos of what appeared to be seventeenth-century Spanish jewelry. She recognized the style easily since she'd done research for a buyer her first year with Sotheby's. She had no idea Trudy had dealt in jewelry. There were also photos of Russian icons, many of which were absolutely stunning. Molly remembered asking Trudy about icons. She had a client in Sacramento who was an avid collector. Trudy had told her she never touched them. Too many fakes coming out of Russia and Greece.

More puzzled now, Molly continued shuffling through the photos, then backtracked, and looked closer at one she'd just passed over. To the side of a display table, almost out of view and in the middle of half a dozen people eyeing Trudy's merchandise, was Milo Kraft. She couldn't believe her eyes. *How could she work with that pig? And why had it been such a big secret?* She'd never seen him at Trudy's estate sales, or even heard her mention him. No wonder he was snooping around her house. He was probably trying to get to those boxes in her office.

The man Kraft was talking with in the photo had

95

his back to the camera, but there was something about him that made Molly pause. Chalking it up to anxiety and fatigue, she set the photo down and gulped down half the mug of espresso. She looked at the photo again and the man with Milo Kraft. Nothing came to mind. Gathering all the photos, she packed them back into the envelope and reached for another.

Quickly glancing at the various cities on each envelope, she tossed Phoenix, Palm Springs, Las Vegas, Houston, Reno, Vancouver, and Portland into the box. When she saw one marked Seattle, she paused, then opened the envelope. Handling each photo as if it were coated in acid, her hands began to shake. Halfway through she saw Carrie, in profile, standing next to Trudy, who wore a shoulder-length blond wig. Molly threw the photos on the floor. Tears scalded her eyes. Wiping them away, she sat quietly for some time. Finally, she returned the Seattle photos to their envelope. Turning it over, she noticed the initials C.N., and set the envelope aside. She didn't have the heart or the will to go through the rest of Trudy's papers, but she knew it was vital that she search for any trail that led to her sister.

Molly quickly went through the stack of paid invoices. The one from Hong Kong Specialties, listing over a dozen pieces of Sèvres and Meissen porcelain figures caught her attention. Noting the date of the invoice, she looked for the total at the bottom. Six thousand dollars? For what was listed, that was chump change! Holding her breath, she scanned each entry. It didn't take a rocket scientist to realize that Trudy was selling fakes. The Milo Kraft connection suddenly made sense.

A lump that felt the size of a grapefruit was quickly growing in her throat. Three of the figures listed were identical to those she had bought from Trudy at her last estate sale in Pebble Beach. And she'd sold all three to one of her best customers from Rancho Mirage! Throwing the invoice on the floor, she shook her head. *This can't be happening. Not to me! How in the hell had I missed that those were fakes?* She'd handled Meissen for years. She knew what to look for. She knew the mistakes forgers made; the wrong colors for the period, the idiosyncrasy of the potters and painters, even the slight variations of the marks. And now she wondered about that Old Paris tea set she'd bought from Trudy just after Christmas. The black and gold service, patterned after the neoclassical French Empire period of 1800–1805, had been so delicious, she'd thought about keeping it for herself. But when a customer walked in the next day and saw it on her desk, he desperately wanted it for his wife. She'd paid Trudy three hundred for it, and sold it for $2,200. There wasn't a dealer alive that would pass that up.

She had no one to blame but herself. She knew better. She'd trusted Trudy, and failed to eagle-eye her buys. Lesson one for all beginners, Max had told her years ago: *Don't trust anyone, friends included. Know the merch, and trust only that. Caveat emptor!* he'd said, waving his arms in the air. *Buyer beware! Etch it on your brain!*

Lost in her anger, Molly jumped when Tiger leaped off the bed and dove into her lap. Catching her breath, she willed her heart to stop hammering and tried to decide what to do.

First things first. She gently put Tiger back on the bed, then began taking the boxes down to the garage. It was two-thirty, and thankfully the fog still lingered. She hoped no one in the second floor apartments across the courtyard suffered from insomnia and would notice her trooping up and down the stairs. She piled the boxes into one of the locked cabinets against the wall, and placed Trudy's answering machine inside the top box. She removed the tape and put it in the pocket of her sweat pants.

Back in her bedroom, she picked up the Hong Kong invoice and the Seattle envelope, then noticed she'd forgotten to add the Pasadena envelope with the others. And the computer discs were still on the floor. Not about to go back down again, she decided to hide everything in the bottom section of her jewelry box. It wasn't the best hiding place in the world, but it would have to do for now. Opening the last drawer of her night table, she removed the jewelry box and placed it on the bed. When she opened the lovely rosewood box, she felt as if she'd been kicked in the stomach.

It was empty. Her Rolex watch, her black jade ring, and the valuable pair of French miniatures she'd so diligently hoarded for a rainy day were gone.

Sinking onto the bed, she looked at a photo of her father on the night table. *Oh, Dad, she did it again!*

CHAPTER 9

Molly awoke Friday morning to find Tiger curled up behind her back and Emma sitting quietly at the end of the bed with coffee on a tray. "How long have you been there?" Molly asked.

Touching the side of the cup, Emma said, "About two minutes. I found the ivy cup. I thought you might like it."

Not used to a cat sharing her bed, Molly sat up carefully. "Are you going to join me?"

"Can I drink coffee?" When Molly nodded, she said, "Yes! I'll be right back. Wait for me."

Back almost instantly, Molly wondered if she'd been conned. Emma must already have had her pansy cup ready to go. It didn't matter. In fact, she thought, it was kind of cute. She needed a smile this morning, and she was pleased it was Emma who provided it. She'd hardly slept at all. It seemed like she spent hours staring at the ceiling trying to decide what to do. They sat together, with Tiger at their side, and had their morning coffee. When Emma finished hers, she seemed distracted and

100

hardly noticed Tiger curled up next to her on the bed.

"You okay?" Molly asked.

"I was just thinking. About us . . . you, me, and a stray cat."

"More like a triad." Molly laughed, hoping to bring a smile to her face. When the telephone rang, she set down her cup with a sigh. "Good morning, Randall. How did I know it was you? Who else calls me first thing in the morning? Daria is still asleep, Bitsy never calls until after lunch, Lucero and I don't have a telephone relationship, and Bennie is busy getting ready for customers."

"Very cute, Ms. Doyle. I need to see you right away. Meet me at Tosca's."

"Now? You've got to be kidding. I just woke up. Wait . . . hold on." Tiger had just decided to lick her cheek. "Get off, Tiger, I'm on the phone."

The silence at the other end seemed an eternity. "Tell your guest this is official business and he'll have to wait."

Molly's jaw dropped, then she almost laughed. "My *guest* is very demanding, and I'm not sure he'll appreciate my leaving so soon."

"Yeah? Tough. And you can tell him I said that."

Before Molly could explain, he'd hung up.

Picking up her cup, she burst out laughing. She could just imagine the look on Randall's face. "I'm in trouble with the law, Emma. Guess we'd better shower and blow this town."

"You're funny, you know that?"

"Yeah, a real comedian." But Molly suddenly didn't feel very funny. Randall's early call could only mean trouble.

"Are we going to Bennie's for apple cake?"

Heading for the shower, Molly said, "Might as well. It might be my last meal as a free person."

Built in the thirties, the shops in the complex had been updated frequently to meet modern needs. The apartment, however, still had ancient plumbing and a small hot water heater. With Emma in residence, Molly had to remember to shower quickly so Emma wouldn't run out of hot water. She was in and out of the shower in less than ten minutes. By eight they were ready to go. Emma wore one of her new outfits, and was thrilled when Bennie complimented her. When Emma noticed Molly playing with her cake, she said, "Go ahead and spill it."

"What?"

"You're not eating. You're just making crumbs and moving them around."

"Oh, it's nothing. I'm just a little tired. Didn't sleep much."

"Is it because of me? Am I a problem for you?"

"No, it has nothing to do with you."

"Honest? Remember what you said about us being honest?"

Molly smiled, and took her hand in hers. "Honest. Okay?"

"Okay. I was just wondering."

"Well, don't. You and I are fine."

"And Tiger too?"

"And Tiger too."

"Yeah, tell me all about this Tiger person."

She should have felt him coming, Molly thought. Randall had some sort of quirky energy field around him that made people squirm. Not bothering to look up, she said, "Tiger is our cat, if you must know."

His laughter nearly shook the small bistro. "Cat? You've got a cat? And you named it Tiger? If that doesn't beat all."

At the counter helping himself to coffee, he looked at Bennie. "Did you hear that? Molly Doyle has a cat named Tiger."

Bennie liked to pretend he wasn't intimidated by Randall, but there were times like this when he wasn't sure. He'd almost spilled a tray of pastries when he heard his laughter. "No kidding? Well, yeah, that's really funny."

Joining Molly and Emma, Randall said, "Okay, now that we got that cleared up, can I have a moment of your time?" Turning to Emma, he said, "How about picking out a pastry for me? Maybe Bennie could help you surprise me, okay? Take your time."

When Emma was out of hearing, he said, "I need you at the station this morning."

"Why?"

"I need your prints."

Molly's stomach rolled. She was going to need

a prescription for acid reflux before the day was over. "Why?"

"I haven't made it public, and I might not. In fact, I shouldn't even be telling you, but since you've managed to end up in the middle, I've got no choice."

Please, God, stay with me on this one. But she knew why he wanted her prints. "Tell me it's not what I think."

He saw her face pale, and looked at her for a long moment, a habit he had that, despite all they'd been through together, still managed to unnerve her. "I've got a homicide to investigate. Trudy was murdered." When she didn't reply, he said, "Your right eye is twitching. Funny, it's usually your left eye. Now, I wonder why that is?"

"Oh, God." Molly shook her head and looked away. "How? Who would kill Trudy?"

"Like they say on TV, when I know why, then I'll know who. I need your prints to—"

"I know. To eliminate me from the house. I guess you got hold of the termite people in time."

"They'd already put the tent up, but that's as far as they got."

Visibly shaken, she said, "Let me get something to eat, then I'll come over."

"Leave Emma with Bennie. She doesn't need to come to the station and see this. She might get the wrong idea. Lucero's got some news for you about her. Daria wants us to come by tonight for polenta around seven. You up for that?"

Molly nodded. "Sure."

"Uh, Molly. I'm . . . I'm sorry about this morning. I was out of line."

Apologies not a big part of Randall's repertoire, Molly almost spilled her espresso. "How nice of you to realize that. I can't believe you'd think I'd entertain someone with a child in the next room."

"Hey, I said I'm sorry. Don't beat me up here."

"You should know me better."

"Yeah? Well, guess what? Sometimes I think I don't know you at all. How's that?"

Before Molly could answer, he was on his feet and headed inside. At the counter, he told Emma, "I gotta run, squirt. You can pick out something for me another time."

Molly watched Randall leave, then clasped her hands to keep them from shaking. She was having a hard time getting past the fact that Trudy was murdered. Why, for God's sake? And how was she going to tell Randall she had all her files? When Emma returned with more coffee, she gulped it down in minutes. The bars of a jail cell floated in front of her eyes. She didn't dare let Randall know she'd gone through Trudy's records last night or heard Carrie's threatening message. Then it struck her. Her prints would be all over them. How was she going to explain that?

Waving Bennie over, she said, "I've got to meet Randall at the station. I, ah, have to give him a statement about Sunday at the antique show. Can Emma stay here while I'm gone?"

Pulling up a chair, Bennie said, "Sure. I've got a new apricot coffee cake, a carrot cake, and a chocolate pudding cake I'm thinking about adding to the menu. How about giving me a taste test, Emma?"

"I'm not very crazy about apricots, but if I like it then you'll know you have a winner." Looking at Molly, she said, "Is this about the lady that died at the antique show?"

"How did you know about that?"

"I heard Mother talking about it to that man I saw the other day. Remember? The one with the dirty hat?"

Molly's heart sank. Carrie might be a bitch, but a killer? No. Absolutely not. Slinging her tote over her shoulder, she said, "I won't be long." Giving Emma a wink, she added, "Small test pieces, okay?"

The short walk to the Carmel police station gave Molly time to think about how she was going to explain to Randall why Trudy's personal records were in her garage. He wasn't an easy man to read, but Molly felt she'd dissected him well enough to know he'd probably think about killing her. Since he'd already been in Trudy's house, she wondered what he'd thought about the wigs. And the minute he got a look at all those envelopes with the photos of Trudy in her different guises, would he simply think she indulged in a little out-of-town play? She also wondered if he'd recognize Milo Kraft in the photos. Come to think of it,

Randall probably didn't even know him. So Milo helped her with shows. So what?

She decided not to tell Randall about the boxes yet. She had to find out how deeply her sister was involved, and the answer might be connected to the invoices. She hadn't a clue how, but she had to take the risk. What had Carrie said on the recording? *Things were beginning to unravel.* She skidded to a halt in the middle of the crosswalk. *What things?* A tourist walking behind her nearly knocked her down. Quickly apologizing, Molly hurried across the street. She knew she had to hear that tape again, and that meant taking it back upstairs. She needed the boxes for one more night. Tomorrow. She'd tell him tomorrow.

Stopping a block short of the police station, Molly paused at the corner. Things were happening so fast, she also wondered if she should tell him about the burglary. She decided to leave it alone for now. Randall knew all about Carrie stealing from her father and his subsequent prison term. In view of her leaving town, he might suspect her. Until she knew more about what Trudy was involved in, Molly decided, and where her sister fit in, she'd keep quiet. How Carrie managed to get into the apartment was irrelevant. She had Emma to think about now, and that was more important.

The Carmel police station, on Junipero Street, a few blocks north of Ocean Avenue, was low-slung, set back from the street by a wide set of stairs. It was well landscaped, and meant to resemble an office building. Unlike most of Carmel, whose architectural heritage ran from Mediterranean to Hansel and Gretel, it was unobtrusive and classy, and only the simple sign on the building indicated this was where they took the bad boys. Not that Carmel had many. In fact, they had very few. Reaching the top of the stairs, Molly took a deep breath and walked in.

Randall was waiting for her. He had a cup of coffee in one hand and a file folder in the other. Glancing at his watch, he said, "As soon as you're done, come over to my office. I've got a meeting in a half hour, but I need to go over a few things with you."

Nodding, Molly smiled and followed the waiting officer. The simple process took little time. Wiping ink from her fingers, she headed for Randall's office.

"Pull up a chair, and yes, you can go ahead and smoke."

"Thanks, but I'm trying to cut down."

"Okay, here's the thing, Molly. You and Daria are the only people that have been in Trudy's house, right?"

Here it comes. The empty office. "As far as I know. Well, except for the estimator from the moving company."

"And you were with him while he was there?"

"Every moment."

"That's what I thought. I'll need his name and

phone number. So, who else could have got in there? Anyone else have a key?"

"I haven't a clue. Well, George, Max's property manager, has one, I guess. Maybe the exterminator had one too."

"No. George said he gave you the only one he had. Do you have it with you?"

Molly thought for a moment, then dove into her tote. "I think I put it in here. I know it's not at the shop. Hang on, I'll just be a minute." Pulling aside her wallet, Kleenex, crumpled shopping lists, and an old garage sale list, she finally found it in her coin pouch. Handing it over, she said, "I have to get it back to the property manager at some point, so don't lose it."

"I don't lose things."

"What's the big deal about the key? Trudy died at the show."

"Routine."

"Randall! Come on!" She was going to take a risk now and ask him a question she knew he wouldn't answer. But if she didn't ask, he'd wonder why. "I still want to know how you know she was murdered."

"It's not for public knowledge at this point."

"Since when am I *public*?"

When he averted his eyes, she slung her tote over her shoulder. It was the best signal she could think to let him know she was angry at being dismissed so commonly.

"Molly, just because you helped us nail that Martyn broad doesn't mean—"

"Can I go now? Emma's still with Bennie, and I've got to get the shop open."

"Look, you're an antique dealer. I'm a cop. We don't cross over, okay? You rip the public, I catch bad people. Got it?"

"Loud and clear, *Chief.*"

"Don't forget tonight. Seven."

"Seven. Got it." She couldn't wait to get out of there. She was about to lose it with him, and she knew if she did, she'd blow it. Those damn pale blue eyes of his were like lasers, and every time she'd had to lie to him, she swore he knew it. Careful not to walk too fast and work up a sweat, she tried to pace herself. She didn't have time to shower again, remember which box the invoices were in, get Emma, and open. Just thinking about all of it made her breathless.

Molly knew the Hail Marys she'd said on the way back to the shop worked. She found the box with the invoices right away. Sneaking up the back stairs without Emma or Bennie seeing her from the courtyard had almost been exhilarating. She quickly shoved the box in her closet, made certain all the doors were locked this time, and breezed into Tosca's looking like she hadn't a care in the world. Now if she could only get visions of throttling her sister out of her mind, she might make it through the day.

Two busloads of tourists arrived in town and a steady stream of shoppers filtered in and out most of the day. Sales were brisk in small items, and she'd sold three pieces of furniture to newlyweds from Santa Cruz. Her good mood quickly vanished when she saw Milo Kraft peeking in her front window. *Just dare to come in here again*, she thought. *Just dare! I'm in the mood for a good rumble.*

CHAPTER 10

Randall didn't have a meeting. He'd told Molly that to get rid of her. If he hadn't, he knew she would have stayed and badgered him unmercifully until he told her how Trudy was murdered. He hadn't liked the feel of Trudy's space Sunday night. He could never put a name to it, but he seemed to *know* when a death scene didn't feel right. It was as if the air was charged. It had happened before, when a death was first thought to be natural, or accidental. It wasn't, as one of his former partners used to say, intuition, or vibes. It was different. It was deeper. Like a calling out. He felt it right away when he stepped into Trudy's space. But for some reason, he'd ignored it. At the time, the heart attack seemed plausible, given Bitsy's remarks about Trudy's heart condition. Big mistake, Randall thought. He knew better. He'd never do that again.

He was a man who loved his work. Piecing clues together to make a whole, and the satisfaction of success, was his life. He'd been one of the best: fair and objective. But he often felt shame that death was the means to make him feel alive. It took a drinking bout—and a deadly hangover—to accept the promotion to Internal Affairs in Los Angeles. Putting dirty cops away became a balm. He could find pleasure in that and not feel the need for confession. But now he wondered if being a cop was worth it if it meant always being suspicious of people. And so he'd ignored the vibes he'd felt in Trudy Collins's space.

When the coroner called him and said they were looking at a possible homicide, Randall kicked his wastebasket across the room. The Collins death, the coroner said, was the result of a vasomotor collapse. Angioneurotic edema, he'd added. "Okay, I got the edema thing. That's still a heart attack, right?" Randall asked.

"It's what caused it," the coroner replied. "I'm faxing the report over now. Take a look and ask yourself why a woman allergic to penicillin would take it with a Coke?"

"Maybe she didn't know," Randall had said. "A lot of people don't."

"It was on her medical alert bracelet, Randall."

"Okay, I'll wait for the report." He'd noticed the med bracelet, but figured it was for a heart condition and didn't look at it. Another mistake he didn't like.

He'd read the coroner's report twice, then did a full search on Trudy Collins on every law enforcement database he had access to. He thought about calling in a few favors at Quantico, then changed his mind. He'd wait and see what showed up first. Besides, he already had a file to think about until the others arrived. Trudy had a jacket right here in Monterey County. When he finished reading it, he called Lucero. "You still going to Daria's tonight?"

"Yeah. Seven, right?"

"Check. Look, we got a situation with that heart attack victim Sunday at the antiques show. Can you stop by here around six?"

Lucero's D.A. mode kicked in and he said, "Give me a heads-up."

"Homicide."

"Got a suspect?"

"Nada. From scratch with this one."

"Who else knows?"

"Just Phillips," he lied. "He alerted me. I've got the tox report in my hands." Lucero didn't need to know he'd told Molly.

"He's a good man. Best coroner we've had in years. I'll be there. Let's keep it quiet for now."

"My lips are sealed."

Randall's first impression of Lucero had not been good. Tall, slim, dark curly hair and blue eyes, he looked more like a waiter in L.A. between acting gigs than a serious and talented prosecutor. D.A.'s rarely got their hands dirty. They usually stuck to being an administrator and a glad hander. Lucero, he soon realized, was a cop at heart and loved the action. But like a rookie, he had to be watched. Zeal was good, but often dangerous. Randall was calling on him before it was necessary, but involving Lucero now would give him access to his team of investigators. Randall's force was small, and he didn't want to tie up manpower when the D.A. had a seasoned roster.

He wondered if Daria or Molly knew Trudy Collins had been arrested a few years back for receiving stolen goods. You never knew what women told each other over a few drinks. He'd bet they didn't know. Being in the restaurant business for years, Daria DeMarco had seen all kinds and wasn't a patsy for a sad story. As for Molly, he felt he knew her well enough to know she'd steer clear of anyone with a rap like that. She'd had enough complications in her life over stolen goods. But he didn't like the way that eye-twitching business was starting up again. A sure sign of stress for most people. For Molly, he'd already figured it was good old Irish temper. Was she holding out on him? He chewed that over for a few minutes, then chalked it up to her sister showing up and then leaving that poor kid on her doorstep. He was certain if Molly knew anything, she'd have said so when he told her Trudy had been murdered.

He called Molly at the shop. "Hey, that info I shared with you today never happened, okay? You don't know a thing, got it?"

"I promise not to utter a word."

Surprised she agreed so easily, he said, "When I go public, faint or something."

"I'll be properly shocked. When are you going to make the announcement?"

"When I'm ready. Okay?" He didn't need an argument from her now. He had a feeling there would be plenty in the days ahead.

Molly hung up and wondered why Randall was being so secretive. Besides, who the hell was she going to tell? She didn't have time to think about it before Bitsy arrived.

Dressed to the nines as usual, Bitsy's step had regained that old saunter, and a big smile lit up her face. "Darling! I'm back, and ready to sell my little heart out. I've decided that mystery herb tea Oliver's been giving me is wonderful! I feel like sixty again. I'm on my way to get my hair done, and I'll be in tomorrow at ten."

Giving her a hug, Molly said, "You look marvelous. Even your cheeks are flushed. Or if that's a new blush, tell me quick. I could use some color."

"It's me, darling. Totally me. I feel grand," she said as she shifted a majolica teapot closer to a lamp. "There, that balances better." Heading for a nineteenth-century Spanish chest by the wall, Bitsy added, "I'd move this armorial plate to the center, dear. Hmm, nice reproduction, but the deep blue would look better next to the yellow roses."

"I like it the way it is," Molly said. "Let's not redecorate just yet, okay? Wait until I'm at the garage sales tomorrow. I'm taking Emma with me. She's never been to one. I'm hoping it will cheer her up a little. She's been a little down since . . . well, since Carrie left."

Glancing toward the stairs, Bitsy said, "She's still here?"

Leading her to a chair, Molly said, "Yes, *Emma* is still here. She's putting her new bed together. Remember that Art Deco bed I found at that sale in Carmel Highlands? I bought a new mattress to fit, and they delivered it when I opened."

"I remember it. You paid too much for it."

"Oh, come on! Fifty bucks for the real thing?"

"Darling, I'm joking of course. You've become a marvelous bargainer. So, the child, er, Emma, how old is she?"

"Twelve going on thirty, as Carrie said."

Bitsy turned her head away. "Don't mention that creature's name to me again."

Molly understood Bitsy's anger. She could only imagine what she might say if she knew Carrie had stolen from her too. "I'll keep that in mind. But please don't act that way in front of Emma. The poor thing—"

"You've decided to keep her, then? What about her father? Wouldn't he have some say in this fiasco?"

Pulling up a footstool, Molly said, "Emma said he died years ago. Lucero is looking into the legalities for me. In fact, I'm going over to Daria's tonight, and hopefully he'll have some information."

"Hmm, well, if you feel you must do this—"

"I haven't much choice. Besides, she's sweet, and has a great deadpan sense of humor, and she *is* my niece. She stays with me, and that's final."

Bitsy smiled. "Well, I wouldn't expect less from you, now would I?" Rising, she said, "I'm off. I'll be in tomorrow at ten sharp. You two get out there and bring back a load of goodies."

Walking her to the door, Molly asked, "Are you sure you're up to it?"

"Absolutely. I feel like a million bucks."

Watching her leave, Molly wondered about Oliver's magical tea. Maybe she ought to call him and find out where to buy it. She could use an extra bounce in her step right now. Between waiting on six customers over the last two hours, ringing up four sales, and faxing a memo to Marvin in the City with a want list for a new customer, she had little time to dwell on the box of invoices upstairs, or her growing fear that her sister's face might soon be on a wanted poster. During a lull around two, she ran upstairs to see how Emma was doing. The bed was made up, and she found Emma curled up with Tiger and *The Call of the Wild*.

"Good book, huh?"

"I love it. I fixed tuna and deviled egg. I was going

to come down and see if you wanted a sandwich, but Mrs. Bitsy was there and, well, I don't think she cares for me, so I stayed up here."

Next to her on the bed, Molly ruffled her hair. "Bitsy thinks you're great. She was just surprised. In fact, she was asking about you."

"Really? I think she's beautiful for her age."

"Oh, honey! Tell her that tomorrow! You'll be her best friend in no time."

"She's coming back tomorrow?"

"Yep, she does Saturday and Sunday for me so I can get to garage sales and auctions."

"Oh, then we won't have to rush around like madmen like they do on those TV shows."

Molly laughed. "Oh yes we will! Wait until you see me in action! You're going to have to run to keep up with me. I've got to get back downstairs, but you did a great job with the bed. It looks super."

Molly made it back down just as a young couple with a small child entered. Giving them a smile, she meandered over to her desk while keeping an eye on the little boy, who'd already left his mother's side. Fiddling with papers on her desk, she watched him run down the main aisle like he was chasing rabbits. She breathed a sigh of relief when the mother caught him by the hand and scolded him. He'd been way too close to knocking over a staggered display of three Spode Blue Italian serving platters. Particularly since they had the old marks and were worth hundreds each. She held her breath once again when he tore away and pulled a French marionette from a bookshelf. About to call out, Molly relaxed when the boy's father took it from his hands. Max would have had a heart attack if he'd been here, she thought. The price on it was fifteen hundred, and he was thinking about keeping it. Seeing the child now in his father's arms, Molly returned to her desk.

Less tense, she pulled out her notebook and that morning's classified ads, and began listing tomorrow's garage sales. She soon had fifteen stops to make between seven and nine. Considering how much she'd sold today, and how little she had in reserve, she hoped tomorrow's treasure hunt would pay off. Still keeping an eye on the couple with the child, she decided to roam the floor and try to imagine what a garden setting would look like toward the back wall. With the tall brick ceilings, she might conjure up a conservatory look. Maybe hang an artificial ivy espalier along the wall, or fill wall pockets with geraniums. Old iron garden furniture was still hot, and two ads in the paper mentioned patio sets. She was running low on lamps too. She'd keep an eye out for interesting vases and have some made.

By the time she and Emma got home from Daria's tonight, she'd probably be too bushed to go through Trudy's invoices and still get enough sleep to be up before six. She knew that was a lame excuse. The truth was, she really didn't want to face more proof of Trudy's duplicity. The invoices had to be examined tonight, and that was that. And she still had to come up with an excuse for having them.

CHAPTER 11

In Randall's office at six sharp, Lucero examined the oversized sales tags that had been scattered over Trudy Collins's desk the night she was killed and shook his head. "Doesn't tell me a damn thing. You got any ideas on these?"

"Not a one. But they're the only thing out of whack at the scene. The only clear prints on the Coke can were hers. A dozen people probably handled the can before she even bought it."

"So who knew she was allergic to penicillin?"

"The killer?"

"Funny, Randall. I'm serious. If she was wearing a med bracelet, she sure as hell wasn't hiding it."

"With all those bracelets she had on? Who'd know except friends? Women like to talk about their health problems."

"Tell me about it! My mother, bless her soul, reminds me every day about her aches and pains. But, hell, she's pushing seventy-five, so she's allowed."

Randall laughed. "She's allowed. My mother was the same. I'd call her every day from L.A. and it was the same story. So I gave her a lot of attention and sent her flowers every week."

"You were a good son. She raised you right."

"An Italian mother," Randall said. "The best."

Picking up one of the sales tags, Lucero said, "What the hell is a Pietra Dura tabletop? I mean, shit, the price is ten grand."

"You're a lousy Italian, Lucero. It's inlaid marble. Very intricate and baroque. Different colored marble is used to make the design. Look at the picture."

Picking up another, Lucero winked. "I did, I was just testing you. So why is a Swedish walnut commode worth eight grand? What's so special about that? It looks like a cabinet, that's all." Picking up two more, he went on. "Or a *pastiglia* cabinet for six grand, or a Spanish oak cabinet for twelve?" Looking closer, he said, "Excuse me, vargueno. Whatever the hell that means."

When Randall didn't reply, Lucero said, "I thought so. We're out of our element."

"Oh, no you don't! We're not getting Molly involved in this. Once was enough. We agreed on it in that mess long ago—that night in the E.R. when we didn't know if she'd make it out alive."

"I remember. But if these things mean anything, she can tell us."

"Who says they mean a thing?"

Rising, Lucero lit a cigar, then said, "Come on, Randall. Like you said, they were the only things out of whack."

Shoving an ashtray toward him, Randall said, "She's got a record. We'll start there."

"There's fifteen or twenty of these tags. Jewelry, Russian icons, you name it. Collins wasn't bored and pasting pretty pictures for fun, then drawing a red circle and a slash across them. They mean something, and you know it."

"We'll see. Take a look at her jacket, and here's a list of agencies I've contacted to see if she shows up anywhere else. I want two of your investigators. Trudy Collins had a wide circle in her life. Besides a local angle, I understand she did a lot of out-of-town shows, and had customers all over the country."

Still reading, Lucero said, "Things are pretty quiet now. I'll give you my top people. Monday morning good?"

Randall hoped so. That gave him time to find Trudy's office files. He didn't want to share with Lucero just yet that they were missing. He had an idea where they might be. "Perfect."

Molly and Emma were already seated in Daria's private room when Randall and Lucero arrived. Emma was engrossed in her book, and Molly was staring into space.

"Caught you daydreaming," Randall said. "Surprised you have time."

By the time a smart remark formed in her brain, it was too late. Daria was right behind them with a platter of antipasto. Manuel, her busboy captain, was at her heels with a large silver tray holding three baskets of garlic bread, a half-dozen bowls of sliced butter on ice, and four bottles of wine from choice Monterey County vineyards.

Pulling up a chair next to Emma, Lucero said, "Hey, kiddo! Got some good news for you and your auntie here."

Grabbing Molly's hand, Emma said, "You fixed everything?"

Pouring wine all around, Lucero said, "Actually, no. The good news is it's going to take a few months to get things sorted out. So, like I said before, you're here on vacation. A lot of agencies have to do their thing." He looked at Molly, adding, "Don't worry, consider it done."

"Thank you. I won't forget this."

"Good! I may have to call on your expertise again someday."

Molly caught a flicker of anger in Randall's eyes. Taking a sip of wine, it dawned on her Lucero might be referring to Trudy.

Assembling a sampling of antipasto for Emma, Randall passed it to her across the table. "Go slow with this stuff. It's pretty spicy. Besides, you gotta save room for the polenta."

"What is polenta?" Emma asked. "I've never had it."

When Randall and Lucero began to speak at the same time, Randall shot him a look and took over. "It's cooked cornmeal. It's what the peasants ate. When going to Tuscany all of a sudden became

125

the in thing to do, tourists wanted to experience the real Italy. So they ate in neighborhood restaurants instead of the fancy places. Then all the cooks who wanted to be a star got on the bandwagon and filled their menus with poor folk food for the cogniscenti."

"So that means it's cool?" Emma asked.

Daria laughed louder than any of them. "Very cool. So we all serve bruschetta and tripe now." Reaching for the garlic bread, Daria said, "By the way, I've been getting calls about Trudy's funeral. Any idea when it can be scheduled?"

"Hey, my mother has a good friend named Trudy. But it can't be the same one," Emma said to Molly. "That was in Seattle."

When Randall didn't answer her, Daria said, "Hello? Was that a tricky question?"

"Sorry. My mind's on the polenta." Shooting a glance at Lucero, he said, "Figure next week sometime. The coroner is backed up as usual. Shorthanded thing."

"So maybe midweek might be good?" Daria persisted.

"I'll call you."

Molly heard little of the exchange. The only words capturing her brain were that Carrie had a friend named Trudy. She'd already figured that, but now Randall knew. And she was certain Randall had told Lucero that Trudy's death was now classified as a homicide. Molly knew Randall wasn't obliged to bring in the district attorney until he had a suspect. But considering how close the two had become, it was a given that he'd told him right away.

When Manuel arrived with a steaming round of polenta covered in gravy and melted cheese, Lucero took center stage. "This is how the real Italians eat polenta. You dump it on a platter, slice it in half with string, then layer it with slices of mozzarella, add a lot of gravy, then put the top on and do it again."

"Gravy? Like you put on mashed potatoes?" Emma asked.

"Pasta gravy," Randall said. "Some Italians call it gravy, and some call it sauce. It's all the same thing."

"That's confusing. They should have one name," Emma insisted.

Staring at Randall, Molly said, "Italians like to be confusing."

"Contrary is more fitting." Daria laughed.

Molly was relieved the conversation had taken a different turn. She'd rather have them talking about food and being Italian than Trudy Collins. It was vital now that she go through those invoices tonight. She already knew what she was going to tell Randall. She just hoped he believed her.

By the time they finished dessert, it was past nine. Emma's eyes were beginning to droop, and Molly took advantage of it. "Emma is about to fall asleep, I'm stuffed, and I've got to get up before six tomorrow and hit the garage sales." Turning to

Daria, she said, "One of the ads mentioned silver serving pieces and flatware, so I'm going there first."

Giving her a thumbs-up, Daria said, "Call me when you get back. I'm running low on forks. Vases too. If you find something interesting, grab it. Glass, pottery, whatever. You know what I like."

When Daria walked Molly and Emma out, Lucero asked Randall, "You want to share our news with Daria? She was a big help last time, and she knew Trudy for years. She could open up a lot of closets for us."

"She's at the top of my list. I was waiting until Molly and Emma left."

"Speaking of Molly, what's with you two?"

"What the hell are you talking about?"

"Hey, come on. Back when she was in Intensive Care, you stayed by her side for damn near three days. And you two spar like an old married couple. Something going on there or what?"

"You're off your ass, counselor. I was worried about her, that's all. You were there too, if I remember correctly."

"Well, hell, I was protecting the county's interest. I didn't want a civilian suing us."

"More coffee, gents? Maybe a little brandy?" Daria asked as she entered.

Randall toyed with his coffee, then said, "I'm fine. Have a seat. I've got some bad news."

★　　★　　★

128

As soon as Molly was sure Emma was asleep, she pulled out the invoice box. After almost an hour, she knew her suspicions had been right. The first thing she should have noticed was that the invoices were made out to four different businesses. Her eyes had been too fixed on the merchandise, and not the details. Not one bill was in Trudy's name. Okay, that was easy. She had multiple entities, and used a Monterey post office box. Over half of the invoices were for reproductions coming out of Hong Kong, Taiwan, Mainland China, Egypt, and Mexico. Molly knew these countries had been exporting fakes for years. Everyone in the trade knew it. It was the scope and variety of goods that astounded her. Trudy's purchases had ranged from so-called Roman antiquities all the way up to nineteenth-century Continental and English pieces. Marble, china, porcelain, furniture; all listed as copied from the best manufacturers and artisans of the periods. The different wigs, contact lenses, eyeglasses, and photos began to make sense. Trudy was a different person for each venue.

A few shots of Jack Daniel's might be in order to calm her shaking hands, she decided. The scope of fraud was overwhelming. *But where did Carrie come in?* She went back to the first stack of invoices and found her answer. Several were addressed to a Tacoma address. That made sense. Seattle was a major port for Asian imports, and Tacoma was just next door.

So here, at last, was the connection to her sister.

All Carrie had to do was ship them to Trudy. Pulling the box closer, Molly rummaged for a recent bill she'd ignored and set aside. It was from a self-storage complex in Tacoma. The phony merchandise was probably taken to the storage unit, and held there until Trudy wanted it. Carrie must have taken it from there to the airport in Tacoma and shipped it to Carmel.

When the phone rang, Molly held her breath. Looking at the clock, she was surprised to see it was already ten-thirty. Scrambling to the phone, she picked it up and prayed it wasn't Randall. When she heard Daria's voice, she felt relief. "Oh, he told you."

"I couldn't believe it, Molly. I just can't get past it. Her death was bad enough, but *murder*?"

Sinking onto the bed, Molly said, "I know. I felt the same. I had to go over and give them my prints since I was in the house helping pack her things. Randall made me promise not to talk. Besides, I didn't want to be the one to tell you." She hated to lie to Daria, but she had no choice. She didn't dare let on about her sister knowing Trudy.

As if she'd read her mind, Daria brought up Emma's comment. "Could your sister have known Trudy?"

"No way. There must be thousands of Trudys in the world. I'm sure of it."

"Maybe not. A woman who was at Lucero's party was in the restaurant yesterday and said she saw your sister at the antiques show and assumed she was a dealer too. She knew you didn't carry Rookwood pottery and wondered if your sister did. I told her that Carrie was an attorney."

Molly slumped against the headboard and closed her eyes. "I'm sure she's mistaken. Carrie told me she'd just got in when she showed up Monday night. True, she's hard to miss, but there are any number of tall blondes around. Besides, if she'd been at the show, she'd have come to see me there instead of waiting until Monday."

"You're probably right. Anyway, don't worry about not telling me. I understand. Randall can be a hard head on occasion."

A vise was closing around Molly's head when she hung up. She wondered if Daria had mentioned all that to Randall.

After setting the alarm for five-thirty, Molly packed up the box and put it in the closet. She'd take it down to the garage tomorrow when they left, and would call Randall when they returned. She couldn't put it off any longer. The spiderweb was growing, and she felt like dinner.

Munching on warm doughnuts from Alberston's, Molly laid out the ground rules for Emma as she drove to the first sale. Snapping her fingers, she said, "We're in and out like that. You stick with me, don't talk to strangers, and when I give you the signal, we head back to the truck like a shot, and get on to the next place."

"Hit 'em hard and roll, right?"

"You got it! You sure you've never been to a garage sale before?"

"Nope. She never went to them. She liked new things."

The fact that Emma continued to refer to her mother as *she* was, for now, understandable, and Molly decided not to make a big deal of it.

Pulling up to the first sale on the list, Emma was out of the car before Molly. The excitement Molly saw in her eyes was worth getting up at five-thirty. The sale was advertised for seven, and while it was six, there was already a good crowd in the driveway. Silver serving pieces and flatware were not a quick sales item. No one wanted to polish the darn stuff anymore, and it was usually ignored. What people didn't realize was that the more you used it, the less you had to clean it. She found several pieces she knew Daria would love. With Emma at her side, they hurriedly picked up four serving trays, two coffee servers, and a mismatched set of sugar and creamers.

"This is like a treasure hunt," Emma whispered.

Molly leaned down and said, "It's a bonanza."

The pieces added up to three hundred dollars, cheap enough, Molly thought, but when she offered two hundred, the owner held out for two fifty. Molly quickly agreed. While the owner boxed the pieces, Molly did a quick tour of the other goods. Emma pointed out some china cups and saucers. "Think Daria would like those? They're only five bucks each."

"Hey, you catch on quick. Yes! Let's get all of them."

"How much are you going to offer?"

"Three."

"Ya think?"

"Watch me."

Laden with bounty, they drove off to the next address. "Can we do this every Saturday?" Emma asked.

"If the ads look good, you bet. Having fun?"

"Yes!"

Remembering that Emma arrived with only a few clothes and books, she said, "Good. Listen, if you see something you like, let me know. Books, or toys, or maybe a stuffed bear?"

"I'm too old for toys, Aunt Molly. Maybe some books."

"Oh, right. Of course. We're also looking for a desk and a few things for your room."

The next three sales had little to entice them. Driving out to Carmel Valley, Molly said, "The next stop should be pretty good. The ad said it was downsizing for world travelers moving to a condo. Let's hope we score a big one."

As soon as they arrived at the sale, Molly bought a desk, night table, and two lamps for Emma's room for an even one hundred. For the shop, she'd found two Birdseye maple side chairs needing new fabric on the drop-in seats, and a slightly soiled cane-backed French chair with some damage to the carving along the legs. Bargaining down to three hundred, Molly knew she'd turn them for eight or nine in no time. The two Oriental rugs she'd quickly grabbed were the real bargains. Worth at least fifteen hundred each, she was ready to bargain, but when she saw one of the rug dealers from Monterey pull up in his van, she agreed to the asking price of five hundred for the pair and handed the owner cash. She didn't want to waste time writing a check and lose the sale.

Emma was in her element, and Molly was wondering if the thrill of the chase for merchandise was genetic. It was wonderful to see her so animated. As hard as Emma tried to hide it, Molly knew she was still hurting. At the truck, waiting for the owners' sons to help load, Molly kept an eye on Emma. When she saw her dragging a box of books and a huge panda away from one of the used book dealers who was angrily saying something to her, she had to clamp her hand over her mouth to keep from laughing.

"I need ten bucks, quick! I'll pay you later," Emma hurriedly said.

Handing her the money, Molly watched her pay then scoot back to her. "What did that man say to you?"

"He told me he had dibs on the box of books, and I told him I was there first and if he didn't back off I was going to scream."

Molly's mouth fell open. "You didn't!"

"Yep, I sure did. And it worked! It's a good thing you have a truck," Emma said as they pulled away. "We'd never get all this merch in a car."

"Merch, huh? You're beginning to sound like a pro. I hated this truck when I first got here. I was ashamed to be seen driving it. Now, I love it. Rust and all!"

Hugging the large panda, Emma said, "I don't usually like stuffed animals." Giving Molly a grin, she added, "I don't consider this a toy, by the way. But this guy called to me. I'm glad he spent his life on a guest room bed and isn't grungy. And oh, the books they had! I could have stayed longer, but I got the Mark Twain set, so I'm happy."

"Is that what you bought? No wonder he was pissed!" Molly laughed so hard, she almost ended up on the shoulder. "Not that they were first editions, but those book people are ruthless. Well, you're learning fast!"

"I think the truck is kind of full. What do we do now?"

"We keep at it. I've got more bungies, and if we find stuff we can't load, we'll go back for it later."

By eleven Molly was feeling the loss of sleep. Emma was still rarin' to go. The rapid in and out of sales, the maniac driving to beat the crowd, and the adrenaline rush were beginning to take effect.

The load in the back of the El Camino truck was threatening to topple, and Molly was in dire need of caffeine. She had two more stops to finish her list. Ever the treasure hunter, a dealer never knew when to quit. And each time she thought about ignoring a sale or two, she invariably found those were the very ones where she made her best buys. But today was different. Fatigue and worry made it hard to concentrate. She'd lost out on an exquisite crystal chandelier by being a half step too slow at the last sale. Distracted by making sure Emma was at her side at another sale, she'd been too late on a pair of lovely Murano glass candlesticks. Like a gambler, one had to know when to quit.

Damn, but she'd wanted those candlesticks! Good quality antiques at affordable prices were becoming endangered species. She had talked like a Dutch uncle to convince Max to let her sell vintage items along with antiques. After all, the name of the store was Treasures, and that alone let them off the hook. As long as tags were honestly marked and the merchandise was attractive, why not? Max agreed, and it made a difference in sales.

At least the silver she picked up for Daria wasn't too badly tarnished. She'd told Daria a while back that she'd keep an eye open for silver, which she used at the restaurant, and wouldn't add a markup. Daria protested, but Molly stood firm. The deal was a free dinner a week if she gave Daria first crack on any new pieces in the shop. Garage sale buys were different, and made up for the frequent times Daria insisted that Molly have dinner with her in her private room.

"I think that's it for today," she said to Emma.

"How about if we stop at Bruno's and get some lunch to go? Then I'll call Bennie's cousin, Robbie, to help us unload."

"You're tired already?"

"Yeah, a little bit. But our work has just begun. I've got to get your stuff cleaned up, and then there's all that silver to polish." *And then*, she thought, *I've got to call Randall.*

"I'll help. I like to clean things. I'll do the silver too, if you want."

"What, and have me arrested for child labor?"

Emma laughed. "You're fun, you know that?"

"That's the nicest thing anyone has said to me in days." She blew Emma a kiss, and added, "And you're fun to have around."

When Molly saw Emma's eyes water, she reached over and squeezed her hand.

Robbie was waiting in the alley when they pulled up. Backing into the garage, Molly was careful to leave room to get to the locked cabinets where she'd hidden Trudy's boxes. It didn't take long to unload the truck. She helped Robbie carry Emma's furniture upstairs and place it in her bedroom. "We'll have to clean it up here. The garage is loaded now." It took three trips to carry the rest to the apartment. When Robbie left, they had a picnic lunch on the balcony outside the living room. "We need a little bistro table and two chairs for the balcony," Molly said. "When the weather gets better, we can eat out there like real people."

"I like us eating on these plastic crates. It's fun. We've got to have a little fun in life, don't you think?"

"You're going to corrupt me, little girl." Getting to her feet, Molly said, "I'm going to run downstairs and see how Bitsy's doing. When I come back, we'll get this silver ready for Daria, and then tackle your desk."

Tossing her baseball cap on the sofa, Molly undid her ponytail and fluffed out her hair. Being on the sales floor in sweats and sneakers wasn't a big deal in Carmel, but she at least wanted her hair to be presentable. Halfway down the stairs, she gripped the iron hand rail so tight, her knuckles were white. Oliver Townsend was sitting at her desk, facing the computer, and she could easily see that her inventory program was on the screen. The database listed every item in the shop; its cost, markup, and purchase source. Information sacrosanct to a dealer. Molly stepped back a few stairs and watched him. The computer was housed in a large 1930s mahogany armoire that wasn't worth much. Fitted out as a computer station and placed against the wall behind her desk, its imperfections were hardly visible, and the burl wood of the accordion doors was actually attractive. Leaning over the railing, she peeked around to the rear of the room, and saw Bitsy with a customer. Hardly the time to make a scene, Molly nevertheless was livid. Backing up farther, she returned to the apartment to cool off and wait for the customer to leave.

She was surprised to find Emma cleaning the

silver pieces. "Started without me, I see. Why don't you relax a little and watch TV? We got up pretty early. You must be a little tired."

"I'm fine. I thought I'd get some of them done while you were downstairs."

"I insist. Take a break. I'm going to call Daria and tell her what we scored." Grabbing the portable, Molly dialed the restaurant. It was a good excuse to kill a little time instead of Oliver. After giving Daria a rundown on what she'd found, she hung up and was about to say something to Emma when she saw her on the sofa fast asleep. Tiptoeing out of the room, she figured Bitsy had either sold something by now or the customer was gone. Standing on the staircase, she saw that Oliver was still at the computer looking over the inventory program. She watched him scroll past several pages. The shop was empty, and Bitsy had her back to Oliver, fussing with another display.

Standing in front of her desk, her arms folded, Molly said, "That's really ballsy of you, Oliver, to be sneaking around my computer."

Oliver's hands literally flew off the keyboard. Molly saw his back stiffen. Turning slowly to face her, he was all smiles. "I was trying to get to solitaire and just kept getting this thing."

"That *thing*, as you well know, is my inventory list, with costs and markups so plain they fairly leap off the screen."

Bitsy, who heard the exchange, was at the desk immediately. "Oh, darling, is there a problem? I didn't think you'd mind if Oliver kept himself amused with a little card game."

"*Mind? Mind* that you let a man I hardly know sit at my desk, use my computer, and then have the nerve to lie to me? If he wanted to play solitaire, all he had to do was click on the shortcut icon." Staring Oliver down, Molly added, "Well?"

"Molly!" Bitsy scolded. "This is uncalled for. Oliver is a dear friend."

"He's a competitor and has no business reading my business files."

"Ladies, please! Oh, this won't do," Oliver said. "I'm not very computer literate. An honest mistake, my dear. I've time on my hands until the painters finish tomorrow, so I thought I'd drop by and keep Bitsy company between sales."

"I'm not your *dear*, and I'm not a twit either. I watched you from the stairs scrolling page after page."

Rising from Molly's chair, Oliver nodded to Bitsy. "I'll see you at dinner. Charles will take me home."

Molly watched him leave, then turned to Bitsy. "Home? And Charles is now his driver too? What the hell is going on here?"

"You were quite rude, Molly. Oliver has had a trying time these past months, and he is my guest. If he wants to refer to my home as '*home*,' I certainly don't mind. And how else is he to get back to Pebble Beach?"

"Drive his own car?"

"Oh, please. Charles drove us in together."

Turning off the computer, Molly ignored Bitsy as she looked over her desk. Nothing was out of place, and Bitsy's sales tags were neatly stacked and covered by a cheap snowball paperweight Molly had found at a garage sale.

"I had a good day so far," Bitsy said. "Twenty-two hundred in smalls alone. I think those Edwardian dining chairs might go this afternoon. The lady will be back with her husband."

"Don't change the subject, Bitsy. I want to know what's going on with this Oliver." Sinking into her chair, she said, "Come on, what's up?"

Sitting next to her, Bitsy sighed. "Oh, really, darling, nothing at all. If you're thinking May-December, forget it. I'm past that stage. Oliver has suffered some horrible wounds, and he needs a new start. I haven't got more than ten years ahead of me, so if I can spread a little kindness around, why not?"

"Touché."

"That wasn't meant for you, and you know it. You are different. Why, almost family. Speaking of which, I've been thinking about little Emma. We need to lay out a plan for the child."

"Plan? As in?"

"Well, darling, she has to go back to school at some date. And I was thinking I could look into getting her into Santa Catalina in Monterey. It's a marvelous school, and the nuns are very progressive."

"I can't afford a private school of that caliber. Besides, I can't really do anything until Lucero sorts out some issues."

"Well, once he does, consider the tuition as my treat." Throwing her hands in the air, Bitsy quickly said, "And no arguments. This is for your mother."

"That's a lot of money. Mother wouldn't expect that."

"Ha! I'm loaded, and you know it. Anyway, what price is friendship? Your mother was my dearest, and I wasn't there when she needed me."

Molly looked away. Still fuming over Oliver, she finally said, "You have an extraordinary talent of changing a subject and turning it around to another problem. This time it may have backfired on you, because I'm going to take you up on the offer once we know where we are with Emma. But I don't want Oliver in here again."

"Understood. Are we best of friends again?"

Molly laughed. "You knew we would be, you old bat."

Bitsy laughed with her, then pointing to the computer, said, "Oh, before you go back up and do whatever you planned, would you show me how to start that thing?"

Molly looked at her for a moment. Swinging around in her chair, she said, "Come a little closer so you can watch. I'm going to turn it off first, so you can follow the steps." Pausing, Molly was about to say something, then changed her mind. Bitsy was never interested in the computer before.

When she rebooted and the screen saver came up, she looked at Bitsy. "Easy, isn't it?"

"Where's the whatchamacalit for solitaire?"

Molly moved the mouse to the icon, then clicked on the game.

Bitsy nodded. "If it was a snake, it would have bit him."

CHAPTER 12

Finding Emma still asleep upstairs, Molly wondered if this was a good time to call Randall. She reached for the phone then changed her mind. Bitsy was still in the shop and might come upstairs with a question. It was better to wait until after the shop was closed, when Emma was deep into one of the Disney videos she'd found at a sale today. She could meet Randall in the garage, so Emma wouldn't be able to hear the lion roar.

Later, waiting for Randall downstairs, Molly thought about the call she had to make to the customers who'd purchased the Old Paris and Meissen from her. She could call them today, but knew she was still too angry, and was afraid she might blow it. Besides, she had to come up with some reason for her stupidity, and then find a way to buy them back. It would make a big dent in what was left of her savings. She'd been brushed with the tar of fraud in New York and got it cleaned off, and she would damn well keep it that way.

Sitting on the open tailgate of the El Camino, she smoked and swung her legs.

"I hope this isn't some new exercise, because you look pretty dumb," Randall said as he strolled in.

"Funny."

"Okay, what's up, and why are we meeting in the garage?"

"I, ah, I have some stuff. I mean, I completely forgot to tell you that I have Trudy's office files here."

Looking around the crowded garage, Randall said, "Oh, she was working out of your truck? I don't see a desk or a—"

"Knock it off, please. You know what I mean."

Leaning against the garage door, Randall said, "Actually, I'm at a loss here. Care to elaborate?"

Jumping off the back of the truck, Molly went to the locked wall cabinet and opened it wide enough for him to see the stacked boxes. "Here," she said, "it's all in here."

Moving in, lighting one of his Cuban cigars, Randall took his time. "Gee, I bet if I opened one of those boxes, I'd find everything nice and neat, right? Probably even color coded."

His calm sarcasm was more deadly than his roar. Molly hated when he pulled that routine. "It was the tent," she blurted.

"The tent?"

"Uh, right. Trudy wanted to get reorganized, and since the house was being tented, she asked if she could move her stuff here."

Looking around at the open beams, the cobwebs,

and the oil-stained cement floor, Randall said, "Oh, sure. Why not? Great ambiance."

"Damnit, Randall! She was going to work upstairs in the apartment."

"Yeah, and you just happened to remember you had her stuff stashed here, right? Wow, lucky me. I also suppose your prints will be all over it too, right?"

"Well, I helped her put it in the boxes. I mean, she just threw stuff around and—"

"Stop, okay? Stop while you're ahead."

"Excuse me?"

"You knew I'd find her office empty and wonder, didn't you? Why didn't you *remember* to mention it when you came in to do your prints?"

"I . . . I was upset. I wasn't trying to *remember* anything."

Pulling out his cell phone, Randall turned his back while he called the station. All Molly could hear was, "Yeah, I'll wait. Six cardboard boxes."

Turning back to her, he said, "I expected more from you."

Molly felt a flush creep up her neck. Folding her arms, she said, "I'm not perfect."

"Neither is murder."

"Maybe if you were a little more upfront with me, I—"

"You'd what?" he broke in. "Not hold back information? You know how important personal records are to an investigation." Randall watched her face, saw her jaw tighten, her chin jut out.

"Okay, Molly, out with it. What are you trying to keep from me?"

He saw a flicker in her eyes as he moved closer. "That Trudy had a past? That she'd been up for receiving stolen goods? Is that it?"

"*What?* When? I mean, where did that happen?"

"You didn't know? Shit, I thought you people knew everything about each other. You antique dealers are worse than a coven. Some years back. Here, in fact. She claimed she didn't know and handed the stuff back like a good citizen."

"I never knew."

"Bitsy must have known. I'm surprised she didn't tell you. Daria too, for that matter."

Molly knew he was watching her closely, so she moved past him and sat on the back of the truck again. When he joined her, she didn't dare let him see her annoyance. She dug in her pocket for her cigarettes and lighter, then lit one. Exhaling slowly, she said, "A onetime mistake is hardly worth mentioning. It happens all the time."

"Yeah, sure. Occupational hazard, right? So what are you hiding, then, Molly Doyle?"

"Oh, please! Stop looking for conspiracies. You're beginning to sound like Oliver Stone. Why would I be hiding anything?"

"I don't know, but you are. A car's coming up the alley. It's probably one of my guys. Stay put, I'll want you to sign a receipt for Trudy's stuff."

Fixing a smile on her face, Molly said, "You're wrong, copper. I don't know nuttin'."

Stopping, Randall turned back. "Yeah? Well, I don't believe you. When you come out with those cute lines, I know you're up to something. You want to play games with me? Okay, you're on. Just don't let me find out you're withholding information. Got it?"

"Got it."

She began to think she should just come clean and give him what she'd hidden upstairs. Seesawing back and forth, she finally decided that as despicable as Carrie was, she was still her sister. Until she knew how deeply involved she was, she'd do whatever it took to protect her. Even if Randall never spoke to her again.

On his way back in with one of his officers, Randall said, "We'll take those boxes off your hands, Ms. Doyle. I appreciate your cooperation. Officer Wilkins will have you sign a receipt."

Officer Wilkins, who knew that Molly and Randall were friends, was surprised by Randall's formality. Handing her a clipboard, he said, "Uh, yes, here we are. If you'll sign here, Molly." Giving Randall a quick glance, he added, "Er, Ms. Doyle. Right by the six boxes of—"

"She's got it, Wilkins, okay?"

Molly barely looked at the paper. She scribbled her name, handed Wilkins back his pen, then went to the cabinet. "There's a dolly you can use," she told him. "It's on the other side of the truck."

Randall relit his cigar and watched Wilkins wheel

the boxes out. At the door, he turned and looked at Molly, then left without saying a word.

Tears started to cloud her eyes. She'd found a haven in Carmel, and people who'd helped mend a broken heart. Randall had become a staunch friend, a wonderful teasing partner, a man she could count on. Daria was already a dear friend. Even Bitsy, as outrageous a busybody one could know, was loved. Bennie and Lucero had been there for her when she needed the warmth of family loyalty. And now, she realized, she might be risking it all for a sister who'd abandoned her child and stole from her family time and time again.

Would she lose all these wonderful people if Carrie had killed Trudy, Molly wondered, and it was discovered that she'd hidden possible evidence? And what about Emma? Would she be able to carry the burden of her mother's guilt for the rest of her life?

Randall was torn between throttling Molly and throwing her in jail. Maybe if he put her in the slammer for a sleepover, he thought, she might get a clue that he meant business. She was holding something back, and he was damned if he wasn't going to get it out of her. What the hell had she come across that she couldn't let him see? She and Trudy weren't that tight. It wasn't as if they'd been lifelong friends. Women didn't have lifelong friends, only men could handle that.

He didn't think Daria knew what was going on. Molly Doyle held a tight hand. He'd learned that lesson the hard way. Then again, he might be barking up the wrong tree. Maybe she was telling him the truth. Maybe she was just frazzled over the sister thing and inheriting a twelve-year-old child. He didn't want to doubt her, but that damn chin of hers was trouble from day one. Stubborn to a fault. His face-reading teacher in L.A. had warned the class to watch out for people with a dimple in their chin. Randall laughed out loud at that memory. He had one, and so did Lucero. And that twitching over her eye thing cracked him up. It was a telltale sign that she was ready to rip.

Molly Doyle was a cop's daughter. She knew how the game was played and won. If she was holding out on him, he at least hoped she knew what she was facing. Now that he had Trudy Collins's personal files, he might be able to find out.

Back in his office, Randall eyed the boxes Wilkins had set on his conference table. He moved the Murder Book to his desk, and faced the Incident board. The three main columns, Motive, Opportunity, and Means, had few notations at this point. Lucero's top investigators were already interviewing, and he expected a report midweek. Without a husband as a possible suspect, and, according to Daria, Trudy wasn't seeing anyone special, he had to consider her business as a prime focus. Unless Lucero's guys came up with a dicey romantic liaison.

Peeling off his sport coat, Randall buzzed for hot coffee, laid out three cigars, lined up an ashtray to

150

his right, and squared off his legal-size notepad. Picking up the phone, he ordered Chinese takeout, joked with the owner of the restaurant a few blocks away, and promised her he wouldn't work too late. When the coffee arrived, he asked not to be disturbed unless it was an emergency or a call from Lucero; then he quickly added Molly Doyle.

Back in the apartment, Molly found Emma in the kitchen scrambling eggs. "I thought maybe we might have a sandwich. I love scrambled eggs on toast with catsup, don't you?"

Looking at the cat clock on the wall, Molly was surprised to see it was already eight in the evening. She hadn't even considered Emma and dinner. Being on her own, she usually ate when she felt like it. Breakfast, lunch, and dinner were dictated by stomach growls. "I'm sorry, I—"

"That's okay. I'm used to taking care of myself."

"I'm just getting the hang of it," Molly said.

Sitting on the floor in front of the television, Molly and Emma watched *Lilo and Stitch,* and spent more time laughing and wiping catsup from their chins than eating. "This is fun," Emma said.

Looking down at her red-smeared jeans, Molly shook her head. "If you say so." She found herself laughing harder at the cartoon than necessary. Even Emma looked at her once or twice. But it was a great break from her encounter with Randall and the worries haunting her.

When the film ended, Emma asked, "Want to see it again?"

"Uh, I don't think so. I'm going to run downstairs and do a little computer work." Picking up their dishes, Molly added, "Don't stay up too late. We've got more sales tomorrow morning, and then Mass at the Mission."

"Mass? You mean church? I've never been."

Molly almost tripped over her feet. "What? Your mother never—"

"No. She said church was for stupid people. Only weak people went there."

Setting the dishes on the coffee table, Molly held her breath, then said, "Do you think I'm stupid or weak?"

Emma's eyes widened at the set look on Molly's face. "No."

"Good. Because I'm neither." Back down on the carpet across from her, Molly took Emma's hand in hers. "For as long as we're together, we'll have a few rules, but I'll never force my likes or dislikes on you. I'll help you any way I can to make good decisions, but ultimately the choices will be yours. I'm going to take you to Mass with me tomorrow. If you want to continue to go with me, fine. But don't ever think religion is for stupid or weak people. I don't fully agree with the Catholic Church, but it doesn't matter. I go to visit God."

"Maybe we better get to the rules? I don't want to make you angry."

"Emma! Stop with the 'make me angry' thing. I'm not Carrie!" When she saw the dead look in Emma's eyes, she hurriedly said, "That was cruel. I'm sorry."

"It's okay. Just habit, I guess."

"Well, break it." Molly grinned. "The rules, then. Number one is homework. It's gotta be done. Number two is clothes. No diva pop queen trash. Number three is music. I will not have—"

Emma was laughing now. "I got the picture. Not my style anyway."

"Not now it isn't, but in a year or two? Here's the big one. Number four. Tolerance. Race, religion, ethnic background, and lifestyle."

Pretending to think, Emma said, "Hmm . . . guess that means not to bug you about smoking."

Molly rolled her eyes. "You too? I'll take it under advisement, okay?"

When Emma nodded, Molly gave her a hug, then headed for the kitchen with the dishes.

Staring at her monitor, Molly had a hard time concentrating. She didn't know which problem to solve first. And she didn't want to know what might be on Trudy's disc. She ought to just hand it over to Randall and let him figure it out. *Yeah, right,* she thought. She could hear him now: *Oh, you forgot to give me her computer discs too? How nice of you to remember. Thank you so much.* And what would she tell him? Another lie.

She was beginning to feel like a magnet, drawing

trouble at every turn. Then there was the loss of her watch and jade ring. That made her angry, but the loss of the miniatures was serious. At today's market, the value of the French miniatures could easily be worth mid-five figures. Her safety net was gone. If Max decided to sell the shop and the complex, she wouldn't have the means to open her own. If, God forbid, something happened to him—and at seventy plus, that was a reality—she'd be in the same boat. Either scenario would be a problem. Now with Emma to take care of, it could be a disaster.

The dark thoughts of her sister flooding her mind brought her up short when she realized she was clutching the small crucifix under her tee shirt again. Looking up at the ceiling, she grinned. *Okay, point taken. I'll lay off with the bad thoughts. But Carrie better be clean, or I get first crack at her, okay?*

Slipping in one of Trudy's discs, Molly hoped the files were on Word. Miracles occasionally happen. It worked. Each file had a city name, much like the envelopes with the photos. Clicking on the Seattle file, Molly blinked, then sat back in the chair. It was filled with line after line of abbreviated words, initials, and numbers. None of it made sense unless you were a cryptologist. She doubted MI5 could decipher it. Scrolling carefully through each page, she finally found two entries with the initials *C.N.* Then *Spns.Nkl.* The number after it was *56.* The next, was *Spns.Cs.Gl.Cn., 77.* On page seven she found another *C.N.* It read: *Spns.Rg.Em.,98.,* and then on page ten, *Spns.Rs.Rb.Em.,62.* There were twelve pages, and none of them made any sense. Next, she clicked on Pasadena. The same story and format for nine pages. The most popular initial there was *T.O.T.* She counted at least eleven entries before she gave up. Clicking through other cities, she began to notice a pattern. While all initials were capitalized, some were in regular text and others were italicized.

Sipping cold coffee, Molly felt she was ready to jump ship. Hieroglyphics would be less trying. At least they were pictures. This was just gibberish. She had an idea it was an inventory code, but why do it so mysteriously? She stared at the screen until her eyes began to water. And then it finally hit her. The fake merch? It had to be. A code of fake merch she'd taken to each show. Feeling revved up now, she began to mumble to herself, "The initials! Sure! The Roman ones are for the fakes, the italics are for . . . the fakes too? Which was which? Shit!"

A tingle ran down her spine. She knew that what she was looking at was more than just a screwball inventory list made in haste. Or maybe that *was* it. Maybe it *had* been made in haste. If that was the case, why? What was Trudy afraid of? Was she being blackmailed and wanted some sort of record? Did the initials belong to the buyers, or the sellers? Trudy's office was a mess. Trudy was not organized. This list meant something.

Pasadena was the closest venue to Carmel. Though hours away, it was still more manageable than Seattle. She knew an interior designer in Pasadena from her Manhattan days, and wondered if she might have some gossip to share. Maybe some rumblings from a show? Or a dealer who'd bought from Trudy? Had any of the fakes been discovered? Chicanery between dealers was rarely reported to the police. They dealt with it among themselves. Make up the loss, don't screw with me again or be exposed and blackballed forever was an unwritten law. But if Trudy wore different wigs and contact lenses, or glasses, she must have worked the shows under different names. How would she know what name Trudy might have used in Pasadena?

Pulling her address book from the desk, Molly looked up Sally Sims. Sally was one of the more renowned interior designers to the movie crowd, and she'd sold her tons of merchandise from Porter's. It was too late to call now, but she'd do it tomorrow. Maybe Davis Wood in Beverly Hills would be better. Davis loved slumming, as he called it, at antique shows. He had an exquisite shop, but he was such a bigmouth. No, she didn't trust him. She remembered telling him a funny story at a party in the Hamptons, and before the evening was over, the entire crowd knew it, and he'd taken credit for it. Davis was out. Sally Sims was it.

Turning off the computer, Molly strolled around

the showroom and noted the holes in her displays. Bitsy had a pretty good day. She couldn't believe she hadn't even looked at the sales tags that Bitsy had left on her desk. When had that ever happened? Sales were life!

Switching off lamps as she neared the stairs, Molly almost shrieked. Milo Kraft was standing in front of her main window, staring at her. Holding onto the wrought-iron rail, she held her breath and stared back. It seemed like hours before he turned and walked away. Then she rushed to the door and shook it to make sure it was locked. She hadn't bothered to check it when she came downstairs. Slipping the old iron bar across the middle, she decided to leave the rest of the lamps on. Racing up the stairs, she checked every door. Satisfied everything was secure, she leaned against the counter in the kitchen and seriously thought about calling Randall. If Milo Kraft was intent on scaring her, he had. Did he know she'd been in Trudy's house and had access to her office? Had he gone around the corner the day she'd seen him at Trudy's, and recognized the El Camino in the driveway? Sure, that must be it. Because he would have seen the moving company truck too. Then there was the Carrie connection. He must know they were sisters, and probably thought she knew what was going on.

She realized that keeping the envelopes, the tape, and disc could put her in serious jeopardy. Not just from Milo Kraft. Words like *obstruction* and *accomplice* came to mind. Even if Carrie didn't kill

Trudy, she still had plenty to worry about. Molly decided she didn't owe her sister a prison term. Her father had already done that. Emma would have to learn to live with her mother's crimes, just as she herself had learned to live with her father's.

Taking a deep breath, Molly punched in Randall's home number. She hoped he'd yell at her this time. She hated it when he played those silent games. All pumped up and ready, she felt like a collapsing balloon when his answering machine clicked on. She paused and wondered if she should just hang up. Maybe his not being home was karmic. Looking up, she blew out her breath and said, "*What? Am I supposed to stay with this? You want me to get in more trouble? Okay, so you work in strange ways, but give me a clue here.*"

Checking on Emma on her way to bed, Molly smiled when she saw Tiger curled up behind the girl's back. The picture of calm in the eye of the storm, she thought.

CHAPTER 13

"Can we get warm doughnuts again?" Emma asked as Molly tore down the deserted streets of Carmel at six in the morning on their way to a big sale near Carmel Point.

"You're playing havoc with my diet," Molly said. "We've got to get to this sale first, then we'll have time for doughnuts."

With so much on her mind, Molly almost decided against going to Sunday morning's garage sales. One part of her wanted to stay and call Randall again, and another demanded relief from worry. Besides, two sales were at Carmel Point, and the enclave of pricey homes just south of Carmel proper had been a treasure trove in the past. In spite of everything, she was still a dealer. The sky could be falling in, but the mania for a *find* was too embedded to be ignored. The hunt for new merchandise and the excitement of the chase were like pirates riding the wake of a Spanish galleon heading for home.

Expecting the street to be filled with people anxiously waiting in their parked cars, Molly was

159

surprised to see she was ahead of the crowd. She parked in front of the house and said to Emma, "Wait here. The sale doesn't start for another hour, and the owners have already moved. I want to do a little snooping before the other scavengers show up."

Peering into the large living room window, she was disappointed to see it filled with Victorian furniture. The heavy style was hard to sell in Northern California lately, and the small items she could see were mostly common and ordinary. Wondering about the other rooms, she hurried around to the side of the house and hoped the gate to the rear garden was unlocked. Luck was with her. She quickly scooted in and walked around to the patio. She was in wrought-iron heaven. Checking out a few chairs and tables, she decided the prices were low enough to work with. She wouldn't have to do much bargaining, and they'd be perfect for the conservatory look.

When she saw the tags were the perforated type—which would allow a buyer to tear off the bottom tag and make a beeline for the cashier—Molly hesitated for a second. House sales were war zones. Only the strong survived. A veteran of many theaters, she glanced around the garden just in case, then tore off tags to two tables and four chairs. Pausing for a moment, she decided to do the same to three plant stands. When she moved under the patio awning toward the house, she saw a gorgeous marble buffet with an iron base. At three hundred, off came that tag too. It wasn't an antique, or even a vintage French pastry table, but it would do. Shoving the tags into her jeans, she moved up to the sliding glass patio door and saw several round tables holding china and glass. She made note of the large urns and vases, which she knew would make fantastic lamps.

Checking her watch, she decided to get out of there before another veteran had the same idea. Sneaking back out the side gate, Molly's eyes roamed the street. The El Camino was still the only vehicle in front of the house. Back in the truck within seconds, she drove off and asked Emma, "Anyone show up?"

"No. I kept my eyes peeled. You're in the clear."

Molly laughed. "You make a good partner. Let's go get some doughnuts."

By the time they stuffed themselves with chocolate doughnuts, they were back at the house and a line was already forming at the front door. Dressed in her uniform of jeans, baseball cap, and sunglasses, Molly easily blended in. Most of the regulars, whom she recognized, were friendly and talkative with each other. She had decided to stay aloof. It wasn't a good idea to get to know any of them. It made bargaining and backing off someone a half step ahead of you awkward. The minute the sale opened, Molly headed for the room off the patio, tore off the tags of the items she'd already decided upon, and quickly paid for everything.

The next two sales were less interesting. The first driveway was filled with pet furniture, poor quality china, stainless steel flatware, baby clothes, and gym equipment still in cartons. Emma, however, was already addicted and pleaded to get out and take a look. Molly hated to spoil her fun, and parked. Handing her a twenty, she said, "You go ahead. I'll wait here."

Molly watched Emma poke her nose in several boxes, and when she saw her lift one and head for the owner, she figured she'd found more books. Molly understood her love of books, and was pleased they had something in common.

When Emma got back, Molly leaned over and opened the door for her. "Want some help?"

Emma quickly shook her head, jumped in with the box on her lap, and said, "Better hit the gas and get out of here before the owner changes her mind and wants this back."

Pulling away, Molly asked, "Why on earth would you think that? Did you pay her what she wanted?"

"Yep. She said she wanted twenty for the box, and that's what I gave her. But a lady next in line said something about these things were hard to find, and when the owner asked her what she meant, I handed her the money and got out of there."

Turning the corner, Molly pulled over and parked. "What kind of books did you buy?"

"Not books." Pulling back the flaps of the

carton, she pulled out a painted bust of an Oriental woman and handed it to Molly.

Molly's mouth flew open. "Emma!"

"There's two of them."

"Two? For twenty bucks?" Molly reached for the box and opened it. She shook her head in amazement. Carefully unwrapping the other figure, she couldn't believe her eyes. Without a word, she wrapped it up again, then put it carefully back in the box. "I've given up looking for these. *I'm crazy about them!* I have two in my bedroom."

"I know. I loved them right away. The faces of the Chinese women were beautiful. When I saw the first one in the box, I kind of thought I'd like to have one too. Did I spend too much? Should I have offered her fifteen?"

"Oh, no. You did fine. Really fine. Well, young lady, you are a true Doyle. You have inherited the eye. You have just bought two Esther Hunt chalkware busts. One is signed, which is fantastic. The other isn't, but that's okay. Whew! You're right! We need to get out of here before the woman who sold them comes chasing after us."

Taking the pretense a bit too far, Molly drove faster than she should have. The residential areas outside the city limits had just as many narrow and twisting streets, if not more. Slowing to a more civilized speed, she said, "These figures have a wonderful history and are very hard to find. I'll tell you all about that later, but the signed ones are worth at least fifteen hundred to two thousand each, and the others . . . oh, hell, anywhere from five or six hundred, depending on the condition. *Emma, you made a major score!*"

Pleased and excited, Emma asked, "Can I keep one? I mean, do they both have to go in the shop?"

"The shop? No, they're yours."

"But you gave me the money."

"That was for polishing all that silver. So it was your money."

Emma hugged the box to her. "I like the way you do business."

"That's a good start for a college fund, honey. I'll make sure you hang on to them."

Calling Robbie on her cell phone, Molly arranged to have him pick up the wrought-iron furniture she couldn't fit in the truck and to meet her at the shop that afternoon. She was already decorating the new section in her mind, and the blistered paint, flaking, and rust on the iron would fit perfectly.

After unloading what they could, Molly told Emma she had a few things to do in the shop before Bitsy arrived, and then she'd tell her more about the Oriental busts. She had two hours. Plenty of time to copy Trudy's discs, set up a password on her computer just in case, get hold of Sally Sims, and then call Randall. Except for building up enough nerve again to call Randall, contacting Sally was the hardest chore to complete. The last number Molly had for her belonged to someone else now. She'd have to call Davis Wood after all. If anyone knew where Sally was, he would. After a half hour of reminiscing and totally insincere compliments about her role in helping solve the art scam, Davis told her Sally had moved to Santa Barbara and that he'd heard she planned to open a fabulous new shop there. Quickly jotting down her number, and pretending she wanted to contact Sally about a client looking for period Italian maiolica urns, Molly promised to stop by next time she was down his way.

Dialing Sally, Molly decided she'd best use the same story with her. This lying game was getting on her nerves. Before long, she'd have to make a list so she could remember what she'd said and to whom. Randall's list was going to be the longest. When Sally answered, the next half hour was almost a word-for-word repeat of her conversation with Davis.

Listening to Sally describe her new life in Santa Barbara, Molly realized that what she needed to know couldn't be handled over the telephone. Gossip, even among the trade, and especially the type of questions she wanted to ask, were best done face-to-face over a leisurely lunch. Glancing quickly at her calendar as Sally went on and on about her newly rich clients and how unsophisticated they were, Molly decided tomorrow would be the perfect day to drive down. Monday and Tuesday were generally slow, and if Bitsy could handle two more days, she'd be able to leave early in the morning and be back Tuesday.

Sally was delighted with Molly's suggestion, and gave her the names of two inns. As Molly jotted them down, she arranged to meet Sally for lunch.

About to call the first inn, she suddenly remembered Emma. She'd have to take her along. Booking a room with twin beds, Molly wrote down the name of the freeway off ramp, then asked how long it would take to drive from Carmel. Four to four and a half hours. Considering she'd never been there and didn't know the road or how heavy the traffic might be, she decided they'd have to leave by six if she wanted to check in at the inn and meet Sally on time.

Carmel had been the southernmost point for Doyle family outings. Disneyland was on the wish list until Molly's mother died. After that, the longing to see the attraction had faded away. Molly had traveled to Los Angeles from New York several times for clients, but it was usually in and out in a few days. Sightseeing was never on the agenda. She looked up Santa Barbara on the Internet and printed out a map. She hadn't realized what a big community it was. In fact, the only thing she knew about it was that it was next door to Montecito, where Oprah had built a mega showplace.

Molly had a cup of instant coffee in the storage room before calling Randall. Slumped in the comfy but dilapidated chair, she tried to remember how she'd planned to word her announcement to Randall last night. Her mind was blank. When his answering machine came on again, she sighed with relief. Looking at the calendar on the wall, she was reminded this was Sunday, not a good day to pile up lies. She still had to go to Mass.

When she tried him at the station and he came on the line, she said, "Got a few minutes? I found some more stuff that belongs to Trudy." When he didn't reply, she knew she was in deep trouble. "A couple of envelopes must have fallen under the seat when she used my truck to bring her stuff over. I'm on my way." She hung up before he could answer. Apparently, the silent treatment plan was in effect. The best thing she could do now was to pretend she wasn't aware of it. She remembered reading somewhere that oblivion was the mark of innocence. She just hoped he'd read the same thing.

At her desk, she put the two envelopes in her tote, and was about to leave when she remembered to tell Emma she had an errand to run. Having her around was taking some getting used to. Coming or going on a whim was now a thing of the past. And real food was in order. She'd have to learn to cook.

Molly decided to just walk over to the police station. The truck was still loaded, and she didn't want Robbie to show up and wonder where she was.

When she got there, Randall was standing in the lobby and motioned her to follow him to his office. She saw the conference table filled with Trudy's records in neat piles. She watched Randall move to the Incident board and pull down a window shade. Turning to face her, he held out his hand. "If you should *happen* to find anything else, I'm sure you'll let me know right away."

She handed over the envelopes and said, "Absolutely."

Nodding, he moved to his desk and opened them. When he didn't invite her to sit, Molly decided to take the offensive. She hadn't expected him to carry it this far. Knowing it was probably a mistake, she turned and began to walk out. She could feel his eyes boring a hole in her back and was almost at the door when he said, "I didn't say you could leave yet."

"Excuse me?"

"Don't start, okay? I got a few questions, that's all." He was angry with her, but knew it was pointless to get her Irish up. Coming around his desk, he pulled out a chair, set an ashtray in front of her. "Can I get you some coffee?"

The grin on his face was too funny for words. Pretending indifference, and tilting her chin up, she sat and pulled a pack of cigarettes from her tote bag. She'd barely put it to her lips when Randall was at her side with his lighter. Nodding her thanks, she watched him as he went back around to his desk, buzzed for coffee, then picked up Trudy's computer disc. "Word, right?"

"Yes." *Shit!* She wanted to evaporate before his eyes.

"You're something else." Randall shook his head and laughed as he pulled up the program. Looking at the file directory, he asked, "Which file do you like best?"

"It doesn't matter. You won't be able to understand it anyway."

Swinging around in his chair, he said, "And why is that? Oh, don't tell me antique dealers have devised a new language and only members of the cult are privy to it?"

"Cute, Randall. Very cute. You won't understand it because it's some sort of code Trudy devised. It didn't make sense to me, so I'm sure you won't be able to figure it out either."

"Yeah? Well, we'll see." He clicked on a file and ignored her for several moments as he scrolled through the pages. When he pulled a cigar from his drawer, Molly's hands turned clammy. Careful not to let him see her wipe them on her jeans, she pretended to be brushing away fallen ash. Looking away from the screen, he said, "Child's play, Ms. Doyle. This is amateur night stuff."

Maybe he was right and her suspicions were off base. Maybe, she thought, she should just leave and not tell him she had an idea the list represented fake merchandise. If he hadn't figured it out already when he saw the invoices from Hong Kong and

Taiwan, then she had time to check it out on her own. "Really? Well, it didn't make sense to me."

Stepping over to the conference table, he picked up a plastic pouch filled with the strange looking sales tags. He'd wanted to keep her out of the investigation, but knew Lucero was right. Molly's input could be invaluable. Going against his better judgment, he set the pouch in front of her and said, "Remember these?"

When Molly nodded, he said, "Go ahead and take them out. They've been processed. See if anything clicks."

Molly emptied the pouch on the desk, and didn't want to touch them. She knew the dark rusty smears were Trudy's dried blood. Seeing her face go pale, Randall opened a drawer and handed her a pair of tweezers. "Here, use this if it makes you feel better."

Taking the tweezers, Molly nodded her thanks. There were several tags, and while her eyebrows rose at the quality of the merch and the prices listed, she finally shook her head. "Great stuff. Wish I had them to sell."

"That's it? What about the fancy necklace?"

Though not similar, it was of the same style as in one of Trudy's Pasadena photos. Molly was puzzled but didn't want to let on. "It looks Spanish. Maybe eighteenth century. Not my field of expertise."

Pointing to the monitor, Randall said, "I think something like it is listed here." When she didn't reply, he said, "Okay, maybe not, then. So maybe this is just some cockamamie inventory list. Probably where she sold the goods, the price, and maybe the initials of who bought it. Most likely done on a laptop at the show, to be revised when she got home. No great shakes, no secret code. Could be homegrown shorthand. These big tags might be something to pass her time."

"You're probably right. Hardly a big clue or smoking gun."

Randall nodded. "Yeah, probably."

"Well, then there's no point in my hanging around." Popping up from the chair, Molly said, "I've got to get back and unload the truck."

"Not so fast."

"Aw, come on! I've got work to do. You've made it abundantly clear you don't need me, so—"

"Why did you keep this from me?"

"I didn't keep it from you! I told you—"

"Knock it off, okay? It's me, Randall, the guy who—"

"Saved my life. Okay, thanks! I won't put you to the trouble again."

Randall stared at her, then shook his head. "That isn't what I was going to say."

The silence between them was suddenly awkward. Molly turned away so he couldn't see her face. She quickly realized what he was about to say, and she didn't know how to apologize for her outburst.

"So, tell me what else you know."

"God, but you're dense," she mumbled. The deep breath she took cleared her brain and helped remind her what she had to do. She knew they were both hotheads, and he'd been with her day and night at the hospital. The bond growing between them deserved honesty. "Okay, but only because I'm going to Mass, and I don't want Him mad at me."

He accepted her apology with a smile. "You taking Emma?"

Molly's lopsided grin was her acknowledgment. "She's never been. Can you believe that? So much for Catholic school training. But then, my sister never listened to anyone, let alone the nuns."

Back in the chair, she finally said, "I think Trudy was passing off repro Sèvres, Meissen, and Old Paris porcelain as period pieces. You probably noticed them on those invoices from Asia. Sad to admit, she screwed me too."

"No. Can that be? You? Molly Doyle? Taken?"

"Do you want to know the rest, or are you just going to—"

"Sorry. I couldn't let that pass. I already figured it, okay? I didn't know you got caught, though."

Lighting a cigarette, Molly waved it around like a baton as she explained how she'd realized she'd been had. "I've got to call the buyers and make up eighteen grand. I bought them from that first estate sale when Trudy let me in early. They were way cheap and I should have known. She said the attorney needed to settle the estate as soon as possible. And when Bitsy and Daria vouched for her, I . . . I let greed get ahead of my brain."

"You got the dough to make those deals right?"

Molly nodded. "I saved the profits for big buys. Well, almost all of it. I'll have to dip into my savings, but what the hell."

"If you get any flak from those buyers, let me know. I'll handle it."

"Flak? I don't think so. Denial most likely."

"Come again?"

"Collectors sometimes don't want to know they've been had. They'd rather pretend they know as much as a dealer. Besides, if they've shown them off, they'll have egg on their face."

"So how are you going to handle it?"

"I'll tell them the truth, and then suggest they pretend they sold them."

Randall gathered up the phony sales tags and put them back in the plastic pouch. "Where do you figure these things come in?"

Giving them another glance, Molly said, "I haven't a clue." Stubbing out her cigarette, she wondered now if she should tell him about going to Santa Barbara. She put that on hold for the moment. "Now that I've leveled with you, I want to know how Trudy was killed."

When he didn't answer, she pushed. "Come on! I thought we were friends again."

His smile told her they were, yet he hesitated. He knew if she was still holding back, he'd never get it out of her unless he told her. It was a gamble, but one he was willing to take. "I'm gonna make you promise to keep a lid on it, okay?"

"Deal."

"I'm not going to announce the homicide. Lucero and I decided to keep it between us for now. Penicillin was found in Trudy's Coke. She was allergic to it. She never had a chance."

"Oh, my God! Her med bracelet! It must have been on there! Anyone who knew her would know."

"Bingo."

Stunned, Molly had to take a moment to absorb what he'd just told her. "Before you ask, yes, I knew. She told me. We were at the La Playa having drinks when I asked about the bracelet. I thought she might be diabetic, and I was concerned." Pausing, she added, "So she knew her killer?"

"Give the little lady a Kewpie doll."

"Milo Kraft!" Molly blurted.

Randall's eyes narrowed. "What do you know about him?"

Molly told him about her very first meeting with him, how he'd offered repros, and that she kicked him out of the shop. She described the day she saw him peeking into Trudy's windows, and then the night he stared at her in the shop. She hesitated for a moment. Her heart and mind were sending so many signals, she wasn't sure which to listen to. Torn between the right thing to do, she realized protecting a murderer—if indeed it was

Carrie—was beyond family loyalty. Reaching into her tote, she pulled out the tape. "I think you'd better listen to this."

"When did you plan to give this to me?" When he saw tears clouding her eyes, he said, "What is it, Molly?"

"Just play it, okay?"

He took a cassette player from the bottom drawer of his desk and slipped in the tape. "This baby plays any make or model. Fancy cop toy. Tell me when to stop."

When she heard Carrie's voice say "it's me," she said, "Stop there."

He watched her face as he listened. "You know this voice." It wasn't a question.

"It's Carrie."

Randall clicked off the machine and sat back in his chair. "Shit."

Molly sat staring at nothing as Randall went to the conference table and pulled open a binder. Returning to his desk, he picked up the phone and hit the speed dial. "You got some time for me?" he said into the phone. "Yeah, now is better . . . Yeah, the Collins thing." When he hung up, he said to her, "Find a sitter. We're gonna have to meet at Daria's again. Make it six."

"You know something about Carrie? You found her? What is it? Tell me, damnit!"

"It'll keep."

"Carrie didn't do it. She's no good, but she's not a murderer."

"Don't count anyone out. Don't ever make that mistake."

Molly slammed her hand on the desk. "It's not Carrie!"

"Calm down. Emma doesn't need to hear it. It's bad enough I gotta bring you into it."

At the door, Molly said, "I'm sorry about the tape." When he didn't answer, she said, "I don't know who to call to stay with Emma."

"Have Bitsy take her home. They can do a little bonding."

"And what do I tell Bitsy? I've got a date?"

"Yeah. Tell her I'm taking you out to dinner."

"Oh, right. She'll have that all over town before she closes up."

"I hear I'm considered quite a catch."

"Really? How nice."

Walking back, she wondered what Randall had up his sleeve. He hadn't been as angry with her, as she'd imagined he would be. Well, she thought, almost. And who had he called? It must have been Lucero. He was the only other person who would know the truth about Trudy's death. She also wondered why she hadn't told him that Carrie had stolen her watch and miniatures. Was further family disgrace too much for her to unburden? Even to Randall?

She wasn't crazy about asking Bitsy to babysit. In fact, she wasn't sure if she'd agree. But maybe Randall was right. A little bonding would do them both good. Especially since Bitsy had offered to pay Emma's school fees. Checking her watch, she realized they were going to be late for Mass.

Robbie had unloaded the truck and was gone by the time she returned. Hustling Emma downstairs, they got to the Mission just as Mass ended. Molly took Emma's hand as they walked into the church against the departing crowd, and guided her into the last pew. Kneeling, she whispered to Emma to sit quietly. Quickly crossing herself, Molly closed her eyes and prayed. She said six Hail Marys after the Lord's Prayer, sat back on her heels and begged for the strength to do what she could to help find out who had killed Trudy.

Passing through the faithfully maintained historic grounds of Mission San Carlos Borromeo, Emma asked, "Is that all there is to it?"

Molly laughed. "No. Just my fast version. Next time we'll do the real thing."

"Do all churches look like this?"

"This is special. It was founded by Father Junipero Serra a couple of hundred years ago. It's one of the oldest in California."

"So this is a history place, huh? I mean here, where we live."

Emma's choice of words were not lost on Molly. It was amazing how easily she'd accepted her fate. "There's so much history here, it would take me a week to show it to you." As they walked to the parking lot, Molly told her about the famous artists and writers who had spent time on the Monterey Peninsula. She smiled when she saw the look of awe on Emma's face when she mentioned that Robert Louis Stevenson wrote *Treasure Island* here, and Mark Twain and Jack London had all lived here for a time.

"And then there's the famous poet Robinson Jeffers. He and his wife built a stone house on Carmel Point by themselves. It's called Tor House. Then they built Hawk Tower next door. We'll have to go check it out one of these days."

"Did they build it themselves?" Emma asked, wide-eyed.

"Stone by stone," Molly said.

"Did they build the Hansel and Gretel houses too?"

"No, a Mr. Hugh Comstock did. If I remember right, he was inspired by his wife, who made dolls. After he built the first two—which by the way, were called Hansel and Gretel—a lot of people in town wanted their own."

On the way to the truck, Molly told Emma about the hundreds of sea otters that filled the wharves on Cannery Row, and the annual migration of millions of monarch butterflies that made Pacific Grove their favorite stopping off place. "Oh, and California's first theater was built in Monterey. It's still there. We'll go see it sometime."

When they stopped for gas, Molly announced she had a few errands to run. "You don't mind being alone, do you, when I have things to do? I mean, you don't have to go with me all the time if you don't want to."

"I'm used to being alone. Besides, you need your space too."

"I don't need a lot," Molly said, then gave her a smile. "But thank you."

CHAPTER 14

Daria wasn't in when Molly arrived. She gave the box of silver to Manuel and told him she'd call Daria later. Next stop was the library, to get a look at a California road map. She wanted to know which highway to take for tomorrow's trip. The best bet was U.S. 101. She could pick it up from nearby Salinas. The coast route was undoubtedly more scenic, but she figured it would add an hour to the trip. Maybe they'd take it on the way home.

Crossing Ocean Avenue from the library, Molly saw Milo Kraft across the street. She couldn't see who he was talking to, but from the way his hands chopped the air, it was apparent he was angry. Anxious to distance herself, she crossed back toward the library, and decided to take a detour to the shop. It was almost ten, and Bitsy would be arriving any moment. She'd ask her about keeping Emma tonight. Robbie would be back soon with the rest of the garden furniture, and she still had to make room in the garage. After circling the block, Molly was a few doors from the shop when she skidded to a stop. She clenched her teeth so hard, she almost bit her tongue. Oliver was coming out of Treasures. Stepping inside a gift shop, she watched him through the window amble up the street. *Damn Bitsy!*

Waiting a full five minutes before breezing into the shop, Molly pretended she hadn't seen Oliver leave. She found Bitsy changing one of her displays again. She had a demonic habit of deciding what went where. It made little difference if Molly was right, which she almost always was, it was just that Bitsy, like any alpha female, had to mark her dominance. With Bitsy it wasn't mean or petty, it was just a dealer thing. It was also a never mentioned superstition. If a chair had been on the floor for more than a week, it was moved a few inches. A lamp might be an inch too far to the right, a vase on the wrong side of the table, three stacked leather books instead of five. During the first few minutes of every opening, many dealers had a compulsive need to rearrange. It was antique feng shui.

After Molly described the garden furniture she'd found, and her ideas for a new section at the back of the shop, she was about to ask Bitsy about taking Emma home with her when Randall walked in.

He was barely in the shop when Bitsy whirled away from Molly and zeroed in on him. "What is holding up Trudy's funeral plans?"

"Hey, can I at least get past the door before you give me the third degree? The coroner's office has been busy, Bitsy. I'm sure he'll release her this week."

"Will you please see to it? It's a disgrace to think that poor woman has been shoved into some cold storage unit and—"

"I'll call him myself first thing tomorrow, okay?" Draping an arm around her, he soothed, "Don't get yourself all worked up. The man has been shorthanded for months."

"Well, then they ought to hire more people. What the hell are we paying taxes for?"

"Good question. I'll bring that up too."

Loving his attention, Bitsy said, "So, darling, what have you been up to?" Giving him a wink, she said, "Can I interest you in some merch? We have a lovely new collection of British toy soldiers under glass that would look fabulous in your living room. You've done such a superb job decorating, and—"

"Whoa," he said. "I'm here to ask you a favor."

"Oh? Well, darling, for you, anything."

"Good. How about inviting Emma over to your place tonight so I can take Molly out for Chinese? She could use a little time off."

Darting a coy look at Molly, Bitsy said, "What a marvelous idea. I'd love to."

Confused about the Chinese thing, Molly went along with him. "That new place in Monterey?"

"Yeah. I hear it's good. Lucero and Daria are going to check it out and wondered if we'd like to join them."

"Great."

As soon as Bitsy headed for the storage room, Molly was at Randall's side. "Chinese?"

"No. We're still going to Daria's. Just through the back door."

Emma spotted Randall then, as she came down the stairs. Her face lit up. "Hey, Chief! Wait until you find out what I scored at a garage sale."

Pretending to give her a stern look, Randall said, "The name's Randall, kid. Got it? So, what's the big score?"

"An Esther Hunt bust. Aunt Molly said it was worth a lot of money."

Bitsy, at Molly's desk now, shot out, "Esther Hunt? What did you pay for it?"

"Twenty dollars," Emma said.

"The legacy lives on!" Looking at Molly, she asked, "Did she know what she was buying?"

"Nope. She only knew she'd seen mine and liked them."

"Way to go, darling," Bitsy said.

"It's 'you go girl,' Mrs. Morgan," Emma said, laughing.

"Thank you, dear. And since you're going to be a permanent fixture around here, you may call me Bitsy."

Pulling a cell phone from the inside of his jacket, Randall said, "Speaking of that—being a permanent fixture, I mean—I've got a present for you, squirt." Handing the phone to Emma, he added, "Keep it with you when you go out."

"Is there a reason Emma needs a cell phone?" Bitsy said. "Really, at her age?"

"Yeah, she needs one even in sleepy Carmel. Times are different, Bitsy."

"Oh, wow!" Emma squealed. "It's one of those camera things. We can send pictures to each other!"

Pleased by her response, Randall beamed. "It's got that text thing too. Or whatever it's called."

Molly was touched by Randall's thoughtfulness and his apparent acceptance of Emma. It was a great idea, and she wished she'd thought of it. Carmel was as vulnerable as any community these days. Taking a look at it, Molly said, "That's awfully generous of you, Randall. But—"

"No *buts,* okay? It was a two-for-one deal, and I didn't know what to do with the other one. Besides, you'll be getting the phone bill, not me."

Molly laughed. "Fair enough. Thank you. It didn't occur to me that Emma might need one."

"Like I said, times are different." Giving Emma a hug, he said, "Just don't pester me with it, okay?"

"I'll send you book reports. I'm almost finished with Jack London, and then I'm going to read the new *Harry Potter.* I always save the best for last."

"Okay, we'll compare notes."

Heading for the stairs, Molly said, "It's been fun, gang, but I've got a thousand things to do. Oh, Emma, you're having an evening with Bitsy tonight while I go out. Better wear that cute jumper and turtleneck we bought. Bitsy dresses for dinner."

At the top of the stairs, Molly almost missed a step when she heard Bitsy say, "You're fine the way you are, darling. Don't bother to change. Now, show me how that damn thing works. I might get one myself."

The first thing Daria said to Molly when she arrived through the back entrance to the restaurant was, "The silver is great. How much do I owe you?"

"Not a thing. It's a credit for my tab."

Daria laughed. "You don't have a tab here."

"I know. That's the problem. Seriously, it wasn't that much, and it's not open for discussion."

"Okay, but just this once."

"What's this all about? I mean tonight?" Molly hoped Randall had told Daria something. She didn't want to be blindsighted. Especially if it concerned her sister.

Moving out of the way of waiters bustling in and out of the kitchen, Daria said, "All I know is Randall said to be available. They're already here."

When they walked into Daria's private room, Lucero nodded to Molly, then said, "This is not going to be one of our friendly get-togethers. This is an informal conference, and will involve some serious issues."

It was very clear Lucero was speaking as the district attorney, not the man they knew as their friend. Not sure how much Randall might have told him, Molly folded her hands in her lap and tried to present a picture of innocence and calm.

"In other words, it's a one-off," Randall said.

Molly was surprised to hear the snap in Daria's voice when she said, "Is that so? Well, let the record show dinner will be served first, and I expect the utmost courtesy from you both until then." With that, she rose and left the room. Molly was speechless, and it was apparent she wasn't alone.

"What the hell was that all about?" Lucero asked.

"You were a little terse there, buddy," Randall replied.

Molly tried to remain silent, but her good sense vanished. "Your tone of voice was a bit much when you're accepting hospitality."

"She's mad at me now," Lucero said.

"Brilliant observation, counselor," Randall retorted.

Daria returned then, with Manuel wheeling in a cart loaded with a large platter of roast duck and steaming vegetables. As Daria began serving, she said, "No antipasto, no garlic bread, no soup or salad. Eat the entrée then say what you have to. I've got a full house out there."

"Shit, Daria!" Lucero said, "Let's not get carried away. I only meant—"

"Save it," Daria said.

When Manuel was about to leave, Daria said, "Two bottles of our best red, and put it on Mr. Lucero's account."

Dinner progressed in silence. Even Molly didn't dare look at Daria. When the table was cleared and coffee served, Daria said, "Speak your piece, and make it quick. I want to get to bed at a reasonable hour for once."

When Lucero cleared his throat, Daria said, "Hold that thought," and turned to Molly. "Oliver Townsend wants to start a tab. He used you as a reference."

"You're kidding, I hope. I caught him snooping on my computer, called him out on it, and now he has the nerve to use me for a reference?"

Daria laughed, then looked at Lucero. "Nerve? I could name a few."

"Bitsy told me he's tapped out," Molly said. "She's fronting him for his new shop. I don't think he has cab money."

Pouring more coffee for Molly, and ignoring the men, Daria replied, "Fine. I'll tell him I stopped taking new charge customers." Sipping her coffee, she said, "Lucero, you had something you wanted to share?"

"My apologies. I didn't mean to come off so—"

"Tough? Yeah, you did. D.A. or not, we're friends here. We've shared a lot of laughs, and a pretty scary episode a while back. I think that alone deserves a little more couth."

"I just meant this is not some Murder Club thing. We're not going to have roundtable discussions everytime a homicide goes down in Monterey County. If Randall and I didn't need you and Molly again, this wouldn't be happening. Like Randall keeps saying, once is enough. It just so happens you're the only one I trust who was close to Trudy, and damn if this isn't another antique mess again, or Molly wouldn't be here either."

Molly didn't miss the flicker of amusement in Randall's eyes. She bet he was getting a charge out of seeing the tough D.A. taken down a peg and having to defend himself.

"And Lucero likes to play cop with me," Randall said, "or he wouldn't even be in the loop yet. So, here's the situation." He shot a warning look at Lucero to let him have the floor. "Trudy's death will remain a heart attack for now. I want her killer to think he or she got away with it. If I announce a homicide, our perp might rabbit."

"Why?" Molly quickly asked.

"Because I'm gambling on the fact that only Trudy's close friends knew about her allergy. And the killer will know that we figured that out."

"We can't do much in the way of interviews," Lucero said. "You don't interview over a heart attack. All we can do is background checks on those close to her. I'm not happy about this little meeting here tonight, but once again, we've got no choice but to reach out to you two. If we bring you both into the station, or my office, someone will know something's up. Too many leaks in the world today. Tabloids pay money for shit that means nothing. I don't want that to happen here. This is our home, and I'm not going to let it be a backdrop for some sleazy reporter looking to dig up dirt."

"What if it's a customer who was pissed off?" Daria asked.

"That's where Molly comes in," Randall answered. "Trudy left some crazy notes and lists on a computer disc. Molly might be able to help us figure them out."

Playing along with the deception, Molly said, "Sure. I'll do whatever I can."

"Have Molly look at those screwy tags she bled all over," Lucero said.

"I'll do that," Randall replied.

"Have you ever dealt with a guy named Milo Kraft?" Lucero asked Daria.

"I've bought silver from him. Why?"

"You didn't know he and Trudy were buddies?" Randall asked.

"He helped her with shows. Packing and hauling, that sort of thing. There was nothing going on between them. Trudy was seeing someone in Portland. Some lawyer. I think he had a pretty big firm. No, wait . . . it was Tacoma."

Molly's head almost snapped off her neck. "Tacoma?"

"She ever tell you his name?" Randall asked.

Daria thought for a moment, then shook her head. "Hell, she went through men like I go through busboys. Sorry, I don't remember."

Molly hoped no one saw her fingers tremble as she reached for a cigarette. Maybe Carrie wasn't the go between. But still, it was her voice on that tape threatening Trudy.

"Think hard, there's gotta be someone she must have bitched about to you," Lucero said.

"I can't. I mean, Trudy was always up, never complained . . . she was just—"

"She was selling fakes," Molly said. "Reproductions. She got me good. I've got to call clients and pay back eighteen grand."

"Oh, no. Jesus! I . . . I never knew," Daria said. "Do you think Milo killed Trudy?"

"Anything's possible," Randall said. "He's got a minor jacket. I'm going to ask him to help us round up the rest of Trudy's merch in case Lucero's investigators can't find out where she stored it. With all the self-storage units around here, she could have easily rented one under a different name. So I'll tell him Trudy was behind in her rent, or owed Max money. He's my problem. We need to nail him with something, and if her inventory is iffy, then I'll see what or who he might give up."

"So when did you figure that all out, Molly? You holding back here?" Lucero asked.

Randall moved right in. "I told her."

"Really. Nice of you to let me know." Turning to Molly, he probed, "What makes you think she sold you fakes?"

Realizing Randall was covering for her, she said, "I, uh, began to wonder after Randall told me." Falling deeper and deeper into the lying pit, she added, "I was a little put off by the color of one or two Meissen figures I bought from her. The blue wasn't quite—"

"Stop!" Lucero said. "Suffice it to say you were had. No long-winded lectures needed."

"Ah, excuse me, Mr. District Attorney. I thought you people were big on detail. And for a new wannabe collector, you've got one hell of a short attention span," Molly shot back.

"Okay, I'm sorry. It's just that we don't have time for—"

"If you're going to collect, you better damn well learn to do your homework. I'm a pro, and I just got taken big-time. So take the warning. The antiques business has been saturated with fakes for hundreds of years. *'Caveat emptor'* is not just a catchy Latin phrase. And in case your Latin is just geared for law, it means buyer beware!"

Trying to calm Molly with a little humor, Lucero turned to Randall and said, "Make her be nice to me, will ya?"

"You're on you own, pal."

Daria's anger with Lucero quickly dissipated as she watched Molly take her turn at setting him straight. "I'll do some checking around with some of the girls," she said. "What about Bitsy, Molly? She's known Trudy longer than I have."

Before Molly could reply, Randall said, "I'm hoping Molly can talk to Bitsy instead of me. If I start asking her questions, she'll know something's up."

"Sure. I'll think of some way to sneak it in."

"Just do girl-talk nosey stuff, okay?" Randall said. "See, we've got another little twist to the thing here." Glancing at Lucero, he continued, "Those Hong Kong invoice people are on a special list, you might say."

"I'd say they were special!" Molly blurted. "I've never seen such quality repros in my life."

"That's not what Randall meant," Lucero said. "It's triad owned. Don't ask how we know, just think about what else they might be shipping in their little teapots and figures."

Molly's eyes flew open. "You're kidding me, right?"

"No way!" Daria shot out. "Trudy wouldn't mess with drugs."

"Really?" Lucero said. "You didn't think she'd sell fakes either, did you? Anyway, Trudy might not have known. She might just have been taking the merch and thinking that was all there was to it. The person who accepted shipment before Trudy is who we're after."

Molly's face turned ashen. She looked at Randall. He didn't have to say a word. They were both thinking about Carrie.

And then Lucero said it. "That person may be your sister, Molly."

Molly heard Daria gasp, and she couldn't meet her eyes. "I realize that now," Molly said. "I'll do whatever I can to help."

"Good enough for me," Lucero said.

"I'm going to Santa Barbara tomorrow to see an old interior designer friend. She's very plugged in down south. I want her to look at some of Trudy's show pictures."

"I can't see what that will accomplish," Lucero said.

"Trudy's wigs . . . the glasses," Molly said. "I found them when I had to meet the moving man."

"So?"

"Trudy did a lot of shows in Southern California. She might recognize her by another name and tell me if there's been any fallout or gossip. If she's been passing off repros out of town, someone must have figured it out by now."

"Just give me this friend's name. We'll check it out," Lucero said.

"Oh, sure. Like they'll just roll over for you. Come on, Lucero, this is my playground."

"Lucero's right, Molly. Let us handle it," Randall said.

"Do you two really think anyone in the trade is going to admit they know about a dealer selling fakes? That's . . . uh, aiding and abetting? Or something? Get real."

"We're not playing your game again," Lucero said.

"Okay, fine. I'm still going."

"Why, Molly?" Daria asked. "Maybe they're right."

Molly looked at Randall and waited to see if he was going to tell them. When he didn't say a word, she knew he was leaving the choice up to her. "Because . . ." she began, "because my sister threatened Trudy. I heard it on Trudy's answering machine."

The silence was overwhelming. Molly felt as if the air had been sucked out of the room.

Lucero was livid. He turned to Randall. "When the hell were you going to tell me *that*?"

"When I was positive. I've just got Molly's say so. Until recently, she hasn't heard her sister's voice for years. She might be wrong."

"It was Carrie," Molly said.

"Oh, God, Molly," Daria said as she reached for Molly's hands.

"I've got to know for Emma, can't you see that?"

"Yes. Of course you do," Daria replied.

"Oh, no you don't," Lucero said. "If that voice is your sister's, then I'll get word out and find her. Forget everything we just talked about. You stay out of this, and I mean it."

"Then tell your friend here to lock me up, because I'm going, and that's final. You can't keep me from taking a trip."

"Jesus, Molly!" Randall said. "Can't you just—"

"*No! I can't just do nothing.* I'm going, and that's final. If I find anything out, I'll come straight to you with it."

"And then leave it alone, okay?" Randall said. When Molly didn't answer, he said, "I *will* lock you up if I have to. Your right rear taillight is out, and I can probably think of something else."

"Okay."

"Okay *what?*" Randall pressed.

"I'll leave it alone. Satisfied?"

Reaching for his coffee, he said, "If I believed you, I would be."

CHAPTER 15

At almost the same time Molly's bedroom light clicked on at five-thirty Monday morning, Randall, only blocks away in his condo, was brewing his second pot of coffee. Reaching for the telephone, he dialed Lucero and caught him as he was leaving for his office in Salinas. "I think I see the pattern on the discs. I need you to call your D.A. pal in Seattle and find out what he can dig up on Carrie Newsome and her old man."

"I'll ask about Kraft too," Lucero replied, "see if the name rings a bell."

"Good idea. He's only been here for five years, so who knows?"

"What bothers me," Lucero said, "is why not just ship here directly? Why Tacoma?"

"Best answer for that at the moment is the goods had to be monitored."

"True. Hey, did your pal get back to you?"

"He called last night after I got home." Randall laughed. "Sure as hell helps to have buds all over the country. If you'd make nice once in a while, you might get your own network going."

"Hey, I'm loved in a lot of quarters. I got the votes to prove it."

"I'm kidding. Anyway, he tells me the Hong Kong connection has a big china manufacturing plant in the New Territories and makes all kinds of stuff. From cheap garden pots to high class repros."

"Shit, you don't know who to trust anymore. So the company is legit, huh?"

"Yeah. And it's perfect for what we're looking at."

"Molly still going to Santa Barbara?"

"She's leaving, all right. Wilkins just called and told me the lights in the apartment are on. She's not up just to watch the early news. Talk to you later."

After assuring Emma that Tiger would be fine for two days in the apartment, making a small detour to Winchell's Donuts, and then to Starbucks to fill Molly's thermos, they were on the road by six-thirty. Molly was surprised by the sense of adventure filling her. Hunting down antiques had always been a rush, but tracking down a killer was something else. Randall and Lucero had opened up so many avenues of thought last night, her imagination was zigzagging all over the place. Fakes and reproductions were one thing, but drugs? Hiding drugs in antiques was not new, but it was a method that had fallen out of favor. With sniffing dogs and new technology, it had been pretty much abandoned except in movies and television cop shows.

Fortified for the four-hour trip with sugar and caffeine, Emma loaded the portable CD with *The Sorcerer's Stone,* then announced she had *The Chamber of Secrets* for the trip back. Molly was thankful Emma had something to keep her occupied. She didn't think the California valley would hold her attention for long.

Emma had been excited when she told her they were going to take a few days off and go down the coast. They could listen to the books on tape Bitsy had bought her. "Bitsy said she'd get the others for me too," Emma said. "Why do you think she's buying me so many gifts? I don't really know her that well."

"Well, she doesn't have children, so maybe she'd like to pretend you're her grandchild. She's a lovely lady," Molly said, trying to drive and keep a sugar doughnut from flaking all over her sweater.

Turning to look out the window, Emma added, "I'd like to have a grandmother. I think it's kind of funny the way she tries to boss everyone around. I think it's an act."

Carrie was right in that she was twelve going on thirty. "I guess your mother told you our mother died when we were very young."

"Yes. Since I never met my father's family, I think Bitsy will do just fine."

Molly smiled. "Just watch her or she'll have your life planned out before you know it."

"I won't ever have to sleep over at her place,

will I? Her home is spooky. I'm not sure I want to go back there at night without you. All those rooms! And that tower thing looks like it belongs in a movie."

Molly grinned, remembering the first time she'd seen Bitsy's home. Perched right on the edge of a rocky cliff in Pebble Beach, the house looked like an old Moorish castle. Three movies had been made there, and Bitsy swore she'd never let them back. It took her months to get her garden and enclosed patios back in shape. Molly had to agree with Emma. The home was a bit scary at night. Jutting out just enough to hear the surf beating against the rocks, it also caught gusty winds that whistled through the old casement windows. The dining room and the huge salon that faced the ocean were ideal settings for an Agatha Christie mystery. Floor-to-ceiling French doors led out to a wraparound stone terrace with a full view of the rocky coast. "I'll be sure to go with you next time."

"That Oliver man is weird. All through dinner he kept ringing a little bell. Every time Josie's helper came out, he complained about something. I thought dinner was pretty good. We had lamb roast, mashed potatoes, and veggies. Oh, and some kind of ice cream dessert that Bitsy didn't like. She said it tasted funny. Oliver said he told Josie to leave off the whipped cream and just put honey on it. Ugh, can you imagine ice cream and honey?"

Keeping her eye on the road and trying to sip coffee, Molly said, "No, and I'm surprised Bitsy ate it."

"She didn't feel so good after dinner, so Oliver helped her up the stairs and then Charles took me home. Your dinner must have sucked too, you were home before me."

"Uh, it was pretty good. Everyone was just tired and wanted an early night."

Except for a few trips to San Francisco for auctions, Molly hadn't done much freeway driving. Huge rigs carrying produce from Salinas to Southern California filled the freeway and smoked past her when she was pushing seventy. When they reached San Luis Obispo, more than halfway to Santa Barbara, Molly stopped for Emma to use a rest room and filled up with gas. She took another look at the road map. They'd be heading toward the coast soon, and Pismo Beach.

"You were going to tell me about those China ladies, remember?" Emma said as they pulled back onto the highway.

"Right, glad you reminded me. Well, let me dig back into my feeble memory and—"

"Feeble? That's funny. You're a real antique dealer, that makes you—"

"Not an expert on everything. Too much stuff to keep up on. So, you have to narrow your field and concentrate on it. An overview is about all most of us can handle."

"Then you don't remember much?"

Molly could see Emma was hoping for a full history, so she tried to recall as much as possible. "I think I can come up with enough for now. Later on you can check it out on the Web. Anyway, I know Esther Hunt, the artist who created them, showed them at the Panama California Exposition in San Diego in 1916." Giving Emma a wink, she said, "How's that for reaching back?"

"Not bad. Go on, what else?"

"Well, she did more than just chalkware busts, she was also quite an artist. She used to hang out in Chinatown in Los Angeles and make sketches of women and children. Some of her busts are of children too. Anyway, they were inexpensive decorations, and her studio put out a lot of them. They became so popular, other people started copying her, and they were often given out as carnival prizes in Atlantic City. She even gave the ladies names. I can't remember them offhand, but yours is called Lotus Bud."

"If so many of them were made, how come they're so valuable now? I mean, I thought antiques had to be rare."

"First of all they're not antiques, but collectibles. You have to be a hundred years old to be an antique, and it doesn't have to be rare. But because the busts were so delicate and chipped easy, there aren't many left now, and they're very valuable. Besides, people love them."

"So how can you tell the difference between hers and the others?"

Molly laughed. "Aha, I was wondering if you were going to ask. Well, the real ones have a different luster than the copycats. She had some secret formula that was hard to discover, and then she usually put a copyright and the name of the lady on the bottom. But others copied that too. So it's the colors and *look* that make the difference. When you've seen the real thing, then it's easier to spot the copy. But you know what? I don't care if I find a copy, I'll buy it. I just love the faces she gave them. They're so mysterious and—"

"Sassy," Emma said. "I like the way they kind of stare at you, like they're daring you to do something."

"Excellent observation, Watson!"

Pleased by Molly's compliment, Emma said, "Whew, it takes a lot of work to be an antique person. Will you teach me?"

Taking her eyes off the road for a brief moment, Molly smiled at her. "I'd love to."

By the time they reached Pismo Beach, Emma had nodded off. Molly turned off the CD and concentrated on the new garden look she was planning for the shop. She tried to envision the wrought-iron furniture with new cushions. The sewing machine she'd bought for ten bucks on a whim would come in handy now. Especially since the following week she'd bought a huge box of sample designer fabrics, yards of lush fringe, and cording from an interior designer going out of business. She had enough silks, velvets, woven tapestry designs, and gorgeous jacquards begging to be pillows to make at least twenty. At a hundred bucks each, she'd make a handsome profit.

Reaching for her coffee, Molly glanced at her rearview mirror and saw a highway patrol car behind her. She checked her speed and was relieved that she was only a few miles over the limit. Easing her foot on the gas, she held her breath as he passed her. That's all she needed now, a speeding ticket. Randall would have fun with that. And then she wondered about her tail light being out. The patrolman had been talking into something when he passed her. Was he checking out her license plate? Maybe a dented rusty old orange El Camino had been stolen somewhere? It was unlikely a twin was still running.

If the weather had been better, the trip might have been enjoyable. Hitting patches of fog, it was now drizzling. Thinking about the shop wasn't working. Her mind was too cluttered. Even when it started to rain, her concentration kept veering between watching the traffic—which was heavier than she'd anticipated—and imagining how much trouble Carrie was finding in trying to sell her miniatures. At auction, in a good house, they'd easily bring thirty thousand. Her safety net, her ace in the hole, and her means to open her own shop someday was destroyed.

And now a big chunk of her savings would be gone once she bought back those cursed Meissen figures. Carrie wouldn't dare expose herself by trying to consign them to a top-notch auction house. Her sister would know that she'd send a theft alert to all of them. Her only hope was to find a private buyer. Whether she had the means to do so was doubtful.

Passing through Goleta, Molly began to relax. She was almost in Santa Barbara, and would have ample time to check into the small inn Sally had recommended, change, and meet her for lunch. Waking Emma, Molly said, "We're almost there."

Stretching and yawning, Emma said, "Bet you were wondering when I was going to ask, 'Are we there yet?' "

"It did cross my mind, smarty."

"I forgot to tell you that Bitsy also got me a head phone thing for this CD, so while you and your friend are talking business, I'll listen to Harry, if that won't be rude."

"That will be just fine," Molly said with much relief. She'd been wondering just how she was going to get Sally to talk openly with Emma at her side.

The charm of the Inn and much of Santa Barbara, which liked to be known as the American Riviera, was not lost on Molly. While her main focus was to get Sally to unload as much insider gossip as possible without realizing she was here for more than a small holiday, it didn't mean she couldn't enjoy the trip. She thought it strange that Sally suggested they meet at a restaurant and not at her shop. Dealers loved to show off their stock. It was a perfect way to say, *Look what I've got, and you'll never know how, or who my sources are. Better yet, my eye is better than yours.*

Could it be possible Sally was working out of her home? Or had her fortunes been reduced and her shop was so small she was embarrassed? Maybe that was why she'd moved here. Antiquedar, the equivalent of radar, said Santa Barbara and its neighbor, Montecito, was the current big hit of Southern California. While always posh, Montecito was now internationally known. Living here told the world you were discerning and had taste even if you were an actor.

It didn't take much effort to find the restaurant. Downtown was easy to navigate, and it reminded Molly of a bigger Carmel. Filled with more historic adobes, it appeared to have as many courtyard shops. And, she explained to Emma, as she tried to find a parking spot, the architecture of the California Mission towns was basically tile roofs, ornate stucco facades, wrought-iron grille work, and towering palm trees. The climate, she added, was much warmer than Carmel. The cashmere turtleneck she wore was already feeling uncomfortable.

She found Sally right away. She hadn't changed one bit. Still tawny blond and chic as ever. Already seated, Sally Sims waved her over. And, Molly quickly noted as she sucked in her stomach, still rail thin. Amid air kisses and a quick hug, Molly introduced Emma. "A niece! How nice. I wish I had one to spoil." Sally laughed. "You look fabulous, Molly! Carmel must agree with you."

Between bites of excellent seafood, Molly and Sally spent the next half hour catching up. Emma concentrated on her gigantic Crab Louis and smiled at all the right places. When she'd finally had her fill, she asked Molly if she might listen to her book on tape. "That way you two can gossip all you want."

"You go right ahead, sweetie," Sally said. "Your aunt Molly and I might forget ourselves and use language too awful for your cute little ears."

When Molly nodded her okay, Emma put on her headset and gave her a wink.

Coffee arrived, and Molly asked, "What made you decide to move up here? Don't tell me you had enough of rock stars begging you to give them some class."

Sally blotted her lips and sighed. "Honey, those people are demented. I will never, ever, do another home for that crowd again. And these new diva bimbos are just as bad. They have absolutely no respect for fine living. One of those little sluts let her dogs shit all over a thirty-thousand-dollar custom rug I had made for her in Turkey, and then her screw of the month puked on another one in her dressing room. Those people are pigs and the scum of the earth. Why any self-respecting mother lets her kids idolize that trash is beyond me. Oh, and remember that fabulous Bureau-plat I bought from you for that actor from Belgium? I hate the man so much, I can't even remember his name."

"Georges Fumere?"

"That's the one! That jerk used that gorgeous desk for a bar and then he had the nerve to call me and tell me the leather top was ruined and he wanted to send it back. That was the straw that broke my back. He claimed something that expensive should have better leather. Can you imagine the stupidity? I mean, I should care, I got my fee, right? But I do, and it just drives me batty."

Molly rolled her eyes and was glad Emma had the foresight to mention the headset. "The stories you and I could tell! No one would believe us. Which reminds me . . ." Pulling some photos from her tote, she went on, "I'm trying to track down this dealer. I was told by a customer she had a treasure trove of Meissen and wants me to contact her. Evidently, she'd met her at a show in Pasadena last fall and lost her card. I remembered when I was packing that you used to hit the antique shows pretty regularly, and thought you might recognize her." Handing Sally the photos of Trudy at the Pasadena show, she said, "I've only got two. My customer's husband was taking pictures that day of various Meissen dealers with some of the merch in their booths, and she sent these to me."

Reaching for her glasses, Sally seemed to take a long time looking at the pictures. When she kept flipping between them, Molly's knee began to jerk under the table. Finally, Sally said, "I haven't a clue, but her Meissen is fantastic. I missed most of last year's shows. I was in Italy staying with friends. I needed a rest after my last job." Throwing her hands up, she said, "Yes, thanks to another one of those mini-divas. But she came with good papers and at least had some style. Let me do some calling around. With merch like that, someone will know who she is."

Taking the photos back, Molly felt deflated. "Great, I'd really appreciate your help. In fact, I've got a client in Pebble Beach thinking about buying a small place here. His wife is going stir crazy with the fog."

Passing their cards across the table, Sally said, "Darling, there are no *small* places here anymore. They're being bought up in twos and threes to make room for *villas*."

"Sounds like Carmel."

"Ah, the new rich," Sally sighed. "God bless them. We'd be starving if not for them. Speaking of which, I've got to run and meet a new client in an hour. How long are you staying?"

"Oh, we'll be leaving first thing in the morning. I just needed to get away for a day or two."

"Long drive just to get away," Sally said.

"Hmm, yes. I didn't realize how far you were. I never could make heads or tails of a map."

"Well, next time plan to stay a little longer. I'll make some calls on your missing dealer. You should hear from me in a few days."

CHAPTER 16

It was almost three in the afternoon when Molly and Emma left Sally. Feeling that the trip had been virtually wasted, and not interested in sightseeing, Molly decided there was no point in staying overnight. Besides, it was a waste of money, and now she was nearly broke again. She wasn't looking forward to another four hours of driving, but if she got too tired, they could pull over in some small town and have a bite to eat and load up with coffee. When they reached San Luis Obispo, Molly decided to switch over to Morro Bay and pick up Highway 1 and take the coast route home. It would be dark soon, but she figured the traffic would be lighter and she'd gladly put up with a few curvy roads if she wouldn't have to contend with all those huge trucks.

She didn't notice the gray SUV until she pulled into Cambria, a small town near San Simeon and Hearst Castle. As she crawled down the main street looking for a coffee shop, the SUV seemed to hover a few car lengths behind, hitting its breaks each time she slowed. Finding a small bistro, Molly pulled into its parking lot and turned off the lights. "Hold on, Em," she said as Emma reached for the door handle. She watched the SUV pull up and then pass the parking lot. She decided she must be more tired than she'd thought to imagine someone was following her. Besides, it couldn't be a car jacker. Who'd want this thing when you were driving a big ticket item?

"I could eat a horse," Emma said.

Molly laughed. "After that huge lunch?"

"I'm really not crazy about seafood. But I love Italian."

"You sure fit into Carmel."

"Think so?"

"I know so."

"Good, then I'll tell you all about Carmel while we have dinner. I read about it at the library when you let me go over the other day."

"I've got a better idea. Tell me while we're driving so I can stay awake."

By the time they finished dinner, Molly's eyes were growing heavy. The thought of driving had lost its appeal. Besides, she reasoned, the fog was getting worse. "Maybe we ought to stay over?" she said to Emma. "It's getting kind of spooky out there. What do you think?"

"It is kinda creepy. I think we should stay."

Molly didn't realize that the small bistro was part of a cottage-type motel when they drove in. The waiter overheard them and said they had a vacancy. Thrilled that she didn't have to go out in the fog and search for a motel, Molly quickly said, "Sold!"

She paid their bill, followed the waiter to a small office off the entrance, and checked in. Within moments, luggage in hand, they were ushered into a charming chintz-filled room with twin beds. The trip and the large plate of pasta had finally taken its toll on Emma. She was no sooner in bed than she was fast asleep. Molly tucked Emma's blanket under her chin and, without thinking, kissed her forehead. She was surprised at how natural that unplanned act seemed. She watched Emma's eyelashes flutter as she slept and said a silent prayer of thanks that Carrie hadn't left her with strangers.

Molly turned off the television, disappointed to hear that the fog was going to hang around for a few more days. Climbing into bed, she decided it didn't matter. They were leaving in the morning, come hell or high water. Besides, all she needed was a good night's sleep. Something she hadn't had this past week since Trudy's murder.

The weather the next morning was more suitable to a Gothic on the Scottish moors than the touted sunny coast of California. The air, as Molly and Emma climbed into the truck, was thick with salty vapors. The flashing neon sign of a gas station up the street seemed to undulate in the dense gray morning. When they reached San Simeon, the home of William Randolph Hearst's famous Hearst Castle, the swirling murk was so thick Molly had to pull over in the small seaside town.

"According to the little map guide in our room, Carmel is only ninety-one miles from here. It's supposed to take two hours, but with this fog, probably a little longer." Sensing Emma was nervous, Molly said, "I sure wanted to show you the castle up on the hill. Too bad it's such a crummy day."

"Crummy is not a good word. Scary is more like it," Emma mumbled.

"Come on, Em! It's only fog. Sometimes you just have to be patient and give it a chance to thin out. We'll park here for a few minutes and see what happens, okay?"

"Good idea. I'll bet that car that's been behind us since we left will pull over too."

Concentrating on keeping the white line on the highway in view, Molly hadn't noticed anyone behind her. "What car?"

"That big gray thing. The one that was behind us last night. Guess he must have decided to stay over too."

"Oh, right, I remember seeing it. It's a Jeep, I think." Looking in the rearview mirror, Molly said, "I don't see it now. Maybe it's someone who lives here and didn't want to travel last night. Probably didn't want to go the extra ten miles. I sure wouldn't have." She dug in her tote for cigarettes and her hand came out empty. She could have sworn she had an extra pack tucked in there somewhere. Pulling away from the parking spot, she crawled up the street in search of a market. Finding one of those quick-stops, she pulled in and asked, "Do you want anything?"

"Nope. Still full from breakfast. Unless," she said, "you'll let me drink coffee with you again."

"With cream, right?" Not waiting for an answer, Molly ran in the shop. Within moments she was back at the truck juggling two plastic cups, and she saw the gray Jeep slowly cruise past. Handing Emma her coffee, she said, "That Jeep just went by. Guess he lives here."

"It was a man?"

Molly finished lighting a cigarette from the pack she'd bought, then shrugged. "I don't know, just a figure of speech. It has those dark tinted windows, so it was hard to tell."

"Oh, I thought it was a woman. A man should be braver."

Cranking the window enough to let the smoke out, Molly said, "Be careful, Em! That remark sounds a little sexist."

"Huh?"

"Never mind." Molly laughed. "I'll explain it later."

After about twenty minutes, Molly started the truck. "No point in staying here all day. We'll just take it slow."

Shortly after leaving the flatter area around San Simeon, the road began to climb toward the higher coastline. It wasn't long before hairpin curves carved into the mountains became the norm. Molly had to brake often in the thick fog, and more than once slowed to twenty just to be able to follow the road. She could hear the thundering waves crashing against the rocky coast below her on the left. With visibility nearly impossible, she had no idea how close to the oncoming lane she might be. Checking the odometer, she was shocked to see they'd only gone ten miles in the past half hour. At this rate, they wouldn't make it home before dark. Too bad the little map guide didn't give estimates for pea soup conditions, she thought. When a highway patrol passed opposite her and blinked its lights, she felt a little better. If he'd made it through, so could she.

"How about some music?" Emma asked. "It might make us feel better." When Molly nodded, Emma turned on the radio, but all she got was static. "Shoot. We can't get a thing. Next time we go on a trip, we can bring some music CDs. I don't think you want to hear *Harry Potter* right now. Would you like to know what I learned about Carmel?" Molly, her eyes glued to the road, nodded, and Emma began, "Well, first thing is the pine trees. Carmel was just a big bare hill next to the beach without trees. So all the huge trees we have now had to be planted. And, uh, sidewalks where people live are banned, and they can't have street numbers, and dogs can run free on Carmel Beach without a leash. Oh, yeah, and after the San Francisco earthquake in nineteen-something-or-other, a bunch of artists and writers moved there and camped on the beach until they finished building their cabins. They used to have bonfires and make big pots of stew."

When Emma realized Molly wasn't listening, she looked over and saw her eyes darting back and forth from the rearview mirror to the road. "What's wrong?"

"That Jeep is behind us again, and I don't like the way it's following so close."

"Guess they didn't live back there, huh?"

Staring ahead now, Molly said, "Guess not."

"Maybe it's a good idea to have company on this road."

"Not that close. He's damn near on my bumper!" With that, Molly tapped her brakes to warn the driver to back off. When the Jeep didn't respond, she punched up the gas a bit more and tried to create a distance between them. Watching to see if the Jeep would stay back, she nearly missed a sharp curve. Swerving away from the jutting boulders hugging the mountainside, she swore, "Shit!" Her hands were turning clammy. She was having a hard time keeping them on the steering wheel. Wiping them on her jeans, she said, "Sorry about that."

"My thoughts exactly," Emma said shakily.

A soft drizzle began, and Molly sighed. "Great. That's all we need now. Fog and goopy roads." Appreciating Emma's attempt at humor, she said, "Guess you've heard all the words, huh?"

"Yep. Even at my age, we know 'em. The girls at school were worse than the boys."

Glancing in the rearview mirror again, Molly was relieved not to see the Jeep. "By the way, you learned a lot about Carmel. I was listening, but I was watching that idiot. In fact, you taught me a few things I didn't know." Noticing Emma was clutching her seat belt, she suggested, "Why don't you put *Harry* back on? He can keep us company."

What should have taken forty-five minutes to reach Gorda, a small one-stop dot on the coast thirty-one miles north of San Simeon, took two hours. When Molly stopped for gas, she was ready to kiss the ground. Still blanketed in thick fog, the lights over the gas pump seemed like a beacon of safety. "Okay, we've got thirty-four miles to Big Sur, and when we get to Bixby Bridge, it's only thirteen miles to home."

"Is that what they told you inside?"

"That's what the man said."

"Did he say how long it would take?"

"Uh, well, he said it's socked in all the way up, but there's hardly any traffic. Come to think of it, we've only seen that highway patrol."

"And that Jeep," Emma said.

"Well, he's long gone."

Back on the slick road, Molly felt somewhat relieved. Her tires looked fine, she had a full tank of gas, and fresh coffee. Still cautious, and watching her speed, they listened to Harry Potter's adventures all the way to Big Sur. Just as they began the approach to the Bixby Bridge, Molly eased off the gas and slowed to a crawl. She hated bridges. Short and shallow bridges were just as menacing to her as long and tall. The man at the gas station had told her that this was one of the ten highest in the world. If the weather were clear, she knew she would have grit her teeth and stood on it. But the fog was thick, and the thought of having to fight through it on a bridge spanning five canyons and 280 feet over the ocean made her queasy.

Trying not to let Emma see her fear, Molly quietly took a deep breath and was about to accelerate when Emma said, "Uh-oh . . . he's back. I can see him in the side mirror."

Like a phantom in a Stephen King novel, the Jeep was behind her once again, and moving fast. A small patch of lighter fog appeared ahead, and Molly took advantage of her greater vision and sped up. "Try to see if you can get a look at the license."

Keeping her eyes moving between the road and the mirror, Molly managed to gain space, but the minute they reached the bridge, the Jeep was only feet from her bumper. The low-slung El Camino was no match for the high grille of the Jeep. When she felt the first hit, her head jerked and her hands tightened on the wheel. "Get my cell phone out of my tote! Dial 911 and tell them a maniac is harassing us!" Pressing harder on the gas, Molly bit her lip and prayed she could outrun the Jeep. The only problem was the bridge, and the hairpin road after it. Half of her brain was helping her zigzag out of the Jeep's aim, and the other heard Emma yelling into the cell phone.

"We're on that monster bridge, the Bix something," she told the dispatcher. "A mean person in a big gray Jeep is trying to crash us! He's trying to run us off the road! Hurry, please, hurry!" Trying hard to show Molly she wasn't in a panic, Emma said, "They'll do the best they can, the lady said."

"Okay, hang on. I'm going to try to get away from him." But before she could, the Jeep was on her tail again, and the next hit knocked her sideways and toward the concrete railing of the bridge. Molly gripped the wheel for all she was worth and pulled out of it in time. She barely heard Emma's squeals when he hit her again. This time the truck started to spin on the slick road. Trying to get out of trouble took all of Molly's concentration. She turned the steering wheel in the opposite direction and managed to straighten up, but the rocking of the truck forced her against the door and she lost her footing on the brake and gas pedal. Heading for the railing again, she turned the wheel and hit the concrete side, grating along it for several feet. By the time she managed to pull away, the Jeep raced past her into the heavy fog.

At a complete stop, Molly tried to catch her breath as her eyes followed the taillights of the speeding Jeep. "Are you okay, Emma?"

Clutching the CD player, she said, "I'm fine."

Pulling back into her lane, Molly inched the truck

slowly across the rest of the bridge. She spotted a wide shoulder on her right and pulled in. Nosing the front of the truck toward the opposite lane, she was in position to jam into the SUV if it returned. She could ram it quick, then hit the brakes and pull the emergency brake to keep them from going over the cliffs. She told Emma the plan and to make sure her seat belt was tight. "Take my jacket out of the back and roll it up like a pillow. If that bastard comes back, cover your head and pray." She checked the gas gauge. She had over half a tank. She could idle for some time and still have enough gas to get them home. She looked at her watch and decided fifteen minutes should be enough. If the Jeep didn't come back by then, they would leave.

Trying to erase the terror on Emma's face, she said, "You're a pretty cool character, Em." Her laugh was a little hollow when she added, "Where's a cop when you need one?"

"Coming around the bend," Emma said, pointing to a sheriff's unit slowing to a stop in front of them. The blinking lights seemed unnecessary now, and the wailing siren was almost an insult to what she'd just been through. Molly's legs were shaking so bad, she pulled up a mass of anger to replace her fear. She jumped out of the truck and yelled, "What took you so long? Did you get him? The Jeep? The bastard that tried to run us off the road?"

The deputy calmly got out of his car and asked, "Are you okay, ma'am?"

"Sure! I'm great! We're having a wonderful time

trying to stay alive. Didn't you get a clue with our SOS or did your dispatch think I was trying out for a reality show? Where is he? I want to get my hands around his neck!"

"Ma'am, please try to calm down. Why don't you tell me what happened."

"I just told you! Didn't you see him go past you?"

The deputy shook his head. "Nothing's gone past me for miles. Nobody's out driving in this fog. Locals know better."

Molly whirled away from him and slammed her hand on the hood. "I don't believe it! He raced past me in your direction and you didn't see him?" Leaning into the truck, she said, "Em, give me that license number."

Handing it to the deputy, she shot out, "Here, now go find him."

Taking the scrap of paper, he returned to his car. With his window up, Molly couldn't hear what he was saying on his phone. When he returned, he told her, "There's any number of side roads the driver could have taken. I've called it in, and we'll do our best to find the vehicle." Walking around the truck, noting the badly scraped driver's side, he asked, "This thing able to get you home?"

"This *thing* is *very* able to get me home, thank you." Leaning back into the truck, she grabbed her tote and pulled out her wallet. Handing him her card, she said, "Here! You're obviously not in a rush to do anything, so call me when you have a moment."

"Just a minute, ma'am, don't take off. I've gotta answer my call."

Climbing back into the truck, Molly tried to steady her shaking hands. Coming down from abject terror left the rest of her numb. She knew it wasn't the deputy's fault that it took him so long to find them. God only knew how far away he'd been when he got the call. But she was still too upset to do little more than scream at him. When both her eyes began to twitch, Emma started to laugh. "I'm sorry, Aunt Molly, but you really look funny with your eyebrows jumping all over the place."

Before Molly could answer, the deputy was back. Stooping down, he said, "Chief Randall would like you to go straight to his office when you get to Carmel. I'm to escort you to Carmel Highlands, then I'll have to turn back."

"Randall? How does he know where I am?"

"I wouldn't know, ma'am. Just following orders from my dispatch."

CHAPTER 17

"Are we going to be in trouble with Randall?" Emma asked.

"No, of course not. He probably just wants to make sure we're okay."

"We could call him."

"Uh, let's not. We'll just drop by and then go home and collapse, okay?" *Great*, Molly thought. That's all she needed today. The first thing he'd tell her was that she should have stayed home like he'd told her to. Then he'd say that because of her stubborn streak, she'd put Emma in jeopardy. Naturally, it wouldn't occur to him that she hadn't invited trouble. It wasn't as if she'd cut the Jeep off somewhere on the road and the driver was filled with road rage. And it would be obvious that it wasn't a case of car jacking. Goddamn bridge! She hated them with a passion. If she'd realized she had to cross that damned thing on their way home, she would have stayed on 101.

Then it struck her. How strange that she hadn't considered it before. Fear had overridden logic. *Who was driving that Jeep? And why did someone want to kill her?*

She and Emma were halfway up the steps to the Carmel police station when Randall came barreling out. "Are you two okay? What the hell happened?"

Stopping just inches from Molly, the strain on his face was so clear, she had to stop herself from reaching out.

He saw her hesitate, and took Emma's hand. "You okay, Em?"

Hugging him around the waist, she nodded, then looked up. "Aunt Molly was wonderful. She saved us from going over the bridge. You should have been there!"

Molly saw Randall's eyes narrow, and she braced herself for a bawling out.

"I wish to hell I had been. She's a champ, Em. One of a kind. Who was it, did you recognize him?"

Almost tongue-tied, Molly shook her head. "The windows were tinted and spattered with mud. Those Jeeps sit up higher than the El Camino, so I couldn't see much."

"What made you decide to take Highway 1 back? You were supposed to stay on 101."

"What do you mean *supposed* to?"

"I think we ought to go inside." Randall's control was monumental. He wasn't sure which he wanted to do first, hug her, or wring her neck. On the front steps of the police station, he knew he could do neither.

Following him, Molly and Emma paused as he asked one of the clerks for coffee and a soft drink for Emma, then added, "How about giving Emma here a tour while I get the info on Molly's hit and run."

Inside his office, with the door closed, Randall said, "Get off your feet, have some coffee and a smoke, then take it from the top."

"I don't have to wait that long. Somebody tried to kill us. It's that simple. Why? I haven't a clue." Putting her hands up to ward off any argument, she said, "I'm not imagining it either. That bastard was intent on knocking us off that damn bridge."

"Okay, simmer down. I believe you. For the sake of argument, we'll figure it's a man. So where did you first spot him?"

"When we pulled into Cambria." Molly told him about the Jeep slowing down while she was looking for a place to eat, then recounted each sighting. "He could have been behind me all the way from Santa Barbara for all I know. Every three cars on the road is one of those big things, and a lot of them are gray."

Randall kept his fear for her as close to his chest as possible, but he knew he had to tell her the truth. "Somebody wants to scare the shit out of you. I know that stretch of the road, and if he wanted to kill you, it would have been easy. He either thinks you know more than you do or just isn't taking any chances. Next time you might not be so lucky."

"Next time?"

"Next time. Come on, Molly. Do you really think this was a one-shot?"

"But why? I mean, what could he think I know?"

"You cleaned Trudy's office out, didn't you?"

"But only you know that. Lucero doesn't even know." Molly sipped her coffee, then said, "Her office was a mess that first day I went there. Papers all over, the tutorial for Word was out and open . . ." She looked at Randall. "Someone was there ahead of me."

"And isn't computer literate so couldn't find what you eventually did. Or didn't have time to look. When did you first notice the messy desk?"

Molly thought for a moment. "The night Daria and I went over. After Daria left, I checked the house to make notes for the movers."

"That's the night Carrie showed up, right?"

Molly stared at him. "No, it couldn't have been her. She had Em with her." When she saw the doubt in his eyes, she quickly said, "Carrie was not driving that Jeep! She'd never hurt Em!"

"I didn't say that, did I?"

"You were thinking it."

"Like I told you before, don't count anyone out. Maybe you'd better find out what they did before they dropped in to see you, huh? She could have left Emma somewhere."

"What about Milo? Maybe he's the one who searched her desk. Maybe Milo was driving the Jeep!"

"Milo would have had a key or he wouldn't have been shaking the door the day you saw him. He wasn't the driver. We've got a tail on him. He was here in Carmel."

"Carrie would need a key too, then."

"Maybe not. We found two windows unlocked. Forensics will have print info later today. And in case you're wondering, I've got Carrie's prints, and an interesting folder on her."

Molly knew somewhere along the line she'd have to face this. And she also knew Randall would have done a full search on her sister. He'd already told her Carrie was in this mess up to her neck. "Are you going to tell me, or keep me wondering?"

"Are you sure you want to know?"

She nodded. "If she's really a suspect, then I think I'd better."

Pulling a file from his desk drawer, Randall scanned it quickly and then put it away. "I can't let you see it, but I can give you an overview. You knew she was a partner in a law firm in Seattle?"

"Yes. She told me she did trusts and wills. Said it was boring."

"Yeah, well, she put some zing in it. She was asked to leave, Molly. Apparently, jewelry went missing from some safe deposit boxes under her control." He saw her face pale, and was suddenly sorry he had to lay all this out. But she had to know. Her life might depend on it.

"Seems she has a weakness for jewelry," Molly broke in.

"I remember. A bracelet put your old man in jail."

Molly got up and walked to the window behind his desk. She folded her arms tight and stared

226

outside. In a voice struggling to stay even, she told him about her missing miniatures and jewelry.

Seeing a faint sheen in her eyes, Randall rose and drew her into his arms. He could feel her bones melt as she slumped against him. "Why the hell didn't you tell me? I could have put her on the wire and brought her in!"

"Don't yell. I was so sick about it, I was numb." She looked up at him and said, "And then there was Em. I couldn't do it, Randall. I just couldn't. Not after she left her on the doorstep."

"Damn it, Molly."

"I know. I'm sorry. I should have come to you right away." Looking away, she said, "It's only money."

"It's all you had. It was your shop dough."

Molly's laugh was dry. "My savings and the miniatures. Poof! Just like that. Wow, what a week, huh?"

"Want to let this file rest? Maybe later?"

She wiped her eyes, and suddenly feeling awkward with his arms still around her, pulled back and gave him her crooked smile. "No. Let's hear it. Great way to cap off an exciting morning."

Releasing her, Randall watched her eyes come back to life. He had to hand it to her. She had balls.

Settled back behind his desk, Molly took a seat in the chair opposite him. He wanted to be sure she wasn't just putting up a brave front. When she nodded, he said, "Okay. In a nutshell, she was asked to leave. Simple as that. No charges, nada.

The scandal was too risky for the firm. And Emma's father? He's not dead. He's Marshall Montgomery, the senior partner of the firm she was with. The Newsome name came from a marriage that lasted a year. Carrie had a long-term affair with Montgomery. His wife found out a few years ago and left him. When Montgomery didn't do the right thing and marry her, she started with the sticky fingers bit. Payback or simple greed? Hell if I know. Montgomery knows about Emma, by the way. Might be a problem with the legal thing for you, but Lucero's handling it."

Molly's mouth fell open. "What? Emma has a father who she thinks is dead? Well, he can't have her! I'll fight the bastard to the end. I'll—"

"Hey, hold up." Randall started to laugh. Despite the seriousness of what he'd just told her and her encounter this morning, he couldn't help himself. "Get that Irish under control, okay? Let Lucero handle it."

"What can he do?"

"Oh, you'd be surprised. Besides, he owes you big-time."

"I want to go home and take a nap. My brain hurts."

"Not yet." Rising, he picked up her empty cup and said, "Relax. I'll get more coffee. We've got more to discuss."

"Could you make it decaf? I'm already a nervous wreck."

When Randall left, Molly picked up her Zippo

and began clicking it open and shut. The sound helped her think. She could still feel the warmth of Randall's arms, and wondered why she felt so calm. He seemed to be inching closer and closer to her, and she didn't know how to handle it.

Returning with a full pot of decaf and a box of cookies, Randall said, "Have some sugar."

Giving a chocolate chip her full attention, she said, "Just don't tell me I have to go into seclusion." When he didn't answer, she looked at him. "I'm kidding."

"It's not joke time. I'm going to insist you keep the alarm on upstairs around the clock. When you're in the shop, keep your cell handy. If you have errands, call me and let me know where you're going. I don't want you two out at night either unless I know about that too, okay?"

"I can't live like that."

"You have no choice."

"But—"

Leaning toward her, he said, "Molly. Look at me." She did. "This is serious. This morning might just have been a warning. If I thought I could convince you to get away, I would."

She had to smile then. "Fat chance, copper."

Frustrated he wasn't getting through to her, he said, "Go home. Get some rest."

They found Emma at the front desk, mesmerized by all the computer equipment. "Time to go, squirt," Randall said. "Your aunt Molly is falling asleep on me. How about I come by with Chinese later?" Looking at Molly, he added, "Maybe while Em's watching a movie, we can talk."

"Very cool," Emma said. "I love Chinese."

After setting the alarm and showing Emma how it worked, Molly said, "Randall is a nervous Nelly sometimes so he wants us to use the alarm when we're upstairs."

"I think it's a good idea." Looking straight into Molly's eyes, Emma added, "I know something serious is going on. Are you going to explain it to me?"

Molly hesitated, then said, "Something serious *is* going on. I can't tell you everything yet, but I will. I promise. Just not now."

"Are you in trouble with someone?"

Molly shook her head. "Not me. Someone I know." Collapsing on the sofa, she said, "I could sleep for two days."

Next to her, Emma clutched Molly's hands. "Is it *her*? Is *she* the one in trouble?"

"No, silly. Your mother has nothing to do with it." Quickly changing the subject, she said, "I've got to go downstairs and check the answering machine, but I think I'll leave the Closed sign on the door."

"Good idea. You look awfully tired. Maybe you should rest."

"You convinced me. Why don't you take a nap too?" Giving her a hug, Molly said, "You were a big help today."

"We're a good team."

She planted a kiss on her forehead. "Yes, Em, we are."

Down in the shop, Molly drank half of a small bottle of water to clear the lump in her throat. Emma's bravery and calm, and her astute reading of the atmosphere surrounding them, left her speechless. Her comment about them being a good team was the clincher. The poor child was taking all this turmoil better than she was. Clicking on the answering machine, she jotted down a few messages, including one from a customer who had a collection of Staffordshire dogs she wanted to sell and one from Bitsy demanding to know why she was closed. Then her droopy eyes shot open when she heard Sally Sims say she had news. She was out of town and would call back on Wednesday.

If only she could manage to hold her curiosity until tomorrow. Turning on the computer, she searched for the names and telephone numbers of the two customers she'd been dreading to call. Jotting them down, Molly decided to call from the storage room. She sat in the old chair and reached for the portable. On the third ring, Mr. Whitcomb answered. After a few moments of pleasantries, she said, "I have horrible news. I've just discovered the Meissen figures I sold you are not genuine." The long pause at the other end made Molly's hands clammy. Hoping to diffuse the expected explosion, she said, "I will refund you fully, Mr. Whitcomb. If you will send them back—"

"Really? Well, how convenient," Mr. Whitcomb

interrupted. "My appraiser verified them as genuine and warned me this might happen when I told him how much I paid for them."

"What? Well, your appraiser is mistaken. Those pieces are—"

When he hung up on her, Molly was stunned. She wondered if Mr. Whitcomb's appraiser was certified or just another know-it-all dealer playing expert. Before she let her temper get the better of her, she dialed the Jacksons in Kentucky. When their answering machine came on, Molly left her name and number and mentioned it was about the tea service.

Staring at the phone, she thought about returning Bitsy's call. She hadn't told her she was going away for a couple of days. When her eyes began to blur and she could feel her heart hammering, she knew aftershock was kicking in. Holding onto the side of the chair, she took a deep breath. It was amazing how much energy survival demanded.

The effort to climb the stairs was awesome. She had to will her legs up each step. Emma was out like a light on her bed, hugging her panda. Curled up next to her, Tiger spotted Molly, then followed her into her bedroom. When Molly lay across her bed, she looked at her father's photo and wanted to cry. *Oh, Dad! It's worse than I thought.* She blinked for a moment, then sighed. *But you'd love Em.* Snuggled next to Molly, Tiger's soft mewing was like a lullaby, and Molly fell instantly asleep.

★　　★　　★

In that singular state of holding onto sleep, to recapture that dreamy realm of escape, Molly's eyes opened slowly. The darkness in her room surprised her. Looking at the bedside clock, she was surprised to see it was six P.M. She'd slept for hours. When her brain came out to play, she recognized Emma's and Randall's voices in the living room, and could smell wood burning. She lifted herself off the bed, rubbed her eyes, and remembered Randall's promise of Chinese food.

Hiding out in the hallway, Molly heard them laughing and saw them setting out a virtual buffet on the oversized coffee table. It must have been Randall who lit the fire, and now, as she watched them, she wondered whose idea it was to prepare everything before waking her. She saw Emma hug Randall's arm and say, "Aunt Molly is going to be surprised. I was kinda sad for a few days, but I'm glad I ended up with her. I think she's wonderful."

When she heard Randall say, "I do too," she stepped back against her bedroom door and held her breath.

"Are you a couple?" Emma asked.

Mortified, Molly wanted to melt into the door. Randall's brief silence seemed an eternity.

"No," he finally answered. "Not a couple."

"Good friends, then?"

"Yeah, something like that."

"You either are or you're not. Which is it?"

"It's kind of complicated, okay? Not something you and I should be talking about."

"Work on the couple thing, okay? I'd really like that. We could be a family."

Molly felt a faint coming on, and quickly stepped into the room. "Hey, why didn't you wake me?" Looking at the coffee table, she said, "Oh my gosh, did you two do all this?"

Randall's laugh was a little too quick, and when he clapped his hands and said, "*Voilà*! A feast for our Grand Prix winner," Molly knew they hadn't seen her lurking in the hall.

"Randall's going to show me how to use chopsticks!" Emma blurted.

Molly was impressed with their quick recovery. Smiling at Randall, she said, "I'll pay attention, then. I still don't have the hang of it. Did you order everything on the menu?"

"I figured you two would be starving by now. I don't guess you had much time to eat since your little adventure."

"It wasn't an adventure," Emma said, "it was scary." Giving Randall a big smile, she added, "But I'm okay now. We're home where we belong."

"Amen," Randall said, looking straight at Molly.

While Emma watched a movie, Molly and Randall took their after dinner coffee into the shop. At the back of the showroom, they sat opposite each other on a pair of matching camel-back sofas. With only three small lamps on, anyone on the street would have a hard time noticing them. "The Jeep that tried to ace you this morning was a rental out of San Francisco and the credit card used was

234

stolen. The highway patrol found it. The driver dumped it over a cliff down by the Highlands Inn. Who knew you were going to Santa Barbara?"

"Just you . . . Daria and Lucero. I didn't even tell Bitsy. She left a message on the answering machine wondering why the shop was closed. She was really pissed. You'd think she still owned it. It was really kind of funny and—" Molly froze. Shaky hands struggled to her mouth. "I was being watched."

"You got it. You're Carrie's sister. She was here and seen with you. If she trusted you enough to leave her kid, she might have trusted you enough to spill her guts. For all they know, you're in on it with her."

"Oh shit."

"Yeah. Something like that."

Molly was silent for several moments. Randall watched her try to absorb the reality of how serious her situation had become.

Finally, she said, "Sally Sims left a message too. She said she'd made some progress and would call me tomorrow."

"How does she know what she's looking for?"

"Huh?"

"You heard me. You didn't know what name Trudy used when she went out of town, so the only thing you could have used were pictures. Let's have them."

Molly went to her desk and pulled her tote out from under the knee hole. He'd caught her so easily again. She purposely sauntered back with the photos, determined not to let him know she was fuming. "I didn't think you'd miss them."

Randall took the photos from her and looked at them. "What else do you have that you don't think I'd miss?"

"Nothing," she said, tucking her feet under her on the sofa.

"Look, Molly, we've been down this route before—"

"How the hell else could I give Sally a means to . . . well, I mean, I had to have a photo, didn't I?"

"You could have asked me."

"Right. Like you'd hand over evidence? You were threatening to lock me up when I said I was going!"

"Okay, point taken. But from now on, you clear anything with me first."

"I tried, but you kept telling me to butt out."

"What the hell do you expect me to do? You wanna be a cop? Sign up for the academy."

"I want to find out who killed Trudy."

Randall pulled out a cigar and gave it his full attention. "Even if it's your sister?"

"But you said—"

"Never mind what I said."

"Yes."

Slowly passing the illegal Cuban Monte Cristo under his nose, Randall avoided looking at Molly. After a moment, he put the cigar back in its case and pulled out his cigarettes. Taking his time lighting one, he turned his attention to a large crystal ashtray on the Tole tray table between the sofas. "Waterford?"

Attuned to his tactics, Molly knew he had more to say and was buying time. She could play the same game, and he knew it. "Aren't you the clever one. And it's a steal at fifty bucks. Hard to sell now. Smokers are becoming an endangered species."

Randall's grin was fleeting. Running his hand over the sculpted rim of the Tole tray, he said, "Nice piece. New or the real thing?"

"Mid-1800s, English, and cheap at twelve hundred. They're going for much more in The City. Be careful with your ashes."

"The minute your friend Sally calls, you get with me. I want to know every word she utters. Even the pauses."

"Okay."

Picking up his cup, he took a few sips, then let his eyes wander the shop. Molly felt like throwing a pillow at him, just to end the game. She hoped the decision he was trying to make was whether to tell her what was really going on. Like it or not, Trudy's death fell smack in the middle of her realm. Even though he hated it, Molly knew he needed her and that he'd never be able to get inside the underbelly of hushed-up bad deals without her. There might be drug smuggling involved, and maybe Trudy was a part of it and used the antique shows to pass on the drugs. It wasn't a new trick, and minor sales were often ignored.

"Okay, here's where we are," Randall said. "I've got a tail on Milo Kraft. I don't want to bring him in for further questioning yet. I'm hoping he'll make some bad moves first."

Molly wanted to jump up and yell *Yes!* But she knew she had to restrain herself or he might change his mind. "Is he your prime suspect?"

"No." When he saw the look of surprise on her face, he said, "He's a minor cog. Guys that swagger and then sweat when a cop looks them in the eye are cowards. Besides, he wouldn't be hanging around if he was the murderer. He's not smart enough to pull that off."

"Then," she began, "you *do* think it's Carrie."

"No again. She's on a surveillance video the San Francisco police made of someone they're looking at up there. They put her in The City all of Sunday up to midnight."

Carrie on a surveillance tape? "How deep is her involvement? Is that what she meant on the answering machine about things unraveling?"

"Not sure yet. I can't talk about their investigation, so don't ask."

"Okay." Molly knew she'd get it out of him sooner or later, but decided to play along. Then she remembered what Daria had said about someone seeing Carrie at the antiques show the night Trudy was killed. She told him about the conversation.

He shook his head. "Already checked that out."

Relieved that Carrie wasn't a murder suspect, she said, "Then she's clear."

"Hardly."

"But you just said—"

"That she wasn't *here*."

"Well, then?"

Leaning in toward her, Randall said, "She's up to her neck in this shit. She's a key player."

"And the San Francisco cops know, right? Oh, great. Another black mark against the family Doyle! Just what do they know?"

Molly's sarcasm wasn't lost on him. He was well aware of her long-held anger for the SFPD. "I already told you not to ask, so knock it off."

Playing with the fringe on one of the throw pillows, Molly asked, "Why kill Trudy, then? Why was it so important to get her out of the way?"

"That's what we have to find out." Randall could have cut his tongue off when he saw Molly's eyes light up. "Lucero and me. *We* have to find out. Present company not included. You're just to funnel me info, and that's it."

"Well, guess what. I'm now part of the *we*, whether you like it or not! Someone tried to kill me today, and that royally pisses me off."

"Goddamnit, Molly! You've got a stubborn streak worse than mine!"

"Flattery will get you nowhere. I'm going to get to the bottom of this if I have to do it on my own. So now you have to ask yourself, do we let her play? Or do we not?"

Randall stood and looked down at her. "I'll think about it."

Rising to face him, Molly put her hands on her hips and stared right into his eyes. "You do that."

"Lucero ain't gonna like this."

"Bullshit. He wanted me in from the beginning. He knows I can help."

Moving away, he strolled toward the door. Stopping every now and then to look something over, he'd pick up a sales tag, give it a glance, then move on. When he reached the door, Molly said, "Thanks for the Chinese."

Turning slowly to face her, he smiled. "Any time."

When he reached for the doorknob, Molly said, "I want to see those screwy tags Trudy made again. I've got some ideas about them."

"We'll see."

"Randall!"

His slow, crooked grin told her she'd won. "My office tomorrow. After your friend calls."

CHAPTER 18

Wednesday morning, Molly pulled the phone away from her ear and let Bitsy drone on about not letting her know she and Emma took off for a couple of days. She apologized and promised to tell her the next time she had the urge to travel. She'd sworn Emma to secrecy about their close encounter with that damn bridge. Bitsy didn't need to know. She would only fuss and drive them both nuts.

Running upstairs, Molly found Emma washing Tiger's food dish. "Bitsy is coming over in an hour with a tutor for you."

"Say what?"

"Oh, we're into street talk now, huh?"

"Only kidding. Vacation's over I guess." Filling Tiger's dish, Emma said, "Well, it had to happen sooner or later." Looking at Molly, she added, "Lessons, I mean."

Leaning against the sink, Molly eyed her suspiciously. "You have a problem I should know about?"

Nodding, Emma said, "I don't do well at school."

Wrapping an arm around her, Molly said, "Let's

sit down and talk about it. Maybe this tutor can help."

Plopping on the sofa in the living room, Emma said, "I don't think so."

"Sometimes it takes a little longer to catch on with subjects. I failed algebra twice. We can't all be brilliant."

"That's the problem. I sorta am. Well kinda sorta."

"Don't play with me, Em. That's not a good way to get out of studying while we get our situation worked out."

"It's true. I've been tested, and I have almost instant recall."

"Are you kidding around again?"

"Cross my heart, hope to die."

Molly didn't know how to fit that into her crowded brain at the moment. Giving Emma a squeeze, she said, "Well, it's not fatal, and the alternative would be worse. So, let's just go along with the program and see what happens, okay? Besides, it will look good on the paperwork when Lucero has things ready. I mean, having a tutor and all. Makes us look serious and conscientious."

"Can we go down to Tosca's before the teach shows up?"

Checking her watch, and then remembering Randall's warning, Molly said, "How about you run down while I watch from the balcony. Get something for us and we'll have it up here, okay? I'm waiting for a call from Sally Sims, and I don't want to miss it. Besides, the tutor will be here soon."

Planting a kiss on Molly's cheek, Emma said, "Thank you for not thinking I'm a freak. I'll be right back."

Watching her run out the French doors, Molly headed for the balcony. As her eyes followed Emma, she touched the spot on her cheek. Had her life taken a different turn, she might have had a daughter Emma's age. Not wanting to think about her runaway husband, or what might have been, the scene she'd witnessed last night between Emma and Randall could have been a ghost of the past. *We could be a family,* Emma had said to him. She shoved those words away. She had a murder to help solve now, and she needed to keep focus.

When Emma returned, Molly said, "I'll take my cake down with me. I've got to do a few things before Sally calls."

At her desk, she tried the Jacksons again in Kentucky. When their answering machine clicked on, Molly hung up. With time to kill before Bitsy arrived with the tutor, and little to do to get the shop ready, Molly decided to plug in the teapot and put some soothing jazz on to slow down her nerves. When the kettle was ready, she fixed tea. She knew she'd have to lay off the espresso. It was making her jumpy and nervous. When the phone rang, she made a dash for the desk and spilled tea on an Oriental rug.

"I'm sorry I missed your call, Sally. We got back late. That damn fog was a real killer." Molly picked up a pen and flipped open her notebook.

243

"The minute I saw that photo, I almost fainted," Sally said. "I recognized her right away. I . . . I didn't want to tell you, Molly. I was too ashamed to let you know the bitch took me so bad. She nearly broke me."

"Oh, my God! You too?"

"Don't tell me she got *you*?" Sally asked.

"We should start a club. Eighteen grand."

"How's fifty-five grab you?"

"Oh, no! What happened?"

"My client, bless his soul, thought it was a great joke. He's a famous comedian, but I can't tell you his name. That was part of the deal. He kept the six Greco-Roman statues and dresses them in togas when he entertains. I tell you, the bitch was good. I was convinced they were the real thing. Whoever did them knew the formula for aging. They looked more authentic than the real ones."

"Same with me," Molly admitted. "The Meissen pieces were exquisite."

"Well, I wasn't the only one here that got hit. Remember the man in the photo? The one in the hat? He was a well-known dealer here in Santa Barbara. Everyone called him Duke. He had so many airs, you'd think he was to the manor born. Anyway, she *really* got him. I doubt you knew him. He rarely went to New York."

"Doesn't ring a bell. Most of our Southern California clients were from Los Angeles."

Sally went on to say how he actually loved his nickname, and even went out and bought a used

Bentley. Molly laughed along with her. "A used one? Oh, how gauche! What was his real name?"

When Molly heard it, she gripped the edge of the desk so hard, she was sure she'd broken her hand. "*Who?*"

Before she could recover, Sally said she had another call coming and had to go. She got off so quickly, Molly wasn't sure if she'd put her on hold or had hung up. When she heard the click, she knew Sally was gone.

Experiencing overload, a condition she feared was becoming normal, Molly almost didn't hear the tapping on the front window. Bitsy and a woman who appeared to be in her late sixties stood outside. What a time to be early. She had to get to Randall, but she couldn't turn them away. Letting them in, Bitsy introduced Molly to Judith Mason. Short and stocky, her short gray hair hastily brushed, and dressed in a warm-up suit, the woman gripped Molly's hand like a wrestler.

"Judith, by the way, is a retired nun," Bitsy announced. "She'll be great for Emma. However, she can't start until next month."

"Oh, well, that's fine. I'm in a bit of a rush, but come right in. You and Sister . . . er, Ms. Mason, can get with Emma. I've got to run over to see Randall. I . . . I had a little fender bender yesterday on the way home and I've got to sign a complaint."

"Can't you go later? We're early because I have to meet Oliver at the new store to sign some papers."

"What kind of papers?" Remembering the tutor, she quickly said, "I'll have Emma come down. Maybe it might be better if we let them get to know each other first."

Running up the stairs, Molly said, "The tutor is here already. I've got to go over and see Randall about something, so will you come down and chat until I get back? Bitsy is with her, but she can't stay."

Back downstairs, she grabbed her tote. "Emma will be right down." She smiled at Ms. Mason. "Nice to meet you."

At the door, Molly turned to Bitsy, "Don't sign any more papers until we talk. I'm serious! I'll explain later."

"Oh, all right. It can wait. I'll pretend I forgot. We'll go over to Tosca's for coffee."

Halfway up the block, Molly pulled out her cell phone and called Randall, "I'm on my way. I just got off the phone with Sally. You won't believe what I just found out!"

Randall was standing in the open doorway to his office as Molly came down the hall.

Barely catching her breath, she plopped down next to his desk and said, "Trudy took Sally for fifty-five grand for some Istoriato maiolica, a Chinese altar table, a Coromandel screen, and several pieces of Flora Danica, and besides that, she sold her six Greco-Roman statues and her client—"

"Whoa! Slow down. What the hell is . . . what did you call it? Isto . . . what?"

"Italian maiolica. Hand painted narrative scenes."

"I thought it was majolica. With a j."

"It is majolica, but the Italians spell it different. You should know that. The Flora Danica alone is—" When Molly saw the blank look on Randall's face, she said, "It's a *very* expensive dinner set. It was originally made for a Danish queen in—"

"Yeah, whatever."

"You don't know what it is, do you? I bet you don't know what a Coromandel screen is either." Ignoring the look on his face, Molly said, "Oriental pictoral folding floor screens made with carved lacquer work. They're called Coromandel, which was the main port in Bengal they were exported from when they started making them in the seventeenth century."

"Wrap it up, okay? I don't care, damn it! I want to know why the Sims woman didn't tell you she recognized Trudy in that photo!"

"Oh, come on. Who the hell is going to admit to being taken that bad? I mean, Sally and I go way back, but still. She wanted to warn me. She said I'd always been up front with her and she never once believed I was part of Derek and Greta's scam. By the way, Sally knew Trudy as Laura Barnes. But wait, you have to hear about the statues and how they're faked."

"Later, okay? So all you got was something we

already knew. Trudy was selling fakes. We've still got an empty page here."

"Nope. I was saving the best for last. Get those pictures I gave you last night."

Moving over to the conference table, he pulled them out of a box and handed them to her. Molly carefully looked both of them over again, then nodded. "I knew I'd seen that hat before." Giving them back to Randall, she said, "The man in the hat? Sally said his name was Duke."

Randall looked at the photo, then said, "And?"

"It's his nickname. He was an interior decorator in Santa Barbara."

"I'm happy for him. Hope he does well. You got more titillating news to share?"

Leaning back and crossing her leg, Molly grinned. "Trudy got him really big-time. He was doing a Hollywood honcho's villa in Montecito and bought a lot of stuff from her. Duke met her at an antiques show in Pasadena, and then later at her warehouse there for more stuff. A few months after the house was done, the honcho had an appraiser catalog everything. The appraiser blew the whistle on Duke's merch, and it cost him over two hundred grand to buy it all back or go to jail. It broke him. Word got out, and his business disappeared. His wife left him, and he couldn't handle the disgrace."

At his desk, with his feet on an open drawer, Randall said, "Drink some water before your throat runs dry." Taking a sip of his, he said, "I'm falling asleep here."

"Remember the initials T.O.T.?" When Randall nodded, Molly said, "Does the name Thomas Oliver *Townsend* ring a bell?"

"*Oliver?*"

"The very same."

Molly had come to recognize Randall's simmering anger, deadly sarcasm, and cool indifference. She realized how controlled this powerhouse could be when he wanted to, but she knew his silence was more telling. Now, seeing his chin jut out as he loosened his tie then yanked it off, her hand automatically reached for the small cross under her sweater.

"I smelled him right away," Randall said. "I figured him for a takedown artist." When he saw the puzzled look on her face, he explained, "Bitsy. I know she's a tough broad, but hell, they're sometimes the easiest mark."

"I didn't like him right off either. But if you think he killed Trudy . . ." Molly shook her head. "I don't buy it. He's sneaky and smarmy, but hardly a killer."

"Don't go there again. I warned you before. Trust no one."

With the photo in her hand again, Molly took another look, then waved it at Randall. "He couldn't know this was Trudy. Look at her. Completely different from what she looked like up here. That seventies bouffant black wig, the glasses, even those dumpy clothes." Checking the photo again, Molly laughed. "I never noticed, but look at how much heavier she looks. I'll bet she padded her clothes! Damn, but she was good."

Taking the photos back, Randall said, "Yeah, good and dead."

"I need to take a look at those tags now. I think I know what they mean."

Laying them out on the conference table, Randall said, "It's stuff she sold the killer. I already figured that."

"And I thought I was so smart."

"You are. But I'm the cop, and I have to be."

Leaning over the table, Molly fanned them out. She spent several moments examining each one. Randall watched her nod at two or three. He left her alone and felt a sudden pride in the way she'd handled herself yesterday. That stubborn streak in her saved her ass, but if she wasn't careful, it might do her in. Taking that trip to Santa Barbara had been smart. She might have made a good cop. He wondered if he ought to tell her that he'd had her watched by the highway patrol, and why. Old friends with many favors to return came in handy. Funny she never picked up on his slip about why she hadn't stayed on 101. They'd lost her when the shifts changed, and by the time the patrols on the coast highway figured she might have gone their way, they couldn't find her in the heavy fog. He decided to leave it alone. She didn't need to know he'd been worried about her. California freeways were a challenge for the most experienced drivers. The fact that she'd been followed was a new problem, and one he hadn't anticipated.

"Okay, we just have to find out who she sold this stuff to," Molly said. "Piece of cake. I'll get right on it."

"You think so, huh?" Randall laughed.

Ignoring him, she said, "I need to make a list of all this. Got a notepad?"

He handed her one from his desk. "We found her local warehouse. It was filled with boxes of stuff from Hong Kong, Egypt, and Mexico."

Her head bent, writing quickly, Molly said, "I'm not surprised." When she finished her notes, she looked up. "I've got to get back. Bitsy hired a tutor for Emma, and she's an ex-nun. She's there now."

"An ex-nun?" Randall grinned. "That could be an experience." Walking her to the door, he said, "I don't have to tell you to keep this between us. Especially the Oliver thing."

Molly hesitated. "I think Bitsy should know."

"I'll bet she already does. Only not the Trudy part. You sit on that. Maybe you're right. Maybe Oliver didn't recognize her."

The walk back to the shop this time was at least enjoyable. The sun had finally come out, the town smelled of pine trees and salt spray, and its freshness was exhilarating. Molly took several deep breaths and smiled. Flower boxes at shop windows overflowed with winter blooms and trailing ivy. The streets were clean. The gutters pristine. A shop owner was sweeping pine needles from his entry. People smiled and walked without haste or hostility. A man was walking a half-dozen beagles, and no one honked their horn. Carmel had become her nirvana, or, as Daria had once called it, Carmelot. For the first time in over a week, she remembered how happy she was here. Randall was going to let her help finally, and she didn't have to lie to him anymore.

CHAPTER 19

Randall pulled up the shade over his Incident board after Molly left. Standing back, he viewed the entries, then added Oliver Townsend under Milo Kraft, and Carrie Newsome under "Motive." Kraft could have any number of motives. Maybe his cut wasn't big enough, maybe he wanted to take over, maybe he wanted out. Carrie's threat had to do with money she had coming. He was sure she wanted out, considering she'd worn out her welcome in Seattle. But Oliver was leading the pack now. Taking a two hundred grand hit put him at the top.

Under "Opportunity," Milo was ranked first. He'd been in the parking lot at the exhibit hall, clearing the van to load Trudy's merchandise after the show. Randall added Oliver under Milo. Oliver had waltzed into Trudy's space to get Bitsy moments after Trudy was discovered. He left Carrie's name on this list. Carrie was iffy, but the surveillance tape she'd reputably been on was not accurate. There were time lapses and a date mixup. And a different set of clothes. The DEA was handling that now, and his contact there had worked with him in L.A. a thousand years ago.

On the Means list, he stared at Milo's name. If Milo killed Trudy, he might be smart enough to think he wouldn't be a suspect since it would be obvious he probably knew about her allergy. Was he working on the theory the cops wouldn't think he was that stupid? The next name was Carrie Newsome. He wasn't sure about her.

Jiggling a marker in his hand, he leaned against the edge of the conference table and thought about Oliver. The homicide wasn't the result of physical strength or a weapon. Only a hand had been needed to drop a tablet in Trudy's soda. So maybe when they first met, Oliver saw the med bracelet and asked about it. People did that. Especially when they were Oliver's age. Health became a new hobby when mortality was knocking on your door. Oliver could be well up on health issues. He'd be keenly aware of medical bracelets, and since Medicare didn't cover prescriptions, he'd know about the free clinics and how to get a pill or two every now and then on the cheap. No paper trail to speak of, no computerized list at your doctor's office.

Back at the board, Randall added Oliver Townsend.

One problem nagged him. The drug angle. Where did Oliver fit into the equation? If he was the killer, then it was simple revenge. But that train of thought led to more questions. How did he know Trudy lived here? How did he recognize her? Where did Bitsy fit into all this? And who tried to scare Molly? It sure as hell wasn't Oliver. He'd seen Oliver having breakfast at the Village Corner when he came back from his run on the beach at seven-thirty in the morning.

And then there was Trudy's financial situation. Healthy, but not enough zeros to account for drug smuggling. But then, she wouldn't deposit that kind of dough. She'd put it offshore or hide it. So far, Lucero's investigators hadn't come up with bank accounts out of the county, and with all the secrecy laws, they might never locate a thing. Gut feeling told him she hid it. They'd already torn her self-storage unit apart and come up empty-handed, except for more phony merchandise. He was betting on her house. Time to go back and do the crawl space under the house and the attic thing again. He'd set that up for tomorrow. There was also a chance she didn't know about the drugs. But he didn't think so.

According to Lucero's investigators, Trudy's reputation with the local lawyers who contacted her for estate sales was good. Her credit was top-notch, and her neighbors all had good things to say. Every antique dealer on her sales call list raved about her. Private individuals who'd hired her for downsizing or moving sales described her as fair, professional, and fun. Randall liked the way one investigator had underlined "*fun.*" The killer sure as hell didn't think so.

Returning to his desk, he had another problem to solve. The driver who played bumper car with Molly. SFPD was doing more legwork on the car rental and stolen credit card. An old high school buddy on the force, a senior homicide detective, promised to get back to him in a day or two. Picking up the phone, he called Lucero and told him what Molly had discovered. Lucero told him Trudy's body was being released and transported to the mortuary Max had engaged.

When Molly returned, she found Bitsy and Emma having coffee and pastries at Tosca's. "Ms. Mason is a *Harry Potter* fan! Can you believe it?" Emma said happily.

"I'm beginning to think I'm the only one on the planet who hasn't read one."

"Ms. Mason told me the Pope said it's a wonderful lesson of good versus evil."

"Oh, did he? Well, that's good enough for me." To Bitsy, she said, "We need to talk about Mr. Oliver."

Bitsy threw her hands up. "Please, not now. I'm already in the doghouse with him. I don't need you on my case too."

"Oh, wow, you missed that!" Emma said. "He found us here with Ms. Mason and was rude to Bitsy. He yelled at her. Ms. Mason told him to leave. Boy, is she something. I'd never figure her for a nun. We're going to start lessons in a few weeks. She's on vacation now."

Molly could tell Emma stories about strong-willed nuns that would curl her hair. Throwing down her tote, Molly asked Bitsy, "What happened?"

"When I didn't show up to sign those papers, thanks to you, he blew a gasket. He shoved them at me here, and I told him I was busy with Emma and Judith and would look at them later." Smiling to Bennie as he passed by with a tray for the next table, Bitsy lowered her voice. "When he insisted, Judith intervened and told him to leave."

"And he did? Just like that?"

"The former Sister Philomena is not to be trifled with, darling. She could stare down Dirty Harry if she had a mind to."

Nodding yes to Bennie when he raised a cup in their direction, Molly was itching to tell her what she'd discovered about Oliver, but she'd promised Randall to keep it a secret. "What's he trying to get you on the hook for now?"

"I have an idea it's for additional remodeling. He hasn't been able to find the type of showcases he wants and mentioned custom cabinets."

"Custom cabinets? How nice. By the way, he tried to start a tab at Daria's, and used me as a reference. She told him she stopped house charges."

"Oh, dear. I'm glad Daria refused him. I got three bills from restaurants last week. And he ran up a bill for clothes at Umberto's and charged them to me. I'll have to speak to him, I guess."

"You guess? Bitsy! What the hell's going on? I can't believe you're allowing this!"

257

"I think he might have misunderstood my offer of hospitality."

Molly began to think Randall was right. It looked like Oliver was out to take Bitsy to the cleaners. He'd lost everything, and now he was in the taking game. And Bitsy Morgan was known for a big heart. She was up in age, extremely wealthy, and had no children.

"Has he, uh, proposed or hinted he'd like to make this arrangement permanent?"

"Oh, Molly, really! Of course not."

"How much is he into you?"

Bitsy looked away for a moment, then fiddled with her pearl choker. "Fifty."

"Jesus!"

"It's a legitimate loan. He gave me a note."

Bennie arrived with Molly's coffee. Setting it down, he pulled up a chair and joined them. "I don't want that jackass here again, Bitsy. If Sister Phil hadn't been with you, I'd have told him to leave myself."

"Sister *Phil?*" Molly said.

"Yeah, she was one of my teachers in high school. You don't mess with that nun." Turning back to Bitsy, he said, "I adore you, and my house is yours, but keep that bastard away."

"I'm so sorry he made such a scene."

"Hey, it's over." He kissed her forehead, then looked at Molly and shook his head.

It was obvious to Molly he too was wondering why Bitsy was putting up with this strutting little prince. It was so out of character. Emma, who had been listening closely, said to Bitsy, "I don't want to hurt your feelings, but I don't think I'd like to visit again if he's going to keep staying with you."

Grabbing her hand, Bitsy said, "Don't you worry, darling. I'll get this problem solved." Giving Emma one of her widest winks, she added, "And you can bet money on that."

Feeling somewhat relieved, Molly said, "Just don't sign a thing. If he gets nasty again, call Randall. In fact, I'd love to set him straight." Thinking about her ordeal yesterday with the Jeep, she added, "I'm in a mood to do some damage."

Bitsy's husky laugh startled the table of tourists next to them. "Oh, darling! How you reminded me of your mother just then. Don't bother. I'll handle Oliver Townsend."

In her first hour open, Molly sold the lovely tole tray table she and Randall had used the night before, and a very nice late nineteenth-century Japanese conical bowl. Buoyed by the auspicious start, she happily listed the sales, amounting to nineteen hundred dollars, into the computer. She'd accepted a one hundred dollar knock on the table, but held firm on the Japanese bowl. The deep green color, as close to jade as Molly had ever seen on stoneware, was delicious, and she didn't really want to sell it. Not terribly knowledgeable with Asian ceramics, she nonetheless had what was called an "*eye*," and knew excellence when she saw it.

The customer wanting to sell her Staffordshire collection was due in shortly. Molly was anxious to see it. Staffordshire figures were always in demand, and she only had a few left. Taking advantage of a lull, she let her mind drift as she strolled through the shop rearranging merchandise, checking for dust, and deciding what to move to accommodate her new garden section. Fluffing up a vintage needlepoint pillow, it occurred to her that maybe Randall was right. Maybe she should stick to selling antiques. Now that she thought about it, finding who Trudy might have sold those sales tag items to was like looking for the proverbial needle in a haystack. Pietra Dura tables were the rage now and would be hard to track down. Swedish walnut commodes were fairly plentiful, as were Russian icons, and Spanish oak furniture was coming into the country daily. And then it hit her. Randall had set her up.

He was going to keep her out of his hair doing research on the tags. He knew she'd just be spinning her wheels for nothing. But he was wrong. And she was going to prove it. *We'll see who outfoxes who,* she thought.

CHAPTER 20

Mrs. Carlson arrived before Molly could decide her next move. The frequent customer set the box of Staffordshire figures on Molly's desk. "I know you'll love to have these. I'm phasing out the English country look for something more elegant. I'm really tired of chintz and plaids." Unwrapping the first figure, she added, "This is Queen Victoria, and I have the Prince of Wales too. There are six all together." Setting the figure down, she pulled a list from her purse. "I have Queen Mary as a young girl . . . the equestrian model. Shakespeare leaning against a pillar, and a matching pair of King Charles spaniels, which I really adore, but, well, I'll let them go."

As Mrs. Carlson continued to unwrap each figure and place them on Molly's desk, Molly's eyes narrowed. "Mrs. Carlson, I'm afraid I can't—"

"Oh, really, Molly, I know you have to make a profit. I won't be asking for the moon. But they are in exceptional condition, and I know you'll be fair."

"It's not that, it's—"

261

"I'll be happy with three thousand for the lot. I paid more, but I'm willing to take a small loss."

"*Three thousand?*"

"They're as good as new!"

Molly held her breath, then said, "They are, Mrs. Carlson."

"I took excellent care of them, and didn't use detergent when I washed them," she proudly said.

"I'm sure you did, but that's not what I meant. They are *new*. They're reproductions."

Mrs. Carlson's lips seemed to disappear. "That's impossible. I have a receipt and I happen to know these are genuine. Made in England in the 1800s. I bought them from a shop in Denver, just last year, and I—"

"Did your receipt list the circa for each item?"

"I . . . I don't remember. What difference does that make? It was an antique shop!"

Molly wondered when people were going to learn anyone could put a sign on their shop and say they had antiques. It was so frustrating for the hundreds of serious dealers to be lumped with dilettantes and less than ethical shopkeepers wanting in on the new American pastime of collecting.

With utmost patience and sympathy, Molly said, "I know you're upset, but let me explain." Picking up the Queen Mary, Molly kept her voice soft, trying hard not to set Mrs. Carlson off. She'd seen dozens of these reproductions sold as genuine, and felt a profound empathy for those who were being duped. "This is as light as a feather, and it shouldn't be. The crazing of the glaze is overdone, and if you look closely, it even has a pattern. Real crazing is random." Turning it over, she said, "Look at the size of the air hole. It's as big as a quarter, and it shouldn't be." Tapping the side, Molly added, "Hear that? If it were genuine, you wouldn't hear a thing. This is a hollow shell made of porcelain. Figures made in the 1800s are earthenware and thicker. And the biggest giveaway is the stamping on the bottom. It says Staffordshire. That wasn't done." Picking up one of the spaniels, she said, "This one says 'Made in England.' Country of origin wasn't used until the early 1900s."

Examining the others, Molly shook her head. "Besides, the colors are too pale, and the faces are too well-defined. The real pieces were made with a press molding method; reproductions are made with a slip casting process." Seeing the glazed look in Mrs. Carlson's eyes, Molly quickly offered, "Let me show you the pieces I have. You'll be able to see the difference right away."

But Mrs. Carlson was not listening. Her hands were flying so fast as she wrapped the figures and shoved them in the box, Molly had to step away from the desk. Picking up the box, Mrs. Carlson snapped, "I think you made all that up. You're not the expert you pretend to be. I'll never shop here again."

She understood Mrs. Carlson's anger, but she still felt a need to explain. Keeping her voice calm and sympathetic, she said, "I'm not an expert, and

I've never pretended to be. I'm very knowledge-able in many fields of antiques, but not all of them. Very few dealers are. But I know Staffordshire, and I'm sorry you've been misled, Mrs.—"

Mrs. Carlson stormed out of the shop before Molly could finish.

She wished she'd had an opportunity to tell Mrs. Carlson about the pond boat she bought when she worked for Max while she was in college. She was sure it was Early American, but when Max saw it, he immediately knew it was a fake. He'd explained how easy it was to dye the sails in tea and use old wood. He hadn't been angry she'd paid three hundred dollars for it. He'd said it was a cheap lesson. The key to buying and collecting, he'd cautioned, was doing one's homework.

After lunch with Emma, Molly was itching to call Sally. But she had to take care of business no matter what. Max might love her to pieces, but he was still her boss, and she owed him a well-run shop that showed a profit. Molly had to hang on to her smile as she waited on two more customers, and she called Ramon, the upholsterer she used, wanting to know when the George III style humpback settee would be ready. Purchased at auction in San Francisco over a month ago, she had an interested customer, and was anxious to get it on the floor. When he'd told her it would be three more weeks, she pleaded for an earlier date. Her customer was leaving for the East Coast soon and she wanted to close the sale. At least the pair of Continental armchairs were almost ready. Mahogany with open sides and high backs, they were the chair du jour of lap dancers. One of the ladies of the profession had given her a standing order after selling her two. Her only requirement was the fabric had to be velvet and Scotch-guarded.

Perfection, Ramon had told her on their first meeting, could not be rushed. She told him she wasn't looking for perfection, just competence.

When Randall called to tell her the mortuary would notify her later about the schedule for Trudy's funeral, she tried to keep her voice even when she told him she'd left Trudy's dress in her house and asked if he'd take her over to get it.

Molly took advantage of another lull and called Sally. She hoped Sally could remember the fake merchandise Trudy had sold Oliver, and added that it would be better to e-mail the info. She didn't want it coming in on a fax. She promised to explain later, but underscored that it was vital.

Just as she hung up, Emma came down the stairs. "Is Trudy the lady who died?"

"Yes. I have to go over and—"

"I heard when I was on the stairs. I came down to ask if I could read some of your antique books."

Seeing the stack in her hands, Molly said, "Read anything you want. Are you really interested in learning about this stuff?"

Nodding, Emma paused, then asked, "Was the lady who died your best friend?"

"No. Just a . . . just a friend."

When Emma went back upstairs, Molly stepped into the storage room for a damp sponge to spot the very expensive carpet she'd spilled the tea on. A Sarouk from west-central Iran, most likely made in the mid-1920s, it was typical of that era, with a central medallion. After World War I, detached floral sprays were more common. Max had sent it down from the City and told her to hold firm on the price of eight thousand. This particular style was becoming hard to find, and he didn't want to let it go for less. She said a prayer of thanks when she saw she hadn't stained it.

Randall arrived promptly at six to take her to Trudy's. Emma may have been thrilled to ride in the police car, but Molly wasn't. She hoped no one saw her. Talk in Carmel vied with the Internet for speed. She could already imagine the chatter. Either she was in trouble or a romance was in the works. She also thought Randall was carrying this protective bit a little too far. The more she was seen in his company, he'd said on the way over, the less likely she'd have another encounter.

"We'll only be a minute," Molly said to Emma. "Lock the door and keep the window closed."

In the backseat with Molly's copy of the *Antiques Roadshow Primer,* one of the first books the show had published, Emma said, "Take your time. This is fascinating."

Randall rolled his eyes. "Is that what you're reading now? What the hell happened to *Harry*?"

"*Harry*," Emma said primly, "is for fun. If I'm going to be a dealer, I have to start early and learn all I can."

Randall looked at Molly and shook his head, "You're corrupting the kid, you know that, don't you? I should turn you in to child welfare."

Inside Trudy's, Randall stood in the foyer as Molly headed for the living room. "I left the dress on the sofa. I'll be right back."

"Just get the dress. Don't touch anything. I haven't released the house yet."

"It's gone."

Stepping into the room, Randall said, "Maybe you left it somewhere else."

"I could have sworn I left it in here."

"Let's check the bedroom. The techs probably put it away when they were done."

As they entered the bedroom, Molly hesitated by the closet door. "I guess they examined those two packed suitcases. I remembered last night that Trudy was planning to stay at the Pine Inn while the house was tented."

"I already know that."

"How did you know where she was planning to stay?"

"It's what I get paid for."

Molly bit back a smart remark, opened the closet door and came face-to-face with Milo Kraft. Only she didn't realize his bulging eyes were lifeless. Or that one of Trudy's belts was wrapped around his neck and cinched to the closet rod. All she felt was Randall's hands gripping her shoulders and pulling her away. Her limbs and her mind seemed to belong to someone else as he brought her back to the living room and sat her in a chair. She didn't know how long she stayed there. It could have been an hour, and it could have been only minutes. The next thing she knew, she was being helped down the stairs and into Randall's patrol car.

Emma was still in the backseat and visibly concerned. "What happened? How come Randall's policemen are here?"

"There's been a little problem," Wilkins said. "Stay here with your auntie, okay?" He leaned into the car and said, "Molly, try to relax. The chief wants you to stay put. He'll be out soon."

"Are you okay, Aunt Molly?" Emma asked as she grabbed her hand.

"Uh, yeah, she's fine. She's, uh, kind of upset, that's all," Wilkins answered.

Molly's eyes fluttered as she turned to Emma. "I'm fine. It's . . . okay. Randall is okay too. There's a . . . a problem in the house." Wrapping the child in her arms, Molly took a deep breath and said, "Randall is handling it."

CHAPTER 21

M olly hardly touched the roast lamb or lasagna Daria brought over that night. They sat in the living room waiting for Randall and Lucero to arrive. Lucero had been at Daria's when Randall notified him. Racing over to meet Randall, he told Daria what had happened, and she immediately made up a care package and rushed to Trudy's to take Molly and Emma home.

"I think you should close the shop and you and Emma stay with me for a few days," Daria said. "Better yet, I'll take a few days off too, and we'll go up to Lake Tahoe." Smiling at Emma, she said, "What do you think?"

"Well, first of all, I think it's a good idea. Aunt Molly has had enough angst to deal with lately. Second of all, I love your food." Hoping to lighten Molly's mood, she added, "Not that Aunt Molly is a bad cook, it's just that . . ."

Trying to grin, Molly said, "That I can't cook. And *angst*? Did you get that? Is that what twelve-year-olds say these days?"

"They hear it on TV," Daria said. "That and

269

'challenge.' We didn't know those terms when we were kids. Today, everything's a *challenge*."

On the floor, her back leaning against the sofa's edge, Molly set her plate on the coffee table and shook her head. "I can't eat. My stomach is still churning. And I won't close the shop. I won't let whoever this person is think I know what's going on. Safety is in pretending ignorance." The minute she said it, Molly saw the look on Emma's face and knew she'd blown it. "What I mean is—"

"I think it's time to tell me everything," Emma said. "If we have to have an alarm on during the daytime and then play bumper car on that bridge, it's kind of easy to figure something's up."

Daria looked at Molly. "She's right. You might be protecting her too much." Daria saw the look of concern on Molly's face and knew she was thinking about Emma's mother. "Maybe just the highlights?"

Molly was silent for a moment. "Okay. The lady who died? Trudy? Well, she was . . . she was selling fake antiques, and someone—"

"Killed her?" Emma said.

Molly's eyes darted to Daria, then she said, "Yes. Well, we think that's what happened."

"Why is that person mad at you? You're the real thing, aren't you?"

"I can make mistakes like anyone else, but yes, I'm the real thing. And I don't know that someone is mad at me. Maybe they're just confused."

"Because you and that lady were friends?"

"Something like that."

Molly hoped that would satisfy Emma. She was about to change the subject when Emma asked, "Then what happened tonight at the house? When the police came?"

Daria saw Molly's face tighten. "Honey, another person died. Your aunt Molly found him, and that's why she's a little upset now. He was a friend of the lady who was killed."

"Was he murdered too?"

"Enough," Molly said. "You don't need to know all this."

Daria shook her head. "You know, I never liked Milo Kraft, but—"

"The man with the dirty hat? Is that who you found?" Emma asked.

Molly and Daria looked at each other at the same time. Both about to speak, Molly raised her hand to stop Daria. "How did you know his name?"

Shoving herself deep into the corner of the sofa, Emma's eyes were huge. "She . . . she knew him. He was at the aquarium, and he was angry with her. And I saw him again one day with you, remember?" she said to Molly.

Daria was perplexed. "*She*? Who the hell is *she*?"

"Mother," Emma said, her voice growing shaky, "and she knew a lady named Trudy. I told you that too, remember?"

"Emma, honey, it's not what you think." Up on the sofa with her now, Molly said, "Your mother wasn't here when Trudy was killed. Remember

271

the night you first arrived? Well, that was the day after it happened. And she's not here now, right? So she isn't involved in this."

"Are you sure?"

"Positive. Do you know why he was angry with your mother?"

"No. I was petting the starfish in the tank. But I could see his face. It was all scrunched up, and his hands were flying all over. He got real close to her one time, and she shoved him away. I got scared, but then he left right after that."

"I'll have to tell Randall all that," Molly said. "He needs to know those kind of things, okay? It might be important."

"But you said she isn't—"

"I just meant so he'll have a fuller picture, that's all."

"How about some dessert?" Daria said, looking at Molly.

Grateful that Daria had changed the subject, Molly said, "You two go ahead, I still have to finish my dinner." She gave Emma a wink. "Why don't you see what Daria brought?" Pulling her plate toward her, Molly made a stab at the cold lamb.

It was halfway to her mouth when Emma got off the sofa and said, "We got here the day before we met you. I guess I better tell Randall that too."

Molly's and Daria's eyes met once again. "Are you sure?" Molly asked.

"Uh-huh, we got here on Sunday. We came to see you Monday night."

Trying not to put too much importance on this news, Molly said, "Oh, well, sure, tell Randall. It's not really that big a deal." Seeing the frown on Emma's face, she added, "Come on, Em. It's not. Just because I misunderstood doesn't mean—"

"I remember her telling you she was tired from driving all day and that we just got here. It was a lie. She lied a lot. It's just the way she is. I stopped trying to figure out why. I guess it's a lawyer's thing."

"God, don't let Lucero hear that," Daria said. Taking the dinner plate from Emma's hand, she said, "Come on, let's get dessert."

Molly closed her eyes and held her head in her hands. If Emma was right—and she had no reason to doubt her—it was imminently conceivable that her sister was a murderer. Worse, Molly thought, she might have been the driver of the Jeep. It was hard enough to think that Carrie had tried to kill her, but abhorrent to imagine she would consider killing her own child.

Daria and Emma no sooner returned with a tray of desserts from the restaurant than Randall and Lucero arrived. Letting them in, Molly tried hard to pretend she had regained some calm. Randall's concern for her was evident, and he made a point of keeping the first few minutes low key. Lucero wasn't as composed, his agitation apparent as he fell into his habit of jingling the loose change in his pocket.

Checking her watch, Molly said, "I think it's to

273

sleep for you, Em. It's been a long day, and Tiger's already curled up on your bed."

"You want to be private and talk about serious stuff." Turning her attention to the tiramisu on her dish, she took a bite, then said to Randall, "Aunt Molly has some things to tell you about my mother. Oh, and I'm going to keep my cell phone with me all the time so you won't have to worry about us."

Randall nodded. "That a girl!" Moving next to her on the sofa, he kissed the top of her head and said, "But don't worry, okay? You got me and Lucero to look after you."

"Yeah, kiddo. We're tough guys. Ain't nobody gonna mess—"

"Okay! I got it!"

"Good kid," Lucero said as he watched her head for her bedroom. "I should have some news soon on her custody." Turning to Molly, he asked, "What have you got on the mother?"

Upset, Molly repeated to them what Emma had said. "I still can't wrap my head around it."

"It might or might not place her at the scene, but it does add her to the opportunity list," Randall said. "You obviously didn't see her at the show, and to try and go back to all the dealers there with a description would take days. We don't have the manpower to chase those people down all over the state."

Lucero agreed, "Randall's right. But like it or not, she's a player here. My gut feeling is she was here for money owed. The meet with Kraft at the aquarium is probably tied to that. The fact that Molly lived here was icing on the cake."

"Would you explain that last remark?" Daria said.

"She was pulling a vanishing act. Emma was excess baggage. I think she planned to dump her here from the first," Randall answered.

Molly didn't want to hear any more about her sister. The earlier rage boiling inside her had suddenly turned to despair. She half listened to Randall and Lucero, and barely saw Daria clear the dessert dishes from the coffee table. Pushing thoughts of her sister from her mind, she asked, "What about Milo? I mean, how—"

"The back door lock was removed, and I'll bet Forensics won't come up with any prints," Randall said. "Fibers will most likely be from a black running suit."

"How did he die? Or can't you tell us?" Daria asked.

"No big secret with those of us here," Lucero said. "I'd guess from the marks on his neck he was strangled."

"I'd bet money on it," Randall agreed.

"I thought he was being watched," Molly said.

Randall looked at Lucero. "He was supposed to be on a twenty-four/seven schedule. Lucero's investigators were handling it."

Lucero waved his hand in the air. "My office blew it. Manpower problems."

Before the two men got going on department budget problems, Daria said, "Boys . . . let's get back to basics. Where does all this put Molly? I mean, safety wise? With Milo out of the picture, that should be the end of it, right?"

When neither of them answered, Molly asked, "Right?"

"Yeah, right," Randall finally said. But he didn't believe it. Kraft's body was still warm when they found him. The killer could easily still be in town, hanging around for Trudy's funeral on Friday. That could mean arrogance, or unfinished business.

"Sure. I'll go with that," Lucero added.

Driving the short blocks back to Lucero's car at the station, Lucero said to Randall, "What about Emma?"

"What about her?" Stopping for jaywalkers crossing the five-way stop at Ocean Avenue and Junipero, Randall looked at Lucero. "She's not an issue. She told Molly she couldn't hear what her mother and Kraft were arguing about."

"No, I mean what she said—the arrival thing. Sunday instead of Monday. You think the mother killed Trudy?"

Staring at the jaywalkers, Randall said, "If they weren't tourists, I'd give them a ticket."

Lucero laughed. "Probably from New York. They do that all the time there."

"Trudy's booth was only a few down from Molly's. Unless Carrie was into disguises like

Trudy, I don't think she'd have taken the risk of being seen by her sister."

"Okay, then who's on your Hit Parade?"

Pulling up next to Lucero's car, Randall gave him a slow smile. "I'm playing with a few scenarios. You'll be my first call."

"Don't pull that mysterious Charlie Chan shit with me. Who do you like for this?"

When Randall didn't answer, Lucero said, "Hey, *Chief,* now's the time to prove what a hotshot cop you are." Giving him a mock salute as he left, he added, "*Ciao.*"

Pulling into the police parking lot, Randall got out, locked the car, and headed to his office, grinning all the way.

CHAPTER 22

Trudy Collins's funeral was in two hours. Molly was relieved that Daria had found something in her closet for Trudy, since she'd made it clear she would never set foot in her home again, even if it hadn't been a crime scene. Now she was unsure if it was a good idea to take Emma. This sudden role of caring for a child left her with dozens of questions. Children today, she'd read somewhere, shouldn't be shielded from the realities of life. Death was a natural occurrence, and rather than mourn a loved one, you celebrated their life. How in good conscience could she tell Emma they were going to celebrate the life of a woman who had cheated so many people? Whose greed had destroyed lives, put others in danger, and now included the murder of Milo Kraft?

She had half a mind to stay home. Until a few days ago, she'd been determined to help find Trudy's killer. When she feared it might be her sister, she'd seesawed back and forth, fighting what was right versus family loyalty. Now, after almost being killed, and then finding Milo's body, she began to realize she was out of her depth. She also had Em to consider. Playing the sleuth put her in danger too.

Molly pulled on a pair of navy hose, slipped on a matching skirt and sweater, then reached in the closet for her raincoat. She wouldn't dignify Trudy's death by wearing black. She didn't mourn her. Nor, she thought, would she celebrate her life.

She'd be late opening the shop today, but she couldn't help it. The church service was at ten, and then on to the cemetery in Monterey. Molly decided just to attend the church service. She'd removed Trudy from a small corner of her heart reserved for friends, and didn't care to watch her casket being lowered into the ground. She now viewed her simply as a thief who'd harmed and deceived so many. Every commission she made would have to go toward what she'd lost on the Meissen and Sèvres Trudy had sold her. When she'd finally reached Mr. Jackson in Kentucky, he said he would return the tea set as soon as Molly's check for six thousand cleared. At least he'd been a gentleman about the problem. The Whitcombs finally came to the conclusion their appraiser was unqualified, hired another, and now they were demanding a refund. While Molly was eager to keep her reputation aboveboard, she nonetheless smarted at the loss of eighteen grand and the humiliation of being fooled. She would put the items in the shop, mark them as reproductions, and take the loss with a smile.

In fact, she thought, as she headed for the kitchen, she might make the Meissen figures into lamps. She could use the vintage silk shades and rococo brass plateaus in the garage and spruce them up, possibly even price them around five or six hundred. They were good-sized and dramatic, and would be stunning.

"Ready?" she asked as Emma came in.

"Do I look okay?"

The pleated tartan skirt, dark blue sweater, and red sneakers definitely made a statement. "You look fine."

"The sneakers are kinda wild, but I didn't think the white ones looked good with the blue leggings."

"We need to go shopping again. Bitsy's going to work the shop this weekend, so maybe we'll go to Target tomorrow."

"Are we still doing the garage sales?"

"Oh, you bet. I've got to run downstairs and check my e-mail before we go."

She hadn't checked her e-mail in a few days, and wondered if Sally had been able to come up with anything. She decided she was out of the sleuthing game, and whatever Sally managed to send, she would give it to Randall and wash her hands of the entire mess. She hated to admit Randall was right and that she should just stick to selling antiques, but just remembering Milo Kraft's face was enough to convince her.

Molly spent several minutes deleting dozens of spams, then lo and behold, came upon an e-mail from Sally with the list she had asked for. The diversity of the merchandise was mind-boggling. She noticed that many of the pieces, in particular the urns, busts, and garden statuary, could easily be drug-concealing vessels. She imagined them packed in straw, batting, and even dung, then heavily wrapped with tarps, cardboard, and wood doused with creosote. She'd even heard that Kevlar, the material in bulletproof vests, had been used to line the inside of crates by drug smugglers posing as antique reproduction furniture makers from Turkey. She saved the e-mail and decided to print it out when she returned from the funeral.

Checking her to do list, she next turned to her calendar and frowned. Oliver's new store was having an opening tomorrow night. She'd completely forgotten all about it, and couldn't bear the thought of going.

And then she began to wonder if she'd judged Oliver too harshly. Given what he'd been through, who was she to throw stones? Those phony Meissen and Sèvres pieces hadn't destroyed her life. Having to return all that money wasn't small potatoes, but compared to what Oliver had lost, it was chump change.

Then she recalled how he'd gone into her computer and pulled up her inventory and cost spread sheet. Despite his misfortunes, that was reason enough to dislike him. But it was more than that. There was just something about him that rubbed her wrong. Maybe it was the ascot he frequently wore. That and the tweed hat, always at a jaunty angle, and the precisely clipped snowy moustache. A slow smile filled her when she realized what annoyed her. Oliver, like many dealers, affected a look. The women in the trade were often flamboyant or starkly simple, and many men seemed to act effete to give the impression they were refined and discerning. Oliver fit that picture.

The service at the Unitarian Church was attended by nearly every dealer in town, as well as others Molly didn't recognize. She and Emma sat with Daria and Bitsy. Oliver, Bitsy informed her, was at his new shop putting the finishing touches together for tomorrow. "He barely knew her, so I told him not to be concerned," she'd whispered. Following small village protocol, Randall made a brief appearance. When Molly quietly told him about Sally's e-mail, he said he'd stop by later. She wondered what the whispering among those here might be like if they knew Trudy had been murdered. Randall still hadn't let that out, or Milo Kraft's death for that matter.

The service was short, and the crowd quickly filed out. Molly and Bitsy spent a few minutes chatting with some of the dealers and shopkeepers, and she was surprised when Ted Banks, the lawyer Carrie had come to see, stopped to say hello. He'd met Trudy, he said, at one of her estate sales when he'd opened his office in Monterey. "I needed good-looking stuff, but didn't have much money then.

When I got on my feet and opened a bigger office, she was a big help steering me to good deals. I'm going to miss her, damnit. She was always upbeat, full of the devil."

"Yes, she'll be missed," Molly said.

"I'm really sorry your sister didn't take my offer to join my firm. But I guess that job in Japan was too hard to resist."

Molly muttered an appropriate reply. and was relieved when he excused himself to talk to someone who'd called him. "Now that's a good-looking man," Bitsy said as she came up to Molly. "He's getting a divorce, you know. Did you give him your card?"

"Oh, please, Bitsy. This is hardly the place to be drumming up business, and I'm not interested in getting to know him."

"Giving him a card would not have been unseemly," Bitsy huffed. "Business is business, no matter where you are."

Ignoring her, Molly waved to a few dealers and watched as they headed to their cars. She imagined many would be going back to open their shops instead of following the hearse to the cemetery. It was Friday, and tourists were already coming in for the weekend. Molly was sure they figured Trudy would understand.

Molly's day had been less than sterling for a Friday. With only three small sales, she decided to hang up the Closed sign when Randall arrived at five. Looking over Sally's list, he said, "How the hell do you fake garden statues to make them look old?"

Handing him a cup of coffee, she said, "Easy. It's been done for eons. Muratic acid is washed over them to remove the slick surface and expose the rougher interior, then rinsed off. The statue is left outside and smeared with yogurt. After about a month, moss is rubbed into the spores and cracks created by the acid, and then given a wash with fish emulsion."

"What the hell is fish emulsion?"

"You're obviously not a gardener. It's liquid fertilizer. The piece is kept moist and out of the sun. When the moss begins to grow, it's carefully scraped away and only left on areas that look natural. Depending on size, statues are sometimes buried in the ground for a few months to get an even more weathered look. It's more commonly done on large urns."

Randall shook his head. "Sounds like too much work."

"Not when you can get thousands for them."

Flipping the list in his hand, he asked, "So what does this Sally think about you being so nosey?"

"I told her I wanted to be on the lookout for this woman and needed to know what kind of phony merch she was pushing."

"Good. That's good. I'd like to keep this, okay?"

"I got it for you. I sure as hell don't want it."

Randall studied her for a moment. "You okay?"

Looking away, Molly said, "I'm fine, considering. You're used to seeing dead bodies. I've had my fill, thank you."

Rising, Randall said, "You never get used to it, Molly. Never. You still want me to meet you at Oliver's opening?"

"Yes. I don't want to have to linger. If you're with me, we can pretend we have to be somewhere else. Bitsy looked a little pale this morning. I'm worried about her. Did you notice, or am I imagining it?"

"I didn't notice, but a spring chicken she's not. Besides, funerals do that to people. Faces have a tendency to droop, you know?"

"I guess. I'll give her a call anyway."

"You still doing the garage sale thing tomorrow?"

"I've decided not to. The ads don't look that promising and I've still got a garage full of stuff I bought last week." Looking around the shop, she said, "I've got to clean it up and move it in here for my conservatory corner."

"Well don't look at me for donkey work. I'm a little busy right now."

When Randall left, Molly called Bitsy. Josie answered and told her Bitsy was resting. When Josie mentioned that Bitsy hadn't been feeling well for a few days, Molly asked if she'd gone to see her doctor. She could sense that Josie was reluctant to tell her the truth but didn't want to lie. When Molly promised not to let on to Bitsy, her housekeeper finally admitted that Bitsy hadn't made an appointment and had brushed off her lack of energy on old age. Molly told Josie she had some shopping to do, but that she would stop by later to check up on Bitsy.

"I can't keep eating Mexican food, Em, and lose weight," Molly said as she took a bite of her second enchilada.

"I know, but it's so good. We only have to eat it when we go shopping, okay?"

"After what I just spent, we won't be doing much shopping for a while." When she saw the downcast look on Emma's face, she hurriedly said, "I didn't mean it like that. I just meant—"

"I'm kind of expensive I guess. I only packed for a few days away. I didn't think it would turn out this way. Well, not for sure, anyway."

"I've been meaning to ask you about that," Molly said as she pushed her dish away. "Do you have any idea what's become of your house or your things? With your mother in Japan, who's going to take care of everything?"

"Oh, she sold the condo and all the furniture before we left. She said she got a buyer right away and that we should pack light until we got settled. She said we'd have a new place real soon. She gave all my stuff to a shelter and said we'd get new things." Taking a sip of her soda, Emma added, "I guess she planned to leave me with you all along."

"I'm glad for that." Molly smiled. "Uh, what did you do when you got here on Sunday? Did you get a chance to see Fisherman's Wharf in Monterey?"

"Nope. She went out and I stayed in our room and watched movies. She said she had to meet some people. But I did have room service for dinner, and it was really good."

"Then you went to Point Lobos on Monday, right? That must have really been fun. I've been meaning to go there."

"Right. It was cold, but she said the hiking around helped her think. Then we had dinner and drove around until we saw the light on in your shop."

Molly wished she could back up time five minutes and hadn't brought up Sunday, but the damage was done, and it only made her more confused. She had to tell Randall, but she wished she'd kept her mouth shut for once.

CHAPTER 23

It was just past eight when Molly and Emma drove through the Pebble Beach Hill gate off the freeway from Monterey. Molly was thankful Bitsy had given her a guest pass, so she didn't have to pay the road fee into the forest. Eight dollars and twenty-five cents each time you wanted to get in could add up quickly. Of course, if one were visiting a resident, there wasn't a charge, but the gatekeeper would have to call first for clearance, and it sometimes was a pain in the neck.

As she waved her pass and drove through, Emma said, "You know, we have to do something about this truck. Your door sticks from the accident, and you have to admit it's pretty grungy looking."

"Ashamed to ride with me, huh?" Molly said, laughing.

"No, but Randall said it was tacky for an antiques dealer to drive this."

"When was that?"

"We talk sometimes on the cell phone. I'm supposed to call him every now and then, remember? So what do you think? Are you going to get a new car?"

"I can't afford one. If Randall doesn't like it, let him buy me one."

"I bet he would if you two were married."

Molly almost missed one of the hairpin turns on Seventeen Mile Drive. "Hey, that's not in the program, young lady. I was just kidding."

"Well, you know he cares about us. He reminded me again at the funeral to check in with him so he knows we're okay. We have a code now."

"Really? Well, that's a cool idea. What's the code?"

"I just say 'Harry Potter' and whatever chapter I'm on. If he doesn't answer, I text it. That lets him know we're fine."

"Does he answer back?"

"Uh-huh, he does the same and tells me what chapter he's on. We can compare notes later, he says."

"Clever," Molly said. "Very clever."

Driving through the Del Monte Forest in Pebble Beach is confusing enough in daylight. Finding your way at night, with only your headlights and occasional starlight, can be daunting. Like Carmel, house numbers are replaced with family names or whimsical titles. The exception was the other end of the forest near Pacific Grove, commonly referred to as Country Club. Molly remembered Daria telling her the home of the famous cartoonist, Jimmy Hatlo, facing the golf course and the ocean, was called "Wit's End." She was further surprised to learn that many of the world's best cartoonists lived on the peninsula, along with several big-time mystery writers.

As they drove to Bitsy's home on Seventeen Mile Drive, Emma said, "It's kind of spooky here at night. It reminds me of those horror movies."

Molly laughed. "It's worse when it's foggy or raining. And then you have to watch out for deer. They live freely here, and you never know when one will jump out on the road."

The usual mini-gusts coming off the bay swayed the cypress trees surrounding Bitsy's home and made the lights in the house shimmer like stars. Molly was surprised to find the iron gates open. When Josie answered the door, she could see that the housekeeper was upset. "I'm so glad you're here," she said. "That woman is driving me crazy. She is growing more stubborn every day."

"What now?"

"She hardly eats, barely sleeps, and she won't call the doctor. See if you can talk some sense into her. She's in her room. You know the way."

"Where's Oliver?" Molly wasn't in the mood to run into him now.

"Mr. Oliver is at the shop."

"*Mr.* Oliver is it now?" When Josie looked away, Molly said, "Stay with Josie, Em. I'll run up and see Bitsy."

Molly could feel the cold of the marble steps through her shoes. Built in the twenties by a lumber baron from Sacramento, the villa was so big and its ceilings so high, the best heating system in the world couldn't combat the constant chill that seemed to follow you through every room. How Bitsy managed to avoid pneumonia was a miracle. The door to Bitsy's room was open, and Molly found her lying on a chaise lounge by the fire. The shadows flickering across Bitsy's face from the flames made Molly stop and catch her breath. Every wrinkle and line on her still striking face seemed deeper, and her skin was almost translucent.

Bitsy's eyes flickered open. "Oh, Molly! I thought I heard someone coming down the hall." Glancing at her watch, she said, "What brings you out here at this time of night?"

"You. You looked ill at the funeral and I'm worried," Molly blurted. "Why haven't you seen the doctor?"

"Oh, darling. It's nothing. Just a little blue funk. It happens at my age."

"Baloney," Molly said as she pulled a chair closer to her. Noting a large glass of pale liquid next to Bitsy on a small table, she asked, "What's that?"

"Hmm? Oh, that's Oliver's magic tea. It does wonders for my aches and pains."

"Josie said you're barely eating and not sleeping well. Since you won't call your doctor, I'm doing it in the morning whether you like it or not."

"Don't be silly. It's just old age reminding me to slow down. I don't think I'll be able to come in tomorrow. Do you mind? With Oliver's party tomorrow night and all, I—"

"Don't worry about me. You rest. I'm not doing

garage sales anyway for a while. I've got too much stuff to get ready as it is."

Molly wasn't sure if Bitsy heard her. Her eyes were closed. "Bitsy?" Moving closer, she gently nudged her. "Bitsy?"

Bitsy's eyes flew open. "Oh, I'm sorry, darling. You were saying?"

"I think you need to get to bed. Let me help you."

"No. I'd . . . I'd rather stay here." Pulling a wool throw closer to her, she said, "It's cozy by the fire. I love sleeping here."

Molly saw how comfortable she was and didn't want to distress her. "Okay." Rising, she added, "Get some sleep." She leaned over and kissed Bitsy's forehead. "Listen, you old bag, I want you around a little longer. I need your help with Emma." Giving her a wink, she said, "We both need you. Got it?"

Bitsy nodded, then said, "Molly . . . wait. Don't go. I . . . I need to talk to you. This isn't easy for me, but it's time I got this off my chest. I've . . . I've been so racked with guilt, I . . . I just wanted to wither up and die."

Alarmed, Molly sank back in the chair. "You're really ill, is that it? Oh, Bitsy, why didn't you tell me sooner?"

"No, it's nothing like that. It's about Trudy."

"Trudy?" Molly didn't want to hear anything more about that woman. She'd had her fill and would just as soon pretend she'd never met her. "Look, I know her death hit you hard, but—"

292

"Harder than you'll ever know," Bitsy said. Her voice was suddenly stronger. "We go back a way, Trudy and I. She was a fine dealer for years in The City, then closed her shop and moved here. That's when we first met. She was tired of being tied to a shop and went on the show circuit. Then she started the estate sale business and did very well."

Molly knew all this history and didn't care, but if Bitsy needed an ear, it was the least she could do to listen. "I remember you telling me."

"Well, that was all you needed to know. But now you should hear the truth. I'm responsible for her death."

Molly couldn't move. Her mouth fell open but she couldn't speak. Her tongue was numb.

"Shocked, are you? Well, I can only imagine what you must be thinking now. It didn't take much effort actually. I'm at least happy to know she went quickly, and somewhat relieved to know she didn't suffer."

When Molly was finally able to speak, she said, "*What*? What could she have done to you to . . . I don't believe you."

"But darling, why would I lie about a thing like that? You see, Trudy became what all dealers abhor and fear. A thief. We all walk that tight line one time or another. Most of us stop and jump back. Trudy didn't. She did the devil's dance on that line. She was ruining our good names, our businesses, and so many lives. I had to stop her. I'd heard rumors, but at first I didn't believe them. When

Oliver called me a few months ago and told me how he'd been scammed so horribly and ruined, I asked him who the dealer was. The name he gave me, and the description, didn't ring a bell, but when he described the merch, I had a feeling it might be Trudy. That's when I invited him here."

Mesmerized, Molly could hardly breathe. She was finding it hard to exchange the love she'd come to feel for this woman with a sudden sense of revulsion. Yet she could do nothing but listen. "Go on," she managed.

"Well, as they say, the truth will out. It did when I showed Oliver photos from a costume party Trudy and I had attended. He picked her out right away. I told him the woman was dead, and he believed me. In fact, he wanted to go out and celebrate. He was that happy. Well, he ran into her one night at the La Playa, and knew right away that I'd lied. It was her laugh that did it. Remember how she—"

"I remember," Molly quickly said. "But why didn't you tell Randall and let him take it from there?"

"Because I wanted the satisfaction of seeing her squirm! Oliver hounded me day and night about her. His bitterness grew by the hour. He began to accuse me of being just like her. My wealth, he said, made me uncaring. He almost had the chance to live like I do, and now it was too late for him to begin again. He just couldn't understand why I was turning a blind eye."

"So that's why you let him play lord of the manor and staked him for the shop."

"It was a small price."

"For what? You didn't screw him over! Damn it, Bitsy! Why didn't he go to the police?"

"I felt responsible. I should have turned her in years ago and I didn't. It was time to make amends and do the right thing."

Molly couldn't look at her. "Oh, God! Bitsy! Why murder?"

Bitsy's neck snapped back. "*Murder?* What on earth are you talking about? You know Trudy died of a heart attack!" Looking away, she calmed down and whispered, "But I brought it on, don't you see?"

Before Molly could find a way to explain the truth about Trudy's death, Bitsy went on to say, "I introduced Oliver to Trudy at the show the night she died. I used her phony name when I did it. You should have seen her face. She turned whiter than clown makeup. I left the two of them staring at each other. Oliver joined me a few minutes later. He told me he felt some sense of justice had been done when she knew she'd been found out. Then she had the heart attack a little later." Reaching for her drink, she said, "So you see, in that sense, I'm responsible." Looking away for a moment, she added, "I paid for a year of Masses for her soul, so maybe God won't look too harshly at me when we meet."

Molly fought an urge to throttle her. Overwhelmed with wanting to tell her Trudy was murdered, the words were nearly choking her. She knew Randall would kill her if she did, and saved by the appearance of Josie and Emma, realized their timing was perfect. Still reeling from what she'd just heard, Molly grabbed her tote and said, "I was just about to come down. It's late, Bitsy needs to rest."

"You will be at Oliver's opening, won't you?" Bitsy asked.

"Wild horses couldn't keep me away."

By the time they reached the foyer, Molly acted on something that had been teasing her brain for days. "Josie, Bitsy told me Oliver's magic tea is wonderful. My back is killing me from moving furniture, do you think I could borrow some?"

Josie was back within moments with a small plastic bag. "I just took a little so he won't notice. I've tried it, and it's great for my arthritis."

Driving carefully out of the forest, she began to think it was a perfect place for Bitsy to live. The rambling Spanish villa was an ideal setting for madness. It was easy to imagine Bitsy wearing one of those flowing silk beaded caftans and descending her winding marble stairway with a long cigarette holder. Her eyes would be lined with kohl. She'd open them wide like Gloria Swanson, and maybe sing something. The director would yell "Cut," and declare it a "wrap."

She still couldn't believe what she'd just heard. What the hell did Bitsy think was going to happen when Trudy and Oliver came face-to-face? Did she really believe she'd caused Trudy's death? She had to call Randall.

"Josie showed me a cool place in the library," Emma said.

"The little reading nook?"

"No. Josie called it a gallery. You get to it from the hall by Bitsy's bedroom through a small door next to those Arabian guys holding torches. When you go in, you can look down on the library and see the whole thing."

"A gallery, huh? I never knew about that."

"It's kinda like those houses in English mysteries. I kept waiting for Lord Voldemort from *Harry Potter* to appear." When Molly didn't respond, she asked, "Is Bitsy sick? Is that why I didn't go in to see her?"

"Hmm, oh, sorry. I was thinking about something. No, she's not sick. Just nuts."

By the time they got home and Emma went to bed, it was almost ten. Tiger had decided to sleep with Emma, and the sight of them curled up together gave Molly hope that maybe all was still right in the world. In her bedroom, she called Randall at home. The answering machine came on. She hung up and tried him at the station. When he answered, she said, "You won't believe what I have to tell you."

Randall listened, then said, "Okay, get some sleep. I'll see you tomorrow."

"Sleep? Are you kidding? I'm wide awake. Who the hell can sleep when some batty old broad tells you she caused a heart attack? And I couldn't tell her the truth! You've got to set her straight, damnit!

You know how dramatic she is, she might even do something stupid."

"Calm down. I'll handle it. By the way, Ms. Doyle, you went out and didn't let me know. I think I told you to—"

"Okay, okay. I blew it. I forgot."

"Yeah? Well, write it on your forehead."

Somewhat assured that he'd find a way to talk to Bitsy without letting the cat out of the bag, Molly decided a cup of cocoa might help her get to sleep. In the kitchen, she found only one packet of instant left. Deciding to save that for Emma, she rummaged in the cabinets and saw she was out of Café Français. A major headache was forming, and the pounding over her eyes was fierce. Eyeing the plastic baggie of Oliver's magic tea she dropped on the counter, she decided to give it a try. Josie swore by it, and so did Bitsy. Maybe it might make the brass band in her head go away.

Molly took two sips and immediately remembered the taste from her college days. So this was Oliver's magic brew! She'd love to see the look on Randall's face if she told him Bitsy and Josie were drinking a mild and somewhat harmless version of opium tea. Well, she thought, at least she'd get a good night's sleep now. Carrying the mug to her bedroom, she set it on the night table and got ready for bed. Turning off the small lamp, she raised the mug in a toast to her father's photo. "You used to say when things get tough, keep a smile on your face and the devil won't know he's winning. But I wish you had been a shoemaker or something. This antique biz is a killer."

Already feeling less stressed, she pulled the quilt under her chin and barely got through her nightly prayers before nodding off.

Randall dumped his ashtray into the wastebasket and wiped it out with crumpled paper. His desk was littered with reports from Lucero's investigators, telephone notes, and faxes from ranking friends at the FBI and DEA. Moving over to the conference table, he dumped the homemade sales tags from the show and began matching them to Sally Sims's list. He'd been itching to do it, but didn't want to waste time running with something only his gut felt. He needed a few more answers from other angles he'd been pursuing. He had most of those now, and it was time to begin fitting the pieces together. The one last bit of information he received a short time ago still bothered him. Why hadn't the killer left town? Arrogance? *Yeah,* he thought. *It fits.*

And now this mess with Bitsy. He had enough on his plate with two homicides to solve. He didn't need a drama queen thinking she was on her way to hell. Randall ran his fingers through his hair, called for more coffee, then stared at a DMV report and shook his head. His smoking gun lay before him, and he still couldn't believe who was holding it.

Hungry for local news in a community that had

little violence except for gang banger shootings in Salinas, the media on the peninsula was no different than a major city when it came to monitoring every police and ambulance call. Acutely aware of this, and the new partnership he'd become part of, Randall had reported Kraft's homicide to Dispatch as a minor scuffle and called for an ambulance for a broken leg. He knew none of the local media would bother with that.

He'd then sent two officers to question the neighbors after they took Kraft away in an ambulance. They were told to use the same excuse and to ask if anyone had been seen going in the house or noticed a car that didn't belong to a resident. They hit pay dirt when the lady across from Trudy said a car had been a foot too far into her driveway and she was worried her husband wouldn't be able to pull in when he came home. Her husband, she'd explained, had a short fuse when it came to his driveway. The kids next door had been a problem lately, and she thought it might be one of their friends again. She'd gone next door, and when no one answered, wrote down the license number in case she had to call the police. By the time she began dinner, the car was gone, but she'd written the number on a shopping list which she still had.

Randall immediately forwarded the info to his contacts, including the Tacoma connection, and wasn't all that surprised when he'd been asked to sit on it. They would put a 24/7 watch on the owner of the car right away. This was the missing link they'd been looking for.

In the middle of aiding a year-long international investigation, and the rush of working on something meaty again, Randall was bothered by Molly's recent attitude. Until she called a few minutes ago, she'd been too compliant. Especially when she'd casually handed over the list from the Sims woman, telling him she didn't want it. This was not the Molly Doyle he knew. Indifference was not in her vocabulary.

Staring at the phone, he felt guilty about not being able to call Lucero. The man had a right to know what was going down in his county. But he didn't dare chance it. Not that Lucero would leak anything, but he'd been told emphatically by the DEA that the information he'd been given was for past favors and his cooperation. No one, absolutely no one, was to know until they said so.

The big guns were coming. He'd be on the front line before they got here. He was sorry Lucero wouldn't be at his side.

CHAPTER 24

Molly slept deeper that night than she had since Trudy was killed two weeks ago. When she awoke, refreshed, she was suddenly hungry. She needed something solid, and quickly. Her pantry was woefully limited, and shopping was in order again. Having Emma to consider now meant keeping all sorts of things on hand she never bothered with. Juice, cereal, milk, fruit, and vegetables rarely made her previous shopping lists. A less than competent cook, Molly was an expert on frozen dinners.

"First thing is Tosca's for breakfast," Molly told Emma. "Then it's to the garage for some clean-up time. Robbie will be here soon to help move furniture in the shop for our new display, and then I've got to work the floor today, so that only gives us three hours. Bitsy's a little under the weather and she needs to rest for Oliver's opening tonight."

"Business as usual, huh?"

"You said it, kiddo. We gotta make some bucks." She'd already mailed the refunds, and her once healthy slush fund was looking skimpy.

They lingered over breakfast longer than Molly

had intended, but she hadn't had much time lately to chat with Bennie. Swearing off espresso this morning, Molly poured more cream than usual into her coffee. When Bennie joined them, he asked, "You going to Oliver's shindig tonight?"

"Yes. If I don't, I'll never hear the end of it from Bitsy. I'm not planning on staying long. Ten minutes max."

"I'm not. I don't like the guy and I don't care if he makes it or not. My dad has ten people lined up for that shop. He only let Oliver in because of Bitsy."

"I didn't know they were that close."

"I think my old man had a thing for her years ago. She must have been something in her day. She's still a pistol." Seeing new customers taking a table, Bennie rose. "I gotta get back to work. *Ciao.*"

Oh, Molly thought, *you have no idea!*

Molly had a problem backing the El Camino out of the garage. The driver's door had been sticking badly since the bridge episode and she could barely open it. She knew she'd have to get it fixed or replaced, but having grown fond of the little orange devil, she almost hated to part with it, dents and all. By the time she had it in the alley, Emma had spread dozens of newspapers over the garage floor. Robbie arrived in time to help set out the wrought-iron garden furniture on the papers. Molly decided the ugly green on the chaise had to go. With paint stripper, it wouldn't take long to remove. A couple hours of physical labor might help her forget what had become a daily diet of chaos. She set Emma up on cleaning the other pieces with soap and water. Pulling on rubber gloves, she was on her knees brushing on the stripper when an article in one of the papers next to her caught her eye.

She set down the brush, crawled closer to the paper, and began to read. The article made her eyes pop. When Emma asked where to find more clean rags, she held up her hand, pointed to a back cabinet and kept reading. Sitting back on the floor, she folded the paper into quarters and jumped up. "I've got to see Randall," she said to Emma. Remembering Randall's warnings, Molly hesitated, then told Robbie, "Keep an eye on Emma, okay? I won't be long."

She nearly ran all the six blocks to the police station. Stopping to catch her breath at the foot of the wide steps, she fanned her face with the papers, then took the steps two at a time. At the next landing she paused again. Only a few more steps up to the front door. Pressing the buzzer to get in, she took deep breaths to calm herself. When she heard the door click, she ran inside and said, "I've got to see Randall right away. It's important."

Running past Sergeant Wilkins in the hall, she gave him a quick smile.

"Hey, Molly, uh, the chief is busy. Let me buzz him, okay?"

"He knows I'm coming," she lied as she ran past him. She couldn't care less if he was busy. She had to see him pronto.

Rushing into his office, waving the paper in her hand, she said, "I've got it! I've got the—"

When Randall whirled away from the Incident board, Molly could see her sister's name in large block letters under Motive, Opportunity, and Means. Her hand flew to her mouth. "You lied to me."

He watched a number of emotions wash across her face, then said, "Yeah. I did. Close the door. Where's Emma? I thought I told you—"

"She's with Robbie." Steam was building inside her. Without a backward glance, she kicked the door shut with her foot, then threw the newspaper on his desk. Then she saw the sorrow on Randall's face, and, just as quickly, a sudden calm filled her. Pointing to the paper, she said, "This is what it's all about, isn't it?"

His eyes still on her, he picked up the paper, then glanced at the article. Flicking the paper with his finger, he said, "You're way off base."

"Stop it. I'm right. Illegal immigrants from Asia to work the sweatshops in Vancouver! They're brought in on freight ships and hidden in containers. Read it, damn you! It says right here fifty were rounded up in a raid and they admitted they came in ships. The reproduction merch was a cover. It was used on the manifest and to line the containers the illegals slept in. Trudy wasn't supposed to sell it. That's what got her killed. That's what Carrie meant by things unraveling. She was probably supposed to junk the merch, and when they found out, she had to leave. Milo was in on it too. That's what Carrie and Milo were arguing about at the aquarium, wasn't it!"

"You through?"

"No, damn it! That's what those wacky tags meant. It was to show Trudy she'd been found out." The adrenaline rush quickly left, and she sank into a chair and held her head in her hands. "I knew it! I didn't want to believe it! Carrie killed Trudy."

"Go home, Molly. You're worn-out. You've had enough thrown at you in the past two weeks to last a lifetime. Close up today. Get some rest."

Wiping tears from her eyes, she shook her head. "I'm not leaving until you level with me."

Randall pulled down the shade over the Incident board, then moved to his desk and sat opposite her. He hated coincidences. Finding that newspaper was one of the worst. "You've got this all wrong," he lied. "If Carrie killed Trudy, then split, who killed Kraft?"

"How do we know she's really gone?"

"She's been tracked to Mexico City. She's been there since she left Carmel." He was lying to her again, but he had no choice. Carrie Newsome had slipped under the radar, and no one knew where she was.

Molly thought about that, then said, "Then

whoever tried to ram me on Bixby Bridge killed Milo."

"Probably."

"Yes, now I see it. A woman wouldn't be strong enough to tie Milo to that closet rod. Even Carrie couldn't have managed that." She asked, "Do you think the killer's still around?"

"Probably."

"Is that all you've got to say?" She nearly screamed it.

"I already said it. Go home. Leave this alone, okay?"

Pointing to the newspaper, she said, "Fine. I'll go home, but I know I'm right about this." Walking to the door, she pulled it open, then turned back. "I won't be opening until noon today. I'm going to Big Five at Del Monte Center and I'm going to buy a gun. If that bastard tries me again, he won't know what hit him."

Randall shook his head. "You can't do that."

"Really? Who's going to stop me?"

"The state of California. It's a ten-day wait for a rifle or shotgun, and fifteen for a handgun. And I'll see to it you won't get a permit."

"You wouldn't."

"Try me."

The staring match lasted longer than usual. Randall finally broke it. "Molly, come back here and sit down for a minute."

"What the hell for? So you can lie to me again?"

"No. Please, I'm serious."

She took a deep breath, then walked back and sat down.

Randall leaned back in his chair. Tapping the newspaper on the desk, he said, "I'm not saying you're right, okay? But, just supposing you are. Have you any idea what kind of people are involved? There are no bounds here. Life is meaningless. Once the fare is paid, they don't give a damn if they make the trip or not. In your wildest nightmare, can you imagine what happens to those who don't? Shark food, okay?"

When Molly didn't answer, he said, "Imagine, if you will, a small-town cop who finds himself in the middle of one of the biggest investigations going on in the country." He began ticking off the agencies. "FBI. CIA. DEA. INS." He watched her face pale as his words sunk in. "Imagine that same small-town cop who can't even tell his D.A. what's going down. Can your stubborn brain absorb that? Then can you cross your heart and hope to die to forget what I just said? Think you can pull that off?"

"Oh, my God."

"And then some," Randall muttered. Stubbing out his cigarette, he said, "But that's not the case here. Just a little Hollywood fun." Abruptly changing gears, he said, "So, what time you dropping in at Oliver's opening?"

"Seattle makes sense. It's a day shorter from Asia than San Francisco."

"Forget it. I just told you—"

"Stop it, will you? I'm tired of you insulting my intelligence."

He was out of his chair in a flash. He grabbed her arm and forced her up out of the chair. Leading her to the door, he snarled, "I'm trying to save your life. Now go home and stay the hell out of this."

Molly's arm shot out to slap him, but he was faster. He held it tight and stared at her. She saw the tight jaw and the angry eyes. Then the sudden pleading in them. "Please, Molly. If not for your own good, then for Emma's."

Her nod was slight, but he saw it and let her go. "Em and I will be there around seven."

Randall watched her leave, then slowly walked to his desk. He opened the bottom drawer and pulled out a fifth of Gentleman Jack and a glass. Pouring two fingers, it was gone in one swallow. He sat down and stared at the newspaper article Molly had left. "That woman is going to be the end of me. Nine in the morning and I'm hitting the booze. Goddamn! How the hell did she figure it out?" Reaching for the newspaper, he crumpled it up and threw it in the wastebasket. Of all the articles she had to run across, it had to be that. Coincidence? He hated the word. Fluke was better. That could work.

Molly felt like a phantom in a Gothic flick as she walked back to the shop. The crisp morning air filled with the heady scent of the ocean was lost to her. Someone waved, but the face was a blur. A horn honked, and it sounded like a broken bell. How she made it across Ocean Avenue without getting hit by a car was a miracle in itself. She stood in front of the shop and blinked. It could have been a tee shirt emporium for all she knew. But it looked familiar, and she didn't move away. Words were forming in her brain and she fought to ignore them. "Oh, Carrie!" she said aloud. "What happened to you? How could you get involved with these people?"

She felt sick. She leaned against the window and held her breath. She said a silent prayer in thanks that at least Carrie had left Emma with her. It wasn't a passport to grace, but it might give her a few points.

She glanced at the display in the front window she'd spent so many hours fussing over. The hours polishing the wood on the Bombe chest in the center of the window, rubbing olive oil into the old leather books, cleaning the brass bases on the lamps, sponging silk lamp shades, touching up the gilding on the picture frames, polishing the silver candlesticks and burning the beeswax candles down just so. It all seemed so frivolous now. She felt like smashing the window and throwing everything in the street.

She gulped for air, then walked through to the courtyard and around to the garage in the alley. She found Robbie helping Emma clean the wrought-iron furniture. "Hey, good job. You're almost done. I'm sorry I took so long."

"We're having fun," Emma said. "I guess you could call this learning from the bottom up, huh?"

Molly smiled. "Something like that."

It was eleven before she unlocked the front door to the shop. A steady stream of tourists flowed in and out until three. Four busloads of German and Japanese tourists were in town, and they seemed to shop in groups. It was all Molly could do to handle the sales by herself. But tourists were generally good-natured, and they were patient with her as she scrambled to handle their purchases.

Just as the last group left, Emma popped down with ham and cheese sandwiches she'd put together. Heading into the storage room, she said, "Should I get dressed up again for Oliver's thing? Maybe I could stay home and read?"

"I'd love to say we didn't have to go at all, but I can't." Molly thought a moment, then decided she'd better explain a few things. "I can't leave you here alone. Even during the daytime. Where I go, you go."

"Not even with Robbie?"

"Nope."

Taking a bite of her sandwich, Emma said, "Is that person in the Jeep still around?"

Molly sighed. "I don't know, Em. But Randall still wants us to be extra careful just in case."

The windows of Oliver's new shop had been covered with brown paper for weeks, and the few times Molly had ventured past for a peek had been wasted. The moment she walked in, she had to catch her breath. *Absolutely stunning* were the first two words that came to mind. Soft classical music filtered through the huge single room. Waiters inched past an already large crowd with flutes of champagne and canapés. Bitsy's wide circle was in attendance, and a photographer was busy taking pictures against backdrops of dazzling Renaissance-style, wall-hung tapestries. French commodes, armoires with doors open offering a sultan's collection of Old World beaded lamps, Tiffany style desk sets, Art Deco ivory and bronze figures of women filled the room.

Molly held Emma's hand as she slipped past a waiter and inched her way toward Bitsy holding court at the back of the room. Pausing every few feet to look over Oliver's merch, Molly was itching to pick up a tag and see what his prices were. She hated to admit the man was inordinately talented. He'd filled the shop with impressive pieces. Her eye, trained to be quick and able to compute and categorize in nanoseconds, took in a number of exquisite French, Italian, and English pieces of furniture. Drawn to a Spanish vargueno—a fall front cabinet enclosing drawers—her eyes narrowed, remembering Oliver swearing he wasn't a competitor the day she'd caught him at her computer.

Still holding Emma's hand, she leaned down and said, "I need to look around a little more before we go over and say hello to Bitsy."

"It's a beautiful store, but I'm checking things out too. We have to know what we're up against, right?"

Molly gave her a wink. "Keep reading those books and I'll have you working the floor before you know it."

Moving behind two figures of six foot Nubian slaves, each holding up a silver bowl of glitter-frosted fruit, Molly zeroed in on a Dutch marquetry chest. The intricate inlay of colored woods was exquisite. Next to it stood a simple Swedish cabinet. Side by side, the two pieces offset each other wonderfully. Farther down the wall was a Pastiglia cabinet from Italy. Two pristine papier-mâché chairs caught Molly's eye. Decorated with swirling gold leaf acanthus, they flanked a stunning Scottish late Regency mahogany tea table priced at $4,500. Taking a close look at the three pieces, she decided they were genuine. And the prices were fair. Even Oliver's sales tags were classy. He used folded over parchment tied to the furniture with a royal blue ribbon. The item's description and price were written in an easy to read calligraphy.

Emma pulled at her sleeve and pointed. "That's a funny-looking clock."

Molly eyed the piece and wondered how Oliver got his hands on it. "It's an astronomical clock. It shows the phases of the moon and stars. You don't see many of them anymore."

"Cool."

Hiding her envy, she said, "Yeah. Very cool."

Moving away, Molly stopped at a glass counter. "Look at this tea service, Em. This is gorgeous." She wished it wasn't in the case. Noting the gilt interior of the sugar and creamer, her hands itched to check the hallmark. "If it's Georgian, it's worth around twenty-five hundred. And that silver saucepan with the hinged spout looks like it might be Georgian too. See the crest and the ivory finial? Pricey, my dear. Very pricey."

"We've got to get stuff like this," Emma said.

"Yeah, well, we will. Don't worry. We will. Let's check out that display case over there." Leading Emma away, Molly stood before a tall case holding a collection of glass goblets. "Now this is the type of merch we might—if we're really lucky—run into at garage sales, so you'll want to take a good look at them."

"Hmm, pretty colors. Is there a name for them?"

"They're called Bohemian glass. Three Bohemian chemists came up with formulas to make the different colors without adding minerals to the glass. On some of the colors, they brushed metal oxides on them to resemble veining. Ruby, amber, green, and violet are the most sought after. Well, there's other colors too, but these are the best, and they're often engraved with stags and huntsmen."

"Are they expensive?"

"Oh, they run anywhere between three hundred to a couple of thousand."

But it was the tall case that interested Molly. It appeared to be Edwardian, painted satinwood with ebony and boxwood. At the top was an oval sphere with a painting of Diana the Huntress. Reaching up on her tiptoes, Molly eyed the quality of the artwork and saw it wasn't authentic for the period. The colors were wrong and the execution up close was wanting. She reached for the tag and blinked. Twenty grand? *No way,* she thought.

Turning away, she tried to see where Oliver was. She didn't want him to see her checking out the tags on the pieces. She finally spotted him with Bitsy's court. Even from her distance, she could see his face nearly glowed. She hoped he choked on every compliment he got tonight. Still, she had to admit he'd expertly mixed the genuine pieces with the fakes. An old ploy to throw off even the most experienced eye, and there were not that many there that night. And where the hell was Randall when she needed him!

Smiling at Gregory Leazer, a dealer she knew, she said, "What a beautiful shop. A great addition to town, don't you think?" Pretense was everything. Especially now. When the dealer grinned, Molly smiled, then said, "Ditto."

Nearly fooled by the tall case, Molly returned to the Dutch piece, picked up the tag and had to bite her tongue. She carefully pulled out a drawer and gave it her special X ray, then shook her head. The dovetails at the side of the drawers were machine made, and the rails showed no wear. Bending at the knees, she examined the feet. Why reproducers didn't do their homework amazed her. They'd put English bracket feet on the damn thing.

Emma said, "This is really beautiful. We should have one too."

Molly's smile was so tight it almost hurt. "Not in my lifetime." Molly's earlier empathy for Oliver—when she'd discovered how much he'd lost to Trudy—was gone. He'd marked the Dutch piece as early eighteenth century, and priced it at sixteen thousand. She moved away, returning briefly to the Swedish and Italian pieces, then turned to face the crowd. She didn't bother to check out the Louis XV vitrine, or the ebonized and boulle two-door one next to it. She didn't have to examine them or look at their tags. She already knew what she'd find.

A soft tap on her shoulder made her start. She turned to see Ted Banks offering her a flute of champagne. "We meet again. Great shop, isn't it? I had no idea all this was lurking behind those papered windows."

Taking the champagne, Molly smiled. "Thank you. Yes, Oliver's done a fabulous job. I'm really impressed."

"Yeah, I like his style. So, who's this young lady with you? I didn't know you had kids."

Molly groaned inside. She hoped to hell he wasn't hitting on her. She wasn't in the mood, and hardly interested in someone her sister knew. "This is Emma, Carrie's daughter. She's staying with me while Carrie gets settled."

"Really?" Giving Emma a wink, he said, "So you're the little gal going on thirty, huh?"

Emma smiled, then looked up at a waiter offering her canapés. When Molly nodded, she took two then looked away.

"I've got my eye on a few pieces here. Think you could help me out? I mean, point me in the right direction? I just bought a town house at Pasadera and I need to fill some empty spaces."

Molly stepped back to let a waiter pass. She didn't want to get stuck with him, but she also didn't want to see him burned by Oliver's deception. "I'd wait. His prices are a little high. I think he overscoped the situation. Many of the new homeowners here are high-powered business people and not easy marks." Realizing she'd been a bit too candid, she added, "Well, what I mean is . . ."

Ted eyed her for a moment, then said, "Is Oliver on the up and up or not?"

"Oh, I didn't mean that. Just . . ." Searching for a way to ease out, she offered, "I'm sure Oliver will do very well."

"Molly, part of being a good lawyer is being able to read between the lines. Misreading the market is one thing, but are you implying some of these pieces are not what they're represented to be?"

"I didn't say that."

Taking a sip from his glass, he said, "Funny, I wondered about some of the stuff I bought from Trudy. Where do these people get this stuff?" Giving her a sly wink, he added, "Being in the business,

317

maybe you could tell me. I don't have to have the real thing. Just the look will do."

Reaching for Emma's hand, Molly said, "I wouldn't know, Ted. I don't deal in high end reproductions."

"I could use someone like you to help me steer clear of a bad buy. What say I drop in the shop and talk about it? I'll bring you a floor plan of my new place. You've probably got a few things I could use."

"Oh, of course. I'd be happy to help. Stop by anytime. Make up a list of what you need, and we'll see what we can come up with."

"Great. I'll come by midweek. By the way, I hear Clint's new golf club and gated development is really taking off. You'll probably get a lot of traffic from that."

Never one to turn away a customer, Molly nevertheless didn't want to jump too quickly and give him the wrong idea. It was apparent he was interested in her personally, but she didn't want to get into a situation that would be embarrassing for both of them. Inching slowly away, Molly replied, "Hmm, yes, I'm hoping too."

Emma's ears suddenly perked up. "Do you know Clint Eastwood?" she asked.

"The most famous question in town. Nope, I don't. I don't move in those circles," he said, laughing.

"Neither do I," Randall said, clamping a hand on Banks's shoulder. "Hey, Ted, how are you? I didn't know you were into this stuff."

Offering his hand, Banks said, "I just bought a new condo and I need a few things. Besides the free champagne and canapés from Daria's, I was hoping to run into Molly."

"Were you now? Well, she's open seven days a week. You ought to stop by."

"We were just making a date to do that. Say, where's your buddy, Lucero? I haven't seen him around the courthouse lately."

"He's been in Sacramento this past week. D.A. seminars and party fund-raisers. You know the game."

Molly spotted Daria coming in and said, "Oh, Daria's here finally." Moving away, she waved, "Nice to see you again, Ted."

"You're not interested in that guy, are you?" Emma asked.

"He's a nice man, that's all. I couldn't be rude."

Exchanging a quick hug with Daria, Molly said, "You didn't tell me you were catering this."

"I almost didn't. I told him he had to pay up front or get someone else. Bitsy paid the tab for him. I stopped by just to be polite. Ten minutes and I'm out of here."

"My ten are already up. I'll leave with you. But first I have to say hello to Bitsy, then find Randall again."

"You've got a look in your eye, Molly. What's wrong now?"

"I've just added two and three and came up with eleven."

Daria and Emma looked at Molly as if she were losing it. "Huh?" Emma said.

All Daria could manage was, "Shit. Not again. Now what?"

"I'll tell you later."

"I can't wait," Daria said dryly. Grabbing hold of Emma's hand, she said, "Come on, squirt. Give me a quick tour while your auntie does her thing. We'll wait for her outside."

Molly made a beeline for Bitsy, who, surprisingly, looked awfully perky. She gave her a hug and said, "I've got to run. Emma's tired. See you later." She totally ignored Oliver and turned away to search for Randall. She found him looking over the Spanish vargueno. Leaning close, she said softly, "If I had a hot needle and stuck it in that ivory inlay, I'll bet it sinks right through."

The look of surprise on his face was worth a million bucks. "Plastic? You're kidding me."

"Probably a high grade. Maybe even super resin."

"No shit. A hot needle, huh?"

"If it's ivory, it won't penetrate. If it's not, it will. Very simple."

"What if it's bone?"

"Bone isn't generally used on pieces like this. I'm going over to Daria's now. I need to talk to you."

"I thought we settled everything this morning."

"This is different." Turning back toward the crowded room, she put a smile on her face in case Oliver or anyone else was wondering about their little huddle. "It's about those tags and . . . something else." Turning back to face him, she said, "And I know who put them there."

CHAPTER 25

Joining Daria and Emma outside, Molly said, "Let's get out of here before I throw something." With Emma between them, they headed for Daria's restaurant a few blocks away. Molly was silent until they reached the corner. "That prick! What's that saying, 'Do unto others as you would have them do unto you'? Is that it?"

"Something like that," Daria replied.

"Well, Oliver likes his own version: 'Do unto others as they did unto you.' Most of those so-called antique pieces of furniture in his shop are phonies and tagged with a fake circa."

Daria stopped in the middle of the crosswalk. "What? Are you sure?" When Molly gave her a look, she apologized. "Scratch that."

"What's 'circa' mean?" Emma asked.

"It means," Molly explained, "around the time of. In other words, if you label something as 'circa last quarter of the nineteenth century,' it means it was made anywhere between 1875 and 1899."

"He's a crook then, huh?" Emma asked.

"No, he's worse. Much, much worse," Molly answered.

When they reached the restaurant, Daria told them to head straight for her private room. "I've got to check on a few things. When Randall gets here, I'll send him back."

Molly and Emma settled themselves at the big table. Molly pulled out her cigarettes and lit one, then stared at one of the French bistro prints on the wall.

"Do you want me to leave the room when Randall gets here? I mean, is this going to be adult time?"

Ruffling Emma's hair, Molly leaned over and kissed her on the forehead. "Have I told you lately what a great gal you are? I think that might be a good idea. Maybe Daria will let you go into the kitchen and watch the chefs. Would you like that?"

"Cool. Maybe I'll pick up some pointers so I can teach you how to cook."

"Funny, Emma. Very funny."

"I thought you might be able to use a laugh. I can tell you're really upset."

"Oh, honey. If you only knew."

"Can't you tell me? Is it about Oliver?"

Hugging her close, Molly said, "Later, okay?"

When Randall arrived, it seemed that Daria had read her mind. With Manuel at Daria's side, and her ever ready tray of coffee and pastries, she said to Emma, "Manuel is going to take you back to the kitchen so you can watch how a restaurant works."

After Emma left, Daria poured coffee and said to Molly, "By the way, Ted Banks was just in looking for you. He said he saw us leaving together and was hoping you might join him for dinner." Giving Randall a quick glance, she grinned, then added, "Considering the mood you're in, I didn't think you wanted to play nice with a guy hitting on you, so I told him you only stayed for a minute. Hope that was okay."

"Nice for my ego, but you're right. I'm not in the mood."

Giving Daria a wink, Randall said to Molly, "Hey, don't let me keep you from your fans."

"Don't worry, I won't. We have more important things to worry about than my *fans*."

Deciding not to aggravate her further, Randall pulled out a cigar, ran it under his nose, then put it back in its case. "Okay, you've got something to tell me, right?"

"Oliver Townsend left those tags on Trudy's desk," Molly said.

Randall played with an ashtray, squaring it with the color blocks on the tablecloth. "Got some proof for me?"

"Yes. His merch in the shop."

"I'm listening."

Molly began ticking off the various pieces, then added, "Okay, so the Dutch piece isn't a mirror image of the tag, but it's the same style and era. The Swedish chest is too. I could name a few others, but from that squinty-eyed look you're giving me,

I know you can see it too. And those pieces match the list Sally gave me."

When Randall didn't respond, Molly said, "I think Oliver threw those tags at Trudy at the show to let her know he recognized her, then slipped the penicillin in her coke. I think—"

"It doesn't matter what you think. You have no proof. No one saw him do that. His prints aren't on anything. I can't arrest the man because you *think* he did it."

"If Oliver's the killer, why leave those tags and then put similar pieces in his shop? I mean, that's really stupid," Daria said. "Wouldn't he know somebody would remember them and he'd be suspect?"

Randall smiled. "Who said killers were smart? You read too many mysteries."

Glancing at Molly, Daria said, "Wouldn't Oliver know you saw them and you'd be at the opening tonight and might put two and two together?"

"No. I don't think he expected me to show up after the way I bawled him out when he was snooping on my computer. In fact, when I went over to see Bitsy, I could tell he was surprised to see me. He probably figured Randall wouldn't put it together either. The little shit is egotistical as hell. Unless Bitsy told him Randall was a collector, he wouldn't figure a cop had an ounce of refined taste."

"Why not pull him in and sweat it out of him?" Daria asked Randall.

"I haven't cause," he replied, deciding it was time to cut this speculation off before the two of them got him in a corner. They were treading on dangerous ground, and he had to pull them away.

"You have the tags!" Molly said.

"I have magazine cutouts. That's all I have." He drained his coffee, then rose. "I'll walk you and Emma home."

Unable to discuss Molly's findings with Emma in tow, they listened as Emma excitedly described her time in Daria's kitchen. "Manuel showed me how the chef sweats garlic. Isn't that a funny way to describe cooking garlic?" Not waiting for a response, she went on, "And then I saw the pastry chef put decorations on a cake he was making for a party. He made flowers and leaves, and even some bees. I didn't get any good tips we could use, though. Except maybe for the garlic. You're supposed to add that last to stuff so it won't turn bitter."

"Great tip, Em," Molly said, her mind still zeroed in on Oliver and the tags.

"Yeah, even I didn't know that," Randall said.

"Huh? You told me you owned a restaurant in San Francisco," Emma said. "You should know all that stuff."

"Naw, I just rake in the dough. I leave my cook alone. He knows his business." Looking at Molly, he said, "I don't interfere with the pros."

When they reached the shop, Randall was

relieved to see that the light outside the apartment was on. Having a clear view of the door, he said, "Okay, you two. I'll wait until you get in, then I'm taking off."

Emma looked at Molly as if expecting her to invite Randall up for coffee. "Do you have to go already?" she asked.

"Yeah, got a ton of paperwork to catch up on." Giving Molly a nod, he said, "You going to early Mass tomorrow?"

Molly's thoughts were miles away. "Hmm? Oh, Mass. Right, uh, I'm not sure which one. I'd like to sleep in a little."

"Town's packed. You might not get a seat, with all the tourists tromping through the Mission."

"Good point. Well then, guess Em and I better turn in early."

Randall watched them climb the stairs, then waited a few minutes after he saw them go in. He knew where Molly's mind had traveled, and he knew she wasn't going to turn in right away. He had a feeling she was up to something, and decided to do a little stakeout just to be sure. Crossing Ocean Avenue, he stood in the planted meridian for a moment, then crossed to the other side. Moving under an awning, he watched as each light in the apartment came on. It was only a little past eight. Since it was too early for bed, he figured they'd watch a little TV first. He would give them a few minutes to settle in, then circle the block, go through the courtyard from the back, and see if the living room or Molly's bedroom lights were on. He could also watch the alley from there and see if she pulled the truck out.

His new partners had promised to keep an eye on her, but plans had a habit of changing by the hour. After his call earlier, he knew they were also busy elsewhere. Satisfied that Molly had time enough to decide to stay put, he walked down to the corner, then crossed Ocean Avenue again. By the time he made it into the courtyard, he saw the living room lights were off and a soft glow from Molly's bedroom. His cell phone rang, and he pulled it out and listened to the agent watching Molly's apartment. The agent had noted the same light changes.

Feeling some relief, Randall crossed the courtyard, cut through the alley, and headed back to the station. Passing Devendorf Park, his cell rang again. He pulled it out and read the message from Emma. *Harry is sleeping.* He shook his head and smiled. Emma was one smart kid.

When Emma clicked the cell phone shut and nodded, Molly said, "We can't leave yet. Go ahead and close your eyes if you want. I'll wake you up when it's time."

Molly sat in the darkened living room as Emma curled up with Tiger on the sofa opposite her. She knew what she planned to do was risky, but after seeing how Oliver had blatantly loaded his shop with items so similar to the tags he'd left at Trudy's booth, she was afraid his boldness might escalate, and believed that Bitsy was his next target. The fact that he'd been giving her opium tea should have set her alarms off. Taken in small doses, and made very weak, as her college roommate from Singapore swore, the tea was harmless and soothing. Generations ago it was common for women to brew it for what they considered "women's problems." She didn't think Oliver was that considerate.

Then Molly thought back to that first night when Carrie showed up with Emma. Just two weeks ago the child was worried about breaking a cup, and now she was going with her to confront a murderer. She realized she was out of her mind to take Emma, but she had no choice. Leaving her alone was not an option. She knew where to hide her in case things got dicey.

When it was time to go, Molly woke Emma. "Put your hood up before we leave. Keep your head low when we go down the stairs and don't make a sound."

Dressed in dark sweats and her baseball cap, Molly went to the French doors in the living room and inched one open. Giving Emma the high sign to follow, she squeezed through and then stooped down by the iron railing. When they made it to the garage, Molly slowly opened the doors and thanked God she'd remembered to spray Armorall on the old hinges. With one finger to her lips, she motioned Emma closer. "I'm going to put the truck in neutral, then we're going to push it out into the alley. We have to go slow, okay? Then we'll ease it out to the street. Once we're there, you get in . . . but don't slam the door. I'll jump in and then we'll take off. Got all that?"

"Ten four."

"You're not scared, are you?"

"A little. If you'd tell me why we're going, maybe I wouldn't be?"

"I need to see Bitsy, but Randall doesn't want us out late at night, so . . . well, it's complicated."

"When is it going to get uncomplicated? I know I'm just a kid, but you're the one who talked about honesty, remember?"

Emma had her there. Molly took a deep sigh. "I'll explain on the way over."

Pushing the truck out of the garage and onto the street was easier than Molly had anticipated. Within moments they were off. Taking the long way to the Carmel gate just in case, she headed for Monte Verde, then turned down Eighth to Carmelo. From there she crossed Ocean Avenue and drove slowly to the gate into Pebble Beach. Waving her pass to the gatekeeper, she drove carefully. She wasn't exactly sure what she was going to do, and was searching for a little inspiration. At least the weather was cooperating. She didn't need a dark and stormy night.

"Here . . ." Emma said, handing her a pack of cigarettes from the glove box. "You're drumming your fingers on the steering wheel. As much as I'm against this, maybe you should have a smoke and calm down. You really need to quit, you know."

Molly took the pack and smiled. "What would I do without you?"

"*Au contraire,*" Emma said with utmost sophistication.

Once again amazed at this wise female in little girls' clothes, Molly checked her rearview mirror, and was relieved to see nothing behind her. On Seventeen Mile Drive now, she kept her eyes open for deer while still trying to decide what she would do.

It was just past ten-thirty. The opening had been between six and nine. By the time the last guests drifted out, Daria's crew would have cleaned up and Oliver locked up the store. He and Bitsy should have left around ten and would be home by now. When Molly saw the lower floor's lights on, she knew she'd been right. Now, the only problem was making sure her visit was enough of a surprise to throw Oliver off guard. Finding the gates open again, Molly wondered if they were broken. Bitsy used to be a harridan about those damn gates. Maybe it was for Oliver's convenience? They had to be opened from in the house, and if he'd been working late at the shop, Bitsy might not have wanted Josie or Charles to wait up. Whatever the reason, Molly was glad they were open. Turning off the lights and the motor, she coasted past the gates and pulled as close to the entry as possible.

"Close the door as gently as you can," she whispered. "Then stick with me."

Moving toward Bitsy's Mercedes, Molly touched the hood. It was still hot. They hadn't been home long. She was glad Bitsy had insisted she keep a key to her house. Pulling it out of her pocket, she whispered to Emma again, "When we get inside, make yourself scarce. I don't want you with me when I—"

"Wait! You said you'd tell me why we had to fool Randall and not let him know we were coming. Are you going to bawl out Oliver for selling fake antiques?"

"Something like that."

"Four-letter words and all that?"

"Probably."

"Cool."

At the massive double doors, Molly inserted the key, then said to Emma, "If the foyer is clear, head for that balcony thing in the library you told me about. Oliver and Bitsy might be in the living room having a nightcap. They can't see the staircase from there."

Molly slowly opened the door, then stepped in. Giving Emma a nod, she pointed to the staircase. "All clear."

She waited until Emma reached the top, then headed for the living room. Lamps were lit but the room was empty. *Shit! They must be in the library.* Back in the foyer, Molly tiptoed across the marble floor toward the double doors leading into the library. They were open enough to hear voices. She listened for a moment, then recognized Oliver's voice. About to push the door open, Molly froze. She was so determined to confront the bastard, she hadn't given thought to what danger she might face. She shoved her hand in her pocket and wrapped her fingers around her keys, praying that her first impression of Oliver as a sneaky wuss was right. If worse came to worst, she could always scratch the hell out of his face. Bitsy had plenty of bronze sculptures in the library; she'd be sure to stand next to one of them.

Taking a deep breath, she threw open the door and walked in. Oliver was sitting at Bitsy's eighteenth-century English partners desk as if he owned it. Bitsy was opposite him, sipping from a china cup. Her head was drooping and she looked as if she might drop the cup. They each had what looked like legal documents before them.

"Molly! Darling! I didn't hear the bell," Bitsy said, pulling up her head in surprise.

"I didn't ring it. I still have my key." At Bitsy's side, she took the delicate cup and set it on the desk. "Are you okay?"

"Oh . . . yes . . . of course, darling." Patting her forehead, she said, "Just tired."

Oliver's face was perfectly haughty. "How dare you barge into our home like this. I won't have it. In future—"

"Excuse me? *Our* home? *You won't have it?*" That was all Molly needed to throw caution to the winds. "*In future?* You don't have a future here." Leaning on the broad desk, her face only a few feet away, she said, "I know all about you, *Duke.*"

CHAPTER 26

Molly let that sink in and saw a deep flush creep up from the top of Oliver's silk ascot to his hardened eyes, now turned to Bitsy. "You told her. You damnable bitch! You promised!"

Before she could respond, Molly quickly said, "Bitsy didn't tell me. I found out on my own." Then she threw the small packet she'd had in the pocket of her sweatshirt at him. It landed just inches from Oliver, on the desk. His recoil confirmed to Molly that she had been right.

"Settle down, Oliver. Go make some tea. You need to mellow out. It's dried poppy bulbs, right? I got some from Josie the other night." Molly shook her head. "Wow, it gave me one of the best night's sleep I've had in weeks. I'd forgotten how great opium tea was. I tried it a few times in college after finals. Slept like a baby."

"You're out of your mind," Oliver finally said. "Opium? Oh, really. It's simply herbs from an herbalist I know."

"Bullshit. You've been feeding this junk to Bitsy for weeks. No wonder she's been going up and

335

down the energy ladder. Slip her some tea, then shove some papers under her nose to sign." Picking up Bitsy's cup, Molly took a sip. "I see you're still at it." She looked at Bitsy and said, "He's been drugging you."

Bitsy gasped. "What?"

"That's a lie!" Oliver shouted.

"Oh, please! You didn't think you'd get away with it, did you? You had to know I'd eventually get her to her doctor for a checkup."

Up above, in the small gallery, Emma was lying on the floor, peering through the rails, her eyes glued to the scene below. When she heard Molly mention opium, she became worried. She was old enough to know this was more serious than Oliver lying about the furniture in his shop. She knew Molly didn't want Randall to know what they were doing, but if Oliver was one of those drug lords she'd seen on TV, this might get ugly. Reaching into her pocket, she pulled out her cell phone, then hesitated. Aunt Molly was pretty righteous. She'd fooled that Jeep on the bridge, and she'd been ready to ram him over the cliffs into the ocean if he came back. Maybe she should wait a few minutes just to be sure. Cocking her ear closer to the rail, Emma tried not to miss a word.

Bitsy stared at the cup for a moment, then shakily pushed it away. Her voice was slurred. "Darling, this isn't really necessary. Oliver and I were just about to finalize ownership of the new shop.

Oliver's decided Carmel is much too cold for his arthritis. I'll be taking it over and—"

"Just decided, Oliver? When?" Molly broke in. "I guess you saw me eyeballing your merch tonight. Darn, I thought I was so careful. You knew I wouldn't keep quiet about your phony tags. Or were you going to let Bitsy get caught with her pants down? She's not a fool Oliver, you should have known better."

"You are mistaken," Oliver finally said.

Snatching up the papers in front of Bitsy, Molly ignored him and quickly read the two-page document. Tearing it in half, she threw it back on the desk in front of him. "You bastard. These papers are a codicil to Bitsy's will. She's so loopy now she wouldn't have known. You'd probably have gotten away with it if you hadn't killed Trudy."

Molly saw both Oliver and Bitsy shrink back into their chairs. "You didn't cause Trudy's death," Molly said to Bitsy. "She didn't have a heart attack. She was murdered. Oliver killed her. He put penicillin in her Coke. She was allergic to it. *That's* what killed her." It was out of Molly's mouth before she remembered Emma was on the small balcony. She glanced up to see if Emma was listening, then caught herself before Oliver saw her inadvertent slip-up.

For a man of advanced age, Oliver Townsend was quick on his feet. He was around the desk and at Bitsy's chair before Molly could blink. He pulled Bitsy up quickly and had a choke hold on

337

her before Molly could move. "The bitch deserved to die! She ruined my life!"

Bitsy's face was ashen. Oliver's arm was just under her chin. Somehow she managed to speak. "Oliver! Don't do this. Let me go. You can have—"

"Shut up, you mangy bag. *I was going to have it all*! This house, your money, all of it, until this know-it-all Molly Doyle figured it out. Yes, Molly, I saw you looking at the vargueno and the other pieces. I worked my ass off like a dog, scrimping to save every penny for top-notch merch. I scrounged and wheedled for years. I was up there with the big boys until that tramp friend of yours ruined me." Sneering at Molly, he said, "I didn't kill Trudy Collins. Bitsy was my target."

Emma's eyes popped open. Scooting back from the rail, she began to bite the nail on her thumb. Reaching for the cell phone, she held it to her and then moved back to see better. Grown-ups argued a lot, she thought, then they usually cooled down. Her mother did that all the time. She learned that the best thing to do was to not talk back and just let her get it out. That's probably what would happen here. But she didn't like the way Oliver was holding Bitsy.

"She left and you didn't alert me?" Randall screamed over the cell phone to the agent at the other end. "What? She's in Pebble Beach and you lost her? Aw, shit, you dumb bastards! That's exactly where she shouldn't be. I'm on my way."

He was already on his feet, pulling on his sport coat. "You should have called me immediately!"

Randall punched in Emma's number, then stopped. If there was trouble, calling her might make it worse. Tearing out of the station, he got into an unmarked car and headed for the Carmel gate to Pebble Beach. He called the gate on his car phone and told them to stop all traffic in and out of the forest. Then he called the Sheriff's Department and alerted them. He gave them Bitsy's location and told them to have two units meet him there without sirens and to stand down unless he called again.

Creeping closer, Molly said to Oliver, "Bitsy? All she's done is try to help you. You should have seen that the merch Trudy sold you wasn't right. Your greed got the best of you, Oliver." Pointing her finger at herself, she said, "I know . . . she got me too."

She had hoped that confession would slow him down. But it didn't. He only laughed. "Well, well. Ms. High and Mighty Manhattan isn't as sharp as we all thought, is she?"

A half heel closer, Molly froze when Oliver pulled out a small derringer and pointed it at her.

"Like they say in the movies, don't move," Oliver sneered.

Molly put her palms out. "I won't! Believe me. I'm rooted to the floor. But put that gun down, okay? If you say you didn't kill her, then . . . then what say you just pack a bag and leave? I mean, we can forget about all the rest."

When Oliver pulled Bitsy tighter and put the gun to her head, Molly was desperate to think of some way to slow him down. "Is that a Ladysmith? My God, last one I saw was at Sotheby's and it went for a mint. Is the handle pearl?" She tried for a laugh: "I mean, your hand is covering it. Pearl ups the value, you know."

When she realized he wasn't buying it, she quickly said, "What pisses me off, Oliver, is that you got to confront Trudy before I could."

"But *I* was thrilled, Oliver!"

Whirling at the new voice in the room, Molly nearly fainted when she saw who was pointing a gun at her.

"You provided me with the ideal suspect. I was at the show purposely to take care of Trudy. When you got into it with her at her booth, I knew the timing was perfect and the cops would be looking at you eventually."

When Emma saw the gun in Oliver's hand, she scooted away from the rail. Too far up to see the new arrival or hear the voice, she eased her way into the hall and punched in Randall's number. He picked up on the second ring. "Come quick to Bitsy's!" she said, her voice shaking. "Oliver has a gun! I'm in the hall upstairs. They're in the library and the front door is unlocked."

"Jesus! Okay, listen close. Go hide somewhere. I'm almost there."

Emma ran down the stairs to the kitchen. She

had to find Josie and Charles. They could help Aunt Molly in case Randall didn't get there in time. She ran out the back door to the herb garden, then across to the small house where Josie and Charles lived. Breathlessly, she pounded on the door. When Charles answered, she rushed in and told them that Oliver had a gun and he was going to shoot someone.

"You?" Molly said, shocked beyond belief. "But . . . but how—"

"Yeah, *me*. I'm glad to know you're so surprised, since you figured out so much already. Move away from the desk, Oliver, and put that girly toy away. Drop it on the floor, then kick it to me."

Stunned, Oliver couldn't move.

"Drop it! Now!"

Oliver did as he was told, then released Bitsy. Sinking in the chair she'd been pulled from, Bitsy said, "Well, I'll be damned. Never in a million years would I have thought—"

"I can't believe this!" Molly broke in. "You killed Milo Kraft too, didn't you!"

"I had to. He knew too much, and like Trudy, got way too greedy."

Leaning back against the partners desk, Molly shook her head in awe. Surprisingly calm, she said, "So she had to go, right? Of course. Why didn't I realize it before? You followed me to Santa Barbara too."

Oliver's neck tweaked. "So that's how you found

out about me! Who told you? Who? I demand to know!"

"Oh, shut up, Oliver," Molly said. "We've got a killer pointing a gun at us, and all you can think about is yourself."

"Okay, kiddies, that's enough. I need quiet. I have to figure out what the hell to do with all of you. Three's a crowd, you know?"

Molly was praying that Emma heard everything. She didn't dare look up again and give her hiding place away. The only thing she could do now was to stall for time in case Emma saw what was going on and ran for help.

Randall drove through the forest like a man who knew every curve, twist, and bump. His radio was open, and he'd had to clamp a cigar in his mouth to keep dispatch from hearing him use every combination of four letter words he'd ever learned. When Bitsy's house was in sight, he doused his headlights and pulled up next to a Sheriff's Department patrol parked down the road. Jumping out, he said, "Stick with me and don't get trigger happy." When the deputy told him about a call that had just come in from Bitsy's driver, Randall ran to the house.

Molly knew she had to think fast, take the power away with surprise. She might buy more time if she told what she knew. "I'm curious," she said. "Correct me if I'm wrong, but I'm guessing Trudy knew it was more than just drugs your cartel was smuggling in those crates with the repro goods. I'll bet she knew about the illegal immigrants and wanted a bigger cut, right?"

"Well, this is a surprise. How did you figure that out?"

"It was easy. I happen to know a little bit about exporting and importing. Seattle was the perfect port for what you were bringing in. Almost next door to Vancouver, which has the biggest Chinese population outside of San Francisco. It was perfect. It's also a day shorter from Asia than San Francisco." Shrugging, she said, "It made sense. Besides, the drug trade isn't as lucrative these days with all the new detection techniques."

Randall found Charles and Emma in the drive. "What the hell are you doing out here?"

"We came out to wait for you. Hurry up! Aunt Molly needs you!"

"The front door is unlocked," Charles said, "but come through the back. They can't hear you. It's carpeted."

Following Charles, Randall told Emma, "You sit tight and don't move."

"What I don't understand—" Molly began.

"Look, I give a shit what you don't understand. Enough chatter. All three of you move to the terrace. We're going swimming."

"Can't we come to some sort of arrangement?" Oliver pleaded.

"Don't whine, Oliver. You'd be the last I might consider."

"One last question," Molly said. Every minute she could stall might make the difference between living and dying. She had to try it. "Please?"

"One. Only one. Then it's outside."

"How did you know I was going to Santa Barbara? And why did it matter?"

"That's two questions."

Molly's laugh was shaky. "Okay, lump them together, then."

"Trudy warned me Oliver was in town. She was sure he hadn't recognized her, since she used those wigs and colored contacts at her shows, but she was getting nervous. Then I saw you at Trudy's with the movers. I knew you'd pack up her office and maybe catch on to what she was doing. I couldn't take a chance on you, so I had you watched. I have to tell you, I drove like crazy to catch up with you. Then when you took the coast route back, I stayed with you. I have to hand it to you, you can handle a car."

"Why did you take off? Another hit or two and I'd have lost control and gone through the concrete railing."

"That's three now. Time's up."

"Yeah, I'd say it was," Randall said. "My Ruger is aimed right at you, Ted."

Not an eyelash moved on Ted Banks's face. With Randall behind him, Molly watched closely, ready to duck in case Ted was crazy enough to whirl around and pull the trigger. His composure was incredible.

"Go ahead, Randall. Shoot me, and my reflex will pull the trigger and one of them will grab it."

"I don't think it would work that way. I'm aiming at your brain. That's instant. Your finger won't get the signal in time."

Molly knew she had to get all of them out of Ted's line of fire and give Randall a free shot if he needed it. The only way to do that was to rush forward and try to knock Bitsy off the chair. If she was lucky, they'd fall onto Oliver, who was standing beside her.

Like a well-choreographed dance, Molly threw herself against Bitsy at the exact moment Ted Banks pulled the trigger. On the floor, her ribs feeling as if the rail of Bitsy's chair had decided to become a part of her body, Molly heard two shots. Nearly deafened by them, she was afraid to see who caught the bullets.

She didn't have to wonder long. When Randall picked her up and held her in his arms, she closed her eyes and sighed, "What the hell took you so long?"

CHAPTER 27

Molly was late for Mass again. She wondered if she'd ever make the full service. When she saw Sister Phil coming out of the Mission gift shop, she stopped to say hello and set a date to begin Emma's tutoring. Holding Emma's hand, she wove through the standing room only crowd at the back. It was easy to spot Randall. He towered over most of the world. He saw them right away. Stepping back, he made room for Molly and Emma. "Get much sleep?" he asked.

"An hour or two," Molly said.

"Sorry I had to keep you and the squirt so long at the station."

"Since I had to give almost every law enforcement agency in this country their own special version, I'm surprised I got any sleep at all."

"Yeah, well, they got their rules. I'm glad to see the last of them. Assholes nearly got you killed."

"Randall!" Molly hissed. "You're in church! Watch your mouth."

Nodding toward the huge crucifix several yards away, he grinned. "It's okay. He understands."

"I thought all those men were very nice," Emma said. "Two of them love *Harry Potter.* When I was waiting for Aunt Molly, we discussed *The Order of the Phoenix.* The one with the beard was the smartest. He's already figured out the next book."

"That was the DEA guy. They're the best read of the group."

When a parishioner next to them asked them to lower their voices, Randall apologized, then steered Molly and Emma out to the courtyard entrance. "I gotta run. I still have some loose ends to tie up and reports to finish. I should wrap everything up in a few hours. How about you and Emma coming by for dinner? I figured a little celebration was called for. Lucero's back from Sacramento. I thought I'd give him and Daria a call."

Before Molly could answer, Emma said, "You know how to cook? I thought you said you left your cook alone."

"I didn't say I couldn't cook. I said I leave him alone because he runs me out of the kitchen when I correct him."

Emma laughed.

"What time, and what can I bring?" Molly asked.

"After you close is fine. Just bring you and the squirt."

"I'm not going to open today. Emma and I are going to the beach, and then we're going to catch up on our sleep. By the way, I've got a lot of unanswered questions."

"I've got the answers." Giving her a wink, he said, "Had them all along."

When Molly and Emma arrived at Randall's condo, conveniently across the street from the police station, Daria answered the door. Emma stepped across the limestone floor of the small foyer and peeked into the living room. "Randall sure doesn't live like those cops on TV. Is his furniture antique? Is he one of us?"

Molly laughed. "He sure is."

"Then why does he tease you so much?"

"That's the way he is," Daria said, grinning. "Oh, by the way, Lucero's a little peeved, so ignore that scowl on his face. He's ticked off that he'd been left out of the loop, and already told Randall so in no uncertain terms."

Following Daria to Randall's state of the art kitchen, they saw him at the Wolfe stove. Lucero, apparently in a better mood now, was leaning against the island chop block trying to tell Randall how to make the vinaigrette for the salad. "Put more balsamic in and some fresh garlic."

When Randall ignored him, Molly and Emma followed Daria to the dining alcove opposite the cooking island, and watched Lucero next to Randall at the stove. Peering over Randall's shoulder, Lucero said, "How much wine did you put in that Bourguignon?"

"Italian men think they are the world's greatest everything," Daria said, "but especially when it comes to food, they are quick to tell the world they are peerless. I'm staying out of the way." Pouring Molly a glass of wine, and a soda for Emma, she said, "I have to listen to this oneupmanship every day as it is."

Noticing Molly and Emma's arrival, Lucero left Randall alone for a moment to give them both a kiss. "Hey, Ms. Marple," he said to Molly, "at it again I hear. I'm still light on the details, but the talk is you really kicked some ass."

"Please, no applause. Bruised ribs again, but I'm getting used to it." Molly smiled as she kissed him back.

Glancing at Randall, Lucero said, "Then plug your ears 'cause I'm not through with him yet." Smiling at Emma, he added, "I heard about you too. Way to go, champ."

Leaning into Molly, Emma said, "Aunt Molly's a good role model."

Joining them at the table, Randall poured a glass of wine and said, "That's a subject that needs some discussion. But not tonight. Come on, Emma, I've got a room of trains you might like to check out."

When Randall returned, Lucero said, "Did you add olive oil to the pasta water so the pasta won't stick?"

"Come on, Lucero. Do I look like I've got a space between my ears?"

"By the way," Molly said, "you told me at church you had answers all along. Mind sharing those little nuggets? Did you know Ted Banks was involved?"

"Knew it for a few days. I got the rest of it from him after they pulled the bullet from his ass."

Lucero let out a yelp. "Is that where you nailed him? Hell, Randall, you're a lousy shot. I'd have put the bastard away."

"Yeah, well that's why you ought to stick to shaking hands and kissing babies. I wanted him alive to talk to us. And he did, in spades."

"And?" Molly pressed.

Pulling up a chair, Randall said, "Check the water, Lucero. See if it's boiling."

"Screw the water. I want to hear this." With that, he got up and turned off the big pot boiling on the stove.

"Check the Boeuf Bourguignon, will ya?" Randall added.

"I did, it's fine. It still needs more wine. By the way, when the hell did you have time to cook this?"

"I started it yesterday. I cook when I have crimes to solve. Helps me think. If I'm into one week, it's a cassoulet. Two weeks, Bourguignon. I hit the two-week mark yesterday. Of course, I knew who the killer was, but I had orders to lay off." Jerking his head toward Molly, he said, "Ms. Lovejoy over there had to butt in and hurry up the ending."

"Damn it, you two! Knock it off. I want to hear what happened," Daria said.

Randall poured more wine, then proceeded to tell them about Ted Banks. He watched their eyes widen at each revelation. He'd become curious about him, he began, when Banks had shown up at Lucero's party with Molly's sister. In case Emma might pop back into the room, Randall chose his words carefully and refrained from using her mother's name. He whispered it once and that was it. Knowing about Carrie's reasons for leaving Seattle—most of which Lucero had uncovered—he wondered why Banks would be interested in her joining his firm. News like that, no matter how hushed up, had a habit of leaking. So, going on the assumption that Banks knew why Carrie had left the law firm, he'd done some reaching out to friends in Washington State. This alerted a few agencies that already had an eye on Banks. They contacted him and made it clear he was to leave Banks alone and not share whatever information he had with any local agency, including the D.A.'s office.

From the DEA, Randall went on, he found out that Banks had a law office under another partner's name, in Tacoma, which Banks had admitted last night was how he met Carrie. Apparently they had a little thing going, and he recruited her when he found out she was light on scruples. "Now, you gotta understand, this is from Banks. Hoping to strike a deal with everyone, he gave up a lot of names. In fact, they couldn't shut him up."

"Trudy's code and those tags!" Molly said. "It just dawned on me. A Spanish necklace was one of the items I couldn't place. Carrie must have given it to Trudy to sell. Remember those letters we didn't understand? It wasn't part of Oliver's tags."

Emma returned and sat next to Molly. Randall paused, then said, "Banks claimed this woman knew Trudy, and it was her idea to use her for a little extra dough. Besides passing her jewelry, she'd lifted from safe deposit boxes where she had power of attorney. So, instead of destroying the repro merch used to pack the containers, they shipped it to Tacoma, and then to Trudy when she had an out of town show. The three-way split worked for a couple of years and they made some heavy-duty dough."

"That's what she meant by things unraveling, I bet," Molly said.

"So she tries to hit Trudy up for more dough because she's on her way to jail if she doesn't skip town, and gets here too late?" Daria asked.

"That's what happened," Randall said.

Molly noticed Emma had left again, and said, "Hold those thoughts. I'll be right back."

"Oh, no," Daria said. "I hope Emma didn't catch on."

"Maybe she's back with the trains," Randall offered.

Passing through the living room, Molly saw Emma outside on the small balcony. "Hey, bored with the trains already?"

Leaning against the railing, Emma's head was lowered and it was clear she'd been crying. "They're talking about her, aren't they?" When Molly didn't answer right away, Emma said, "Remember the honesty thing?"

"I remember. Yes, they're talking about your mother. And, my sister." Bending down, she put her arms around Emma and said, "It's not a nice story for either of us, but at least we have each other. So that's a pretty good ending, don't you think?"

"And we'll live happily ever after?"

Hugging Emma to her, Molly said, "Count on it."

Back with the others, along with Emma, Molly gave them a thumbs-up. "Emma's okay. She knows who we're talking about."

"What about Kraft?" Lucero asked. "I'm still way behind on events. Who aced him? Ted?"

"Right again," Randall said. "Kraft knew too much, and was hitting him up for more dough. When I told Banks a neighbor wrote down his license when his car was close to blocking her driveway, he damn near bit his tongue. I couldn't help but rub it in."

"Why did he take Carrie to Lucero's party?" Daria asked. "I don't get it."

"It was a fishing game," Randall answered. "Banks said he was curious if Molly was involved, seeing that she shared the same occupation as Trudy. Carrie claimed Molly didn't have a clue, but Banks didn't believe her. The, uh, relation-ship was too close. He tried to scare Molly off when he went after her on Bixby Bridge. He had an idea she might have found out about Oliver and figured out Trudy's gig. But he didn't dare go any further. He knew if something happened to Molly, the cat would be out of the bag. That Jeep was a getaway car his partners delivered in case he had to split. Besides, he had to shut Kraft up first. The stupid thing was to kill him at Trudy's. He should have done it somewhere else and make it look like an accident. That's the trouble with corporate lawyers—they don't mix with violent criminals enough."

"Whoa! Back up. Oliver?" Lucero said. "That wimp hanging around Bitsy? What's he got to do with any of this?"

"Oh, right, counselor. I forgot you didn't hear about that." Looking at Molly and Daria, Randall said, "When Lucero showed up this morning, the station was crawling with DEA, CIA, and INS people. The main agenda was the illegal immigrant operation out of Seattle. Oliver was cooling off in a cell. I've got a shopping list of charges I can use. I could use his trying to defraud Bitsy, but the opium tea thing is iffy. Doesn't matter, he's facing attempted murder. When he put that gun to Bitsy's head, he pulled down the big one. He's my problem, not theirs."

Rising to turn the burner under the pasta pot back on, Randall said to Lucero, "You get him next, pal." Randall then told Lucero what Molly had discovered, and about the scene at Bitsy's when Banks showed up. "In some ways, we owe Oliver a lot. His coming to Carmel started a domino effect that blew an international cartel the big boys had been watching for months."

"I'll keep that in mind," Lucero said.

"I almost forgot to ask about Bitsy," Daria said. "How's she holding up?"

Molly began to laugh. "You won't believe this. She's packing for Rome. She's going to see the Pope to ask forgiveness for her lax ways."

Daria's eyes flew open. "You're kidding, right? Think she can get an audience with him?"

Lucero, at the stove watching Randall again, said, "Hell, I'll bet money on it." Poking him in the arm, he asked, "Hey, did you tell everyone about all the dough your guys found under Trudy's house, and her will?"

Randall grinned, as if he'd been saving the best for last. "Oh, yeah. There was ninety-something grand in one of those mini safes." Giving the pasta a stir, he said, "And she left everything to the local drug rehab group, and instructions for a qualified antiques dealer to hold a sale for her merch. Guess it was her way of saying mea culpa, huh?"

Lucero nudged Randall. "Qualified, huh? Got anyone in mind?"

Randall thought for a moment, then shrugged. "Hell, I don't know." He looked at Molly and said, "Think you can handle it?"

"I'll have to check with my assistant. How about it, Em?"

When Emma popped up with "Kaching!" she broke up the room.